SIDE *by* SIDE

We gratefully acknowledge the support of the Canada Council for the Arts and the Ontario Arts Council for our publishing program. We also acknowledge the financial support of the Government of Canada through the Canada Book Fund.

Side by Side is a work of fiction. All the characters and situations portrayed in this book are fictitious and any resemblance to persons living or dead is purely coincidental.

Cover design: Val Fullard

Library and Archives Canada Cataloguing in Publication

Kushwaha, Anita, 1980–, author
        Side by side / Anita Kushwaha.

(Inanna poetry & fiction series)
Issued in print and electronic formats.
ISBN 978-1-77133-545-4 (softcover).-- ISBN 978-1-77133-546-1 (epub).--
ISBN 978-1-77133-547-8 (Kindle).-- ISBN 978-1-77133-548-5 (pdf)

        I. Title. II. Series: Inanna poetry and fiction series

PS8621.U839S53 2018   C813'.6   C2018-904364-4
                                                                       C2018-904365-2

Printed and bound in Canada

Inanna Publications and Education Inc.
210 Founders College, York University
4700 Keele Street, Toronto, Ontario, Canada M3J 1P3
Telephone: (416) 736-5356 Fax: (416) 736-5765
Email: inanna.publications@inanna.ca Website: www.inanna.ca

MIX
Paper from
responsible sources
FSC® C004071

SIDE *by* SIDE

a novel

ANITA KUSHWAHA

Inanna poetry & fiction series

INANNA PUBLICATIONS AND EDUCATION INC.
TORONTO, CANADA

To N and J
For brotherly blessings

And I know you feel isolated
And I feel what you won't say
I don't care if the disbelievers don't understand
You're my pretty boy
Always

—"Pretty Boy" by Young Galaxy

PART I: FALL

There is an hour, a minute—you will remember it forever—when you know instinctively on the basis of the most inconsequential evidence, that something is wrong. You don't know—can't know—that it is the first of a series of "wrongful" events that will culminate in the utter devastation of your life as you have known it.
                    —Joyce Carol Oates, *A Widow's Story*

1.

KAVITA SLUMPS BESIDE HER HUSBAND on the curb outside her parents' home where hours earlier an Ottawa police car had idled. A mild late-summer breeze, as light and downy as dandelion seeds, grazes across her skin. A bright half-moon hangs in the clear night sky. Crickets and grasshoppers chirp their nocturnal music. The kind of velvety, soul-sighing evening that reminds her of countless others spent with her brother Sunil, jogging through the quiet streets of their neighbourhood under the buttery glow of streetlights, hearing the beat of their even strides against the pavement and the rhythmic huff of their synchronous breath. As she sweeps away her tears, she knows running through the streets is futile now. The time for searching is over.

Her brother is gone.

The police came on the tenth day after Sunil's disappearance. A Thursday. The day of the week dedicated to the worship of Lord Vishnu, the peace-loving deity of the Trimurti. For her mother, a day of fasting, of quietly holding a prayer in her heart, and yellow offerings, such as marigolds, since they are in season and can be plucked from the garden, those blooms that burst with the colour of happiness and peace. A day that used to end with prayers and halwa by the light of a diya. On this Thursday, however, the Guptas were not graced with the blessings of a gentle god. This Thursday, they felt only the quake of Shiva's destruction.

"I can't think straight," she says, pressing her knuckles into her swollen eyes. Curtains of dark curls hide her face. Despite the mild evening, her bare arms and legs swell with a fine layer of goose bumps like textured leather. Although hindsight has no power over their present fate, she scours her memory of their last days together for clues, the way a detective might link scattered bits of evidence on a cork board with tacks and string in an effort to uncover relationships, causality, reason—to make sense of chaos.

"Shall we go in?" Nirav asks. He tucks a few strands behind her ear. "You're knackered, love. Going over it won't change anything. You're going to drive yourself mad if you carry on like this."

"Going over it is all I can do now," she says, staring at the pavement. He is still dressed in his office clothes. He had left work as soon as she called him that afternoon. He had rushed to be with her. Yet, somehow, she can't help but feel insulted by his proper appearance, the even tone of his voice, his dry eyes.

"Come, my love. Let's go inside and I'll make you some tea."

"I can't." She turns away from him. "I can't breathe in there."

Inside the house, her parents have retreated into the solitudes of their grief and separate bedrooms. She had fixed each of them a toddy before helping them to bed, where they had withered into their mattresses, drained by weeping and a week of erratic sleep.

Afterwards, she had poured the rest of the brandy typically reserved for company down the kitchen sink without letting a drop touch her lips. The contents of her parents' modest liquor cabinet went the way of the brandy. A diminutive yet self-preserving voice inside her head made a salient point: any substances that might be overconsumed as a remedy against the pain of bereavement had to be removed immediately. That same voice knew if she started down the path of forgetting—of numbing—then she would not stop until she reached oblivion.

Earlier, while administering the toddies, she had detected a similar precarious wish for oblivion in her parents' deadened eyes. These ripples of Sunil's suicide threatened to overwhelm them all. No matter how much she craved an end to the hurt, the survivor in her whispered with a meditative calm unique to the shock of trauma, reminding her of her duty to care for her parents; she was their death doula now. *You're all they have left*, the voice told her.

"You can't stay out here all night." Nirav rubs circles on her back, a conciliatory gesture. The warmth of his broad palm soaks through the knit of her tank top. Rolling her shoulders back, she shrugs him off, rejecting his sympathy. She knows she doesn't deserve any. He lifts his hand away as though in slow motion. Resting his forearms over his knees, he sighs.

"I know we have to go in eventually. But I can't face it yet." The reality of entering the house and not finding Sunil. Never again finding Sunil. Kavita gazes across the street at the flicker of television reflected in her neighbours' front window. She pictures them sprawled on the couch, snacking on chips, chatting during the commercial breaks. Spending an evening blanketed in the comforts of banality. Taking it for granted the way fortunate people have the good fortune to do. The way she had lived until about a week ago.

She hugs her knees in for warmth. "I still can't believe it."

"It must be the shock."

But that wasn't it. "No, it's this," she says. "This is really happening." But it wasn't supposed to.

Why, Bear? she thinks to her elder brother, invoking her ancient nickname for him, which she hasn't used in years but somehow comes back to her now, her version of *bhaiya*, a word which had been too knotting to her toddler tongue. Bear always felt more befitting of Sunil and Kavita meant it with no less affection than the Indian endearment. *What changed your mind?*

Sunil had called her at work, which alone surprised her. But when he asked her to leave early and come home without delay, she knew something wasn't right.

The four of them gathered in the living room.

With his gaze fixed on the dusty rose carpet, Sunil began to tell them about his plan to end his life, all at once, mechanically, as though playing a cassette, as though he had rehearsed the lines too many times before. That he would drive far away, somewhere secluded, somewhere they would never find him. Swallow the sleeping pills he had been hoarding for weeks. Wait for the coma of a poisonous sleep.

As he spoke, Kavita's body hardened as if his unreal words were an icy fog trying to leach into her marrow, but every part of her refused to absorb it. She couldn't speak. But the first thought to enter her frozen mind was, *He doesn't mean it*. How could her Sunil—her beautiful brother, the kindest, gentlest person she had ever known—want to cause himself such harm? Shock soon dissolved into fear like ice into puddles. Her next thought was a silent declaration to her brother: *I won't let you hurt yourself, Sunil*. And finally: *I'm going to save you. And that's all there is to it*. That was the power Kavita thought she possessed—the magic to dissolve terror in a potion of resolve. Simple. Done.

"I'm sorry," Sunil went on, as their mother wrung her hands, and their father gripped the carpet with his toes. He hadn't meant to hurt them, but he needed them to know. He was scared of himself and what he might do.

"What happened?" Kavita asked him. "How did it come to this?"

A few months earlier, the anti-depressants he had been taking since adolescence to manage his condition had stopped working. His doctor had prescribed him new medication. Those pills made him feel worse, even worse than before he had started treatment. The noise in his head was as loud and fast as his adrenaline heartbeat. He couldn't settle. He couldn't sleep. He wasn't eating. The noise in his head grew louder and louder.

He was sick of it. The noise in his head. The troubles of his body. The pills. Having to accept words like *managing* and *coping* as poor substitutes for what he really wanted: to live, with ease, like a normal person.

So, he made up his mind. He was done with being broken. He was going to fix himself.

About a month ago, he had started weaning himself off his pills. He hadn't consulted his doctor, whom he had lost faith in after his last experience. He decided he was through with being a lab rat. He researched the weaning process thoroughly online. It seemed straightforward enough. He felt empowered. He knew it was going to be a challenge, but he chose to believe in himself for a change. His will to live med-free, in and of itself, seemed like more than enough to carry him through the rough patches.

As he weaned, he replaced the pills with all the advice that had been bestowed upon him over the years, solicited and unsolicited, welcome and unwelcome, alike. He went for power walks in the sunshine. He tried laughter yoga. He ate turkey, salmon, and dark chocolate to the point of revulsion. He took his vitamins. He even considered eliminating gluten. Every day, he wrote a list of the things that were worrying him, followed by a list of all the things he was grateful for. He tried to stop taking life so seriously. He got into the habit of smiling, even when there was nothing to smile about, as a way of tricking his brain into thinking it was happy. *Fake it till you make it* became his personal credo.

At first, he had felt optimistic. He was doing it. He was his own placebo. He was fixing himself. By the third week, the false homeostasis began to fail. As the last traces of medication dwindled from his bloodstream, his symptoms had resurfaced. The noise in his head was the same as it had always been. He couldn't settle. He couldn't sleep. He stopped eating again.

He had tried to fix himself, with everything in him, but he had failed.

It was crushing.

The noise started to whisper he would always be broken.

Bear, Kavita thinks to him now. *I'm sorry I just sat there. I should've said something reassuring. I was about to, but I pulled back. I'm not sure why. You were always so private about these sorts of things. I knew how hard it must have been for you to let us in. I didn't want to make you feel even more uncomfortable. But that seems stupid now. How could knowing I was there for you make you feel worse? That's what I wanted to tell you. That I was there for you, no matter what, no matter how long. I felt every word you said, and I believed you.*

"He probably thought I was ashamed of him," she says.

"He would never think that."

"He might have. There's so much we didn't know." An awful thought occurs to her. Maybe she never really knew Sunil at all. The closeness she felt between them was all in her head. One-sided. Can it be true? And if so, what can she do about it now? *Sunil,* she wants to yell at the sky. *Tell me it isn't true.*

"Who knows what to say in these situations? You didn't want to push him farther away, that's all."

"I should've risked it." Kavita lifts her gaze to the night sky, to the gaps between the strobe light stars. "He couldn't be farther away from me than he is now."

After a while, their mother said, "We should go to the hospital."

"There's no way. I'm not going to emerg. It's too fucking humiliating."

"But *beta*—"

"Mom, I'm serious. No hospital." There was a panicked look in his eye, and it spread through them all, as they sensed his unspoken threat to flee.

"Okay, okay. No hospital. Just settle down, *beta*, please?"

No one spoke for half a minute. "Can we at least call your doctor?" their mother asked, gently. "It's not too late. They might still be able to see us."

"Can we go tomorrow? I'm exhausted."

"I think we should go now," Kavita blurted. They needed to keep him safe, and they needed help, fast.

"I'm not going to do anything."

"We should at least get your doctor on the phone," Kavita pressed. "He needs to know about this." Maybe the doctor would have better luck convincing Sunil to go to the hospital.

"It took everything I have just to tell you guys. I can't do it all over again."

"Sunil—"

"Kavita, I just want to go to bed."

She reached for her parents for support but both looked as bewildered as she was.

"Okay," their mother said. "Tonight, you rest. Tomorrow we'll call."

Kavita shook her head. Her gut was telling her waiting was the wrong move. But what could she do? She couldn't force him. And she didn't want to scare him into doing something reckless.

Sunil rose to his feet. "Come on, narc," he said to her. "I've got some pills for you to confiscate."

Kavita wanted to reprimand him then, for making light of their terror. But fear kept her expression placid. As they descended the stairs to his basement bedroom, the connective tissue that held her knees together felt slackened, overstretched. Kavita gripped the railing like a crutch. While he fetched the pills, she stood outside his bedroom, not peering inside, not giving him a reason to withdraw. He needed to feel safe, in control—with his condition, control was essential. That much, at least, Kavita understood about his condition.

Sunil emerged from the doorway and swung a white plastic bag at her. "Trick or treat?"

"Not funny." Her hands felt weak as she caught the bag. "Is that all of them?"

"You want to search my room?" He meant it as a joke, but could probably tell from the look on her face, Kavita was considering it. "That's all of the them, okay, Little One? Don't you trust me anymore?"

"Of course I do." But the truth was, part of her couldn't, not yet. "You know I have to ask." She hesitated for a few seconds. "Sunil, are you sure you don't want to see the doctor now? Why not get it over with? I'll be right there with you. Come on, let's just jump in the car and go." As she watched his face closely, the panicked look she had seen earlier charged his features again.

"So, you *don't* trust me."

"N-no, I do. I just ... I don't know what to do. I'm scared. I want to help you and I don't know how."

"Then listen to me," he said. "That's what I would have done for you."

"Sunil—"

He started walking towards his room. "I'm going to bed."

"Let me know if you need anything, okay? I'll be right over there." She pointed behind her, to the orange and brown velvet couch in the family room. She wouldn't sleep that night. Instead, she planned to sit vigil until morning, within earshot of Sunil's bedroom, monitoring access to the front door, just to be on the safe side.

"You're staying over?"

"Where else would I be?"

He gave her a faint half smile. "I'll leave my door open." A second later, she heard the creak of bed springs.

Acting quickly, she rushed to the bathroom and started flushing the sleeping pills, while keeping an eye on the stairs. As she emptied the last bubble pack, she felt as though she were diffusing dozens of little bombs that would have destroyed them.

Then she called Nirav from her cell.

"Don't tell me," he said. "I've won an all-inclusive trip to Jamaica!"

It was a game they played sometimes, especially in the afternoons, when each of their cubicles felt particularly prison-like.

"Niru—"

"Well, I'm sorry to tell you, miss, but I won that trip *last* time. Any chance for Cuba?"

"Nirav, please stop."

"Sorry love," he said, apologetic. "I was just having a laugh. Is something wrong?"

"It's Sunil." Something about hearing her husband's voice weakened her. Kavita felt her belly fill with tears. But now wasn't the time to fall apart. Sunil needed her to be strong. She willed the tears into a block of ice, and told Nirav the details of Sunil's plan, mechanically, realizing there was no other way to deliver such news.

"He can't be serious?"

"He handed me a bag of pills a minute ago. I flushed them."

"I don't know what to say, darling. But really, I'm sure he doesn't mean it."

"Can you bring over a bag of my things?"

"I'll come right after work."

"Will you stay over too?"

Now, as Kavita rubs heat into her arms, she feels her belated anger rise, degree by degree. Would an extra pair of eyes have made a difference the next day? Eyes that could have helped her keep watch over Sunil. Eyes that still remain offensively dry.

"Why didn't you spend the night when I asked you to?"

"I told you, I had a meeting early the next morning."

"You didn't believe him."

"No, I did."

"If you had believed him, you wouldn't have been able to stay away, meeting or no meeting."

"I—"

"Why haven't you cried?"

"I don't know," Nirav shrugs. "Maybe it's shock."

Kavita shakes her head. Where was her husband's sympathy for her brother? Why wasn't he slowly crumbling like she was?

"If I do feel anything right now, it's awful, for you and your parents. That you have to go through any of this at all."

You, Kavita notes. Not us. Not we. Married only a year, and already, there they were, facing a crisis that would have strained even the longest and strongest of marriages.

"Because of Sunil? Is that what you mean? Are you trying to blame him?"

Nirav averts his eyes. "It might seem foolish now," he offers, after a brief silence. "But honestly, I didn't think he meant to go through with it. I believed he was in distress, but since he came to you, I thought that meant he didn't really want to hurt himself in the end. I thought he was reaching out."

The heat rising inside of Kavita stops. She can't be angry at her husband for this reasoning, at least. She knows it is possible to believe someone is in as much danger as they insist, and also believe the danger will not come to pass. The conceit of it sickens her now. Or is it the ignorance? What can she say in her defence, other than, she didn't know what she was really up against at the time. After a few moments, when her larynx softens, she manages to mutter, "So did I."

Kavita sat vigil on the basement stairs—the couch was too comfortable—watching Netflix on her iPad, the waterline of the coffee pot, slowly lowering, as daylight rose.

They were the GP's first appointment of the day. Kavita sat with Sunil in the examination room, while their parents waited outside.

He dangled his legs back and forth over the edge of the examination table, rustling the crisp white sanitary paper. Over the years, he had confided in her about his aversion to doctor appointments, a hostility he had carried since childhood. He hated the undressing and weighing and measuring. Having to stick out his tongue, breathe deeply, endure the pricks of needles. The power of doctors made him nervous. A relative stranger who told him if he was too heavy or too light, if his blood pressure was too high or low, if he needed to be switched to this or that medication. Always, the doctor judged if he was normal or abnormal, within the curve or an outlier.

Fifteen minutes later, Dr. Jones tapped on the door. He was a silver-haired, middle-aged man with a sombre countenance. Not unfriendly exactly, just to the point, like a hastily written prescription. Sunil saw him every few months. The GP made him fill out quizzes to verify that his symptoms were still in remission and wrote him new prescriptions and told him to keep doing what he was doing—eat right, exercise, take his pills, get enough sleep. Sunil had thought of him more as a pharmacist than a doctor, really.

"So," Dr. Jones said as he took a seat at the desk. "What can I do for you today?"

Sunil spoke to the tiles.

"You shouldn't have tried weaning off your medication by yourself," Dr. Jones said. "By the sound of it, you did it too quickly. It can take months to wean properly. And you did it in, what? About a month?" Dr. Jones shook his head. "Some people have to stay on medication for their whole lives."

"I know."

"Of course, having said that, you can come off them at any time. They aren't the problem."

There was a puzzled pause. Anyone with Internet access could look up the side effects of the drug online, which Kavita had done last night while evading sleep. Oh, there were problems: blurred vision, high blood pressure, chest pains, chronic sleeplessness, excessive sweating, anxiety, depression, suicidal thoughts, and on and on.

Kavita was about to ask for clarification when the doctor asked, "Have you had any suicidal ideation?"

"Yes."

"Do you have a plan?"

Sunil nodded.

The doctor crossed his arms and tucked his chin, emitting a hint of disapproval. "Tell me what it is."

Kavita went rigid, not only from having to bear witness to Sunil's plan for the second time in less than twenty-four hours, which would have been reason enough, but also because as her brother—her private, gentle, careworn brother—confessed to the cold doctor the darkness of his desperation, Kavita could feel Sunil's vulnerability, his nakedness, as though disrobed herself. The way he spoke, with his eyes down and his shoulders slumped, as if he had something to be ashamed of, made Kavita want to scream at the doctor for his disapproving looks, and cry with her brother, as she reassured him that being in crisis was nothing to be ashamed of, so he should hold his head up, because he was brave, he was doing what most people didn't, he was putting himself out there, and asking for help. Could the doctor see the courage sitting in front of him through his narrowed eyes? Did he ever stop to consider what it cost?

"Do you want to be admitted to the hospital?" Dr. Jones asked.

"To be honest, the thought of it scares me."

"Why?"

"I'm not sure, exactly. It just scares me."

"Hmph," Dr. Jones grunted. For a second, it seemed to Kavita that the doctor was more perplexed by Sunil's aversion to psychiatric wards than by his plan to end his life.

Regardless, now was her chance to speak up. Pushing her displeasure aside, she said, "Going to the hospital might be our best option, though, isn't it?"

"I really don't want to go."

"What do you think, Doctor?" she asked.

Dr. Jones gave Sunil an appraising look. "Well, there's a big difference between thinking about suicide and acting on those thoughts. Have you ever attempted?"

Sunil shook his head.

"No, chances are if you had, you wouldn't be sitting here with me now. Well, in that case, I suppose you might as well wait for your appointments at home. At least you'll be comfortable there. You seem to have a good support system around you." Dr. Jones shifted his attention to Kavita. "Just keep an eye on him."

"Are you sure?" she asked. "I mean, he might not have made any attempts, but he has a plan. Isn't that supposed to be a red flag?"

"I've seen worse," Dr. Jones said, flat. Then he turned away from Kavita and started tapping at the keyboard, adding a few lines to Sunil's file. "I'll write you a new prescription, since you didn't like my last recommendation."

"It's not that I didn't like it."

Dr. Jones jerked his head to look at Sunil, his gaze a piercing challenge. "Pardon me?"

Sunil seemed to shrink. "Never mind."

"As I was saying," Dr. Jones went on, once again facing the computer. "We'll try something else, and I trust you'll stay on the medication this time. We don't want to go through this again, now do we? I'll also write you a script for some sedatives to help you sleep, to be administered by your family, of course. After a few solid nights of rest, you're bound to feel better. You should probably take some time off work, too, if you can. Do you have benefits? Okay, good. Well, I'll write you a note for that as well."

Dr. Jones arranged appointments with a social worker and a psychiatrist for the following week.

"Are these the earliest appointments we can get?" Kavita asked. "I was hoping for something today or tomorrow." But according to the cards, Sunil wouldn't see the social worker, the first of his appointments, until next Wednesday, six days from now. Keeping Sunil safe for six days felt like an epic task. As Kavita thought about the length of time between now and then, by some cruel magic, time expanded, days becoming longer than days, hours longer than hours.

"What can I tell you? The waiting lists are long, even for cases like yours. There's always someone who's worse off."

"When will Sunil see you again?"

"Oh, well, I think we could touch base in about five weeks or so. We should know if the medication suits him by then. The ladies at the front desk will help you arrange a follow-up on your way out. And try to get in before I go on vacation." Dr. Jones rose from his chair, signalling that their allotted time was up. They had already backed up the rest of his appointments for the day. "Hang in there, Sunil," the doctor said as he opened the examination room door. "It's a good sign that you came in today."

As they left the doctor's office with the appointment cards in hand, despite the bumps during the consultation, Kavita nevertheless felt a lightness swell in her torso, a buoyancy that could only come from their new course of action, their new plan of hope, which they would use to replace that of Sunil's hopelessness.

Kavita winces against the glare of a passing car's headlights.

"Maybe I shouldn't have gone along with it."

"What?"

"Not admitting Sunil to the hospital."

"But he didn't want to go."

"He was scared. But I should've found a way to reason with him."

"Didn't the doctor say he would be fine to wait at home?"

"The fact is," she says, numb. "If Sunil had gone to the hospital, he would be alive right now."

"Kavita—"

"It's the truth, isn't it?"

That moment in the doctor's office was pivotal. An instant that could have changed their fates. But they chose another path, which at the time, seemed like the right one.

"When we left the doctor's office, I swear to you Sunil seemed more optimistic. I didn't just imagine it."

"I suppose none of us really knows what goes on in another person's head. You can't blame yourself for that, though."

"I must've missed something."

"What do you mean?"

"We left the doctor's office on the same page. Sunil seemed more at ease. But then something happened. Something changed his mind."

But what?

From the doctor's office, they drove to Sunil's work, so he could fill out the paperwork for his leave of absence. Being there reminded Kavita she needed to work things out with her own office, too. She had taken a week of personal leave, but she would have to talk to her manager about a more long-term arrangement.

They sat in a couple of chairs outside of the HR department cubicles. As Sunil filled in the forms, he said in a low voice, "It won't be long before everybody knows."

"They wouldn't talk about you behind your back. Would they?"

"HR is the worst. Cathy in particular has a bad rep for gossip."

"That's so toxic? How is that even allowed?"

Sunil bounced his shoulders.

"Well," Kavita told him, "who cares what they think, right?"

"It would make it a lot harder to come back to work."

"Then we'll find you a better job." In a better place.

"Yeah," he said, doubtful. "'Cause that's so easy. I've worked hard here. It's taken me a long time to get to where I am now with my job."

Kavita could see his point, perhaps in the sharpest relief she ever had. He had spent the last five years climbing the company ladder, and now he was finally the supervisor of the IT department. Why should he have to start over?

"I can't stand the idea of people looking at me differently or treating me differently after this."

"Don't worry about that now," she said. "First, we need to get you healthy. We have time to figure out everything else." Maybe there was an opening in IT at her office. Kavita made a mental note to look into it later that day, when she planned on calling her boss.

As she watched him fill out the paperwork, Kavita sensed his hesitation. He had created clear boundaries between his professional and personal lives. And to him, his life with his condition, while not a source of shame, was nonetheless, personal. It was his to talk about, or not talk about, as he chose. He had never bought into the idea that people living with mental health issues should out themselves in order to change mainstream perception. The mainstream could broaden its own mind, as far as he was concerned: his hands were full. Now, it seemed, the cost of accessing the help he needed in order to heal, would come at the expense of his right to privacy.

Reason for absence, she read on the form. He reached into his pocket, pulled out the doctor's note, and scanned it. Kavita noticed his expression darken. Then he hastily folded the paper in two.

He hovered his pen over the empty black line. She wondered what the doctor had written, what prognosis could make Sunil reluctant to even write it out. *Medical,* he scribbled finally. *See doctor's note.*

On the way home, they stopped at the pharmacy to fill his prescriptions. They were about to pull out of the parking lot, when Sunil asked, "Can we go somewhere?"

Kavita looked at him, surprised. "Aren't you tired?"

"I just don't feel like going home yet."

"What do you want to do?" their mother asked, watching him from the rear-view mirror.

"How about the marina?"

It was their family's favourite picnicking spot from when Sunil and Kavita were little. They would pack a cooler of drinks, a tiffin of *aloo jeera* and *puris*, and spend the day collecting clam shells, building sand castles, and skipping stones. "We haven't been there in ages," Kavita said.

"I think it's a good idea," their father agreed. "Some fresh air might help you sleep, *raja*."

"Marina it is," their mother declared, and they were off.

The marina was about thirty minutes away. Stepping out of the car, Kavita took in the view. The river glimmered in the distance as though flecked with mica. Gazing at its gleaming waters, she remembered the stories their parents had told them about the rivers in India—the Ganga, Yamuna. About people who would travel to bathing *ghats* to dip in the sacred waters in search of absolution and the healing powers of *gangajal*. She wondered if the river in front of them flowed with mysticism too. If her brother bathed in its waters, would it cleanse him of his troubles?

They strolled towards the pier as if drawn by the lighthouse. Along the way, they passed an old man fishing, a young family of four feeding fries to seagulls, a woman sitting on a bench reading a book. At the end of the pier, their parents stopped to rest on a bench and watch the sailboats. Kavita was impressed by how well her parents were tolerating each other. They were even sitting at the centre of the bench, not at either end, as they tended to, which to her exemplified the separate togetherness that defined their marriage. Maybe it was true that crisis drew people together. Maybe their family was on the brink of a new beginning too, just as Sunil was.

"Feel like skipping stones?" Sunil asked her.

A flood of childhood memories made it impossible for Kavita not to smile. "Let's go."

At the lighthouse, they hobbled around the pebbled shore, rummaging for stones, as they had done countless times before. When they were young, Sunil had taught her which stones had the right thickness and weight, how to flick rather than throw.

Holding a handful of rocks, Kavita stood a step away from her brother and watched as he cast. The pebble skipped once, twice, three times.

"Not bad," she grinned.

"Let's see you do better."

"Challenge accepted."

They fell into a tranquil rhythm, their snug silence punctuated by the occasional *plim plim plom* of their stones on the water.

After a while, Sunil stopped casting stones. He gazed at the water with a faraway look, at the ship sails in the distance like triangles of paper.

"What's wrong?" she asked. She was glad her parents had stayed behind.

"I'm just thinking."

"About what?"

He flicked a glance at her, then resumed his watch of the sails. "The doctor's note."

"Do you want to talk about it?"

He pressed his lips together.

"You know you can tell me anything."

"I know." He lowered his gaze to the shoreline, and the gentle push and pull of the water's edge over the slick pebbles. "He said I'm completely debilitated. Those were his exact words in the doctor's note."

She blinked. "Oh."

"Yeah, *oh*." He launched a stone. "How am I supposed to come back from that?"

"Well," scrambling for something comforting to say, "I bet that's just doctor speak. Something they say all the time. Remember, he wrote you that note so you could get time off from work. You know what insurance companies are like. He probably had to make it sound worse than it is."

"Maybe."

"You're not convinced."

"Maybe he wasn't just saying it. Maybe he really thinks I'm totally fucked."

"Stop it, Sunil." Kavita hobbled over the pebbles and held his shoulders, firm. "You're not fucked." She waited for a sign of recognition. "You're not. People come back from these sorts of setbacks all the time. You need to cut yourself some slack, okay? And be patient. It'll happen. We'll get there."

His dark eyes were soft and dull. "You're so naïve, Little One."

"Not so naïve, Sunil. And not so little anymore, either. I'm right about this. You have to trust me. Things are already working themselves out. Can't you see that?" He shrugged out of her grasp. Inch by inch, she felt him retreating inward. "You know everything's going to be okay, right?"

He stared at the horizon with a firm look, clear and resolute. "I know," he said. A few long moments passed. "Come on, let's head back."

She stuffed her hands into her pockets and followed him. Then she felt it—the *rakhi*.

Reaching into her pocket, she pulls out the bracelet made of crimson thread she has been carrying since then. It was her gift to Sunil for *Raksha Bandhan*, brother-sister day. The day they reaffirmed their bond, their promise to protect each other. Normally, while she tied a *rakhi* to Sunil's wrist, their mother would retell the old story of the mythical twins, Yami, the goddess of the sacred river Yamuna, and Yama, the God of Death. How Yami had tied a *rakhi* to Yama's wrist thus making him immortal. Yama, touched by his sister's gesture, had declared any brother who received a *rakhi* from their sister would be blessed with long life.

"I thought you gave that to him," Nirav says.

Kavita twists the bracelet around her forefinger so tightly

that her florid fingertip pulses in unison with her heart. "I meant to after his appointment, but with everything going on, it kept slipping my mind. Then at the lighthouse, things got so tense, the timing didn't feel right." Her throat aches. "I thought I'd get another chance." She twists the bracelet around her fingertip once more, focusing on the heat and the pressure, which feels only right to her, feels like the least of what she deserves. "Maybe if I had given it to him, he would have remembered us. He would have known he wasn't alone." In his darkest moment, he might have glimpsed the thin red thread and remembered how much she loved him. She thinks of Yama and Yami, and the sacred bond between brother and sister. "I didn't protect him like I was supposed to."

"You were with him all the time."

Kavita thinks this is how people must feel in confession. "Not all the time."

On the ride home, Sunil began to withdraw. Kavita had never seen him retreat so deeply inside himself. The look of preoccupation on his face was startling, impenetrable. The hopefulness she had felt as they left the doctor's office vanished. Terror took its place. Her gut told her in hammer-like knocks that something was very wrong.

When they got home, Kavita knew she had to do something. Sunil went down to his bedroom without a word. She watched him go and waited for the click of his door. Then she unpocketed her cell phone, sickened by what she was about to do. One day she hoped he would understand. But her cell was dead. She had forgotten to charge it the night before. She hated to take her eyes off the front door, ordered herself to be quick, as she rushed to the kitchen for the cordless, but it wasn't in its dock, nor was it in her father's room, or her mother's, or the dining room. At last, she found it tucked into one corner of the couch. All of her searching had amounted to half a minute. As she dialled 9-1-1, she slipped out the front door so no one would hear her talk to the police. The operator had just come on the line, when Kavita noticed the empty space in the driveway, where Sunil's car was usually parked. For a moment, she stood motionless, her mind slow to absorb the immensity of the situation, a computer unable to process an overwhelming amount of data.

"Oh my God," she whispered, chilled.

She felt kneeless.

"I took my eyes off of him for less than a minute and he slipped away." Even as she hears herself mutter these words, they don't seem real. But they are. She sees herself running to the corner of their street, then the next, her eyes desperately reaching along the cracked pavement, in search of Sunil's sky-blue sedan, and not finding it. In an instant, the geography of their small world mushroomed to an ungraspable size. Where did he go? How was she ever going to find him?

"You couldn't have known he would take off," Nirav says.

"I should have taken his car keys." Why hadn't she thought to take his car keys? Stupid. Stupid. Careless.

"His appointments had been arranged, for goodness sake. Anyone would've let their guard down a little."

Yes, that was it. She had let her guard down. Because they had left the doctor's office on the same page, but then something changed, only she hadn't known how hazardous the change would turn out to be. "I think it must've been the doctor's note."

"What about it?"

"Sunil mentioned it when we were at the marina. He was trying to put on a brave face, but I could tell he was devastated by what the doctor had written."

"What did the note say?"

"That he was completely debilitated."

"Anyone would take that to heart."

"I think he took it more than to heart. I think he took it as a sentence. Something he could never overcome."

Nirav lowers his brow.

"I told him to forget about the note," Kavita explains. "I said it wasn't important. The only thing that mattered was that he get better. And he would, in time. I told him everything was going to be all right. He said he knew." She remembers the look in his eye, distant, resigned. "But now, I think we were talking about different things." Why, why couldn't she tell what she was seeing then? "I think he had been weighing his options, and after our conversation, he made his choice."

Her zigzagged journey along the mess of tacks and string has brought her here. This is the answer to the enormous WHY. But is this really The Answer? Will she ever really know Sunil's reasons? She wants to ask him. Hear his beautiful voice. But she can't. Because he's gone. Forever. How can he be gone, forever? He has always been there, her whole life. What is life, even, without him? She doesn't want to know. Doesn't want this life. She wants the one they had, together. Wants another chance to make things right. She knows better now. Knows what to do. Please, dear God, wake her up. Let this be a dream, and let it be over.

Kavita begins to shake. Fault lines cover her like veins. She feels close to breaking.

"People always say once they've made up their minds, they seem at peace but that's bullshit." The person who sat beside her in the backseat was unrecognizable. He wasn't her Sunil, her gentle brother. Now she understands why: his face was a portrait of inner war.

"The last time I saw him was when he went to take a nap. I didn't even get a chance to give him a kiss. Mostly, I remember the back of his head as he went downstairs. That's it." A nothing moment.

Nirav wraps his arm around her back. "You loved him more than anyone, Kavita. And he knew that."

"But it wasn't enough."

Lifting her gaze to the night sky, Kavita lets the ache seep in. As she stares at the gaps between the stars, she asks him: *Where are you? Are you safe? Are you at peace now? Did you see how we searched for you? To us, you died today. But only because we were the last to know.* How naïve she was to think the police would visit them with good news. But she had. So had her parents. When one of the officers said they had found Sunil, the joy she felt, the relief she saw shining in her parents' eyes, at last, not tears of dread, but tears of celebration. The nightmare was over. They had found him. How naïve she was to not let the officer finish his sentence. Yes, they had found him. That is, they had found his body. What remained of it. They were so sorry.

With those simple words, their world detonated, and fell apart around them—a private apocalypse.

"Come on," Nirav says. He rises to his feet and reaches out one hand. "It's time to go inside. Long days ahead."

A day longer than this one? Nirav helps her to her feet, and holds her around the waist as they walk up the driveway, a sharp pang through her belly as they cross Sunil's empty parking spot. They are halfway to the house, when she realizes it is no longer her home. If the house is anything now, it is a keepsake box robbed of treasure, a music box without a song, a shell that forgot the sound of the ocean. Without Sunil to give it a warm, beating heart, what was once home has now become nothing more than a painful memory of what home used to be.

When she finally makes it to bed, still dressed in her clothes, Kavita cocoons the duvet around her, and gives her body of stone to the mattress. A black lake of exhaustion seals itself around her. At last, she closes her aching eyes to this awful day, expecting that when she opens them again, she will be greeted by the white glow of the hereafter, and Sunil's beautiful face.

2.

HELL ISN'T FIRE. It's waiting. It's the ticking of a clock. An incessant metronome that lasts for ten days. Every dash of sound, a measurement, like a step, that marks the distance between the last time you saw your loved one and wherever they are now.

Ten days of rationalizing where he might be. Of searching those places and not finding him. Of calling the police station for updates and getting nothing. Of calling everyone he knows but no one knows where he is. Of pacing. Of having hope, losing it, and then gathering up what's left, like a barrier of sand that gets smaller and smaller every time you give into your subterranean fears and wash it away a little more with your private weeping. Of telling yourself stories to keep your loved one alive, the stories, a tattered safety net that loosely holds what remains of your sanity. Of watching your mother cry. Of praying.

On and on it goes, that broken highway line of time and sound, until the moment the ticking abruptly stops. Which coincides with the moment you realize you were wrong about the meaning of hell. That there is a hell worse than waiting.

And that hell is occupied by people like you, the wretched, whom have nothing left to wait for.

3.

THE NEXT MORNING, Kavita wakes in bed with a sharp throb needling the right side of her head. With slow blinks she clears away the cobwebs of sleep. Her eyes feel bulbous, as though reacting to an antigen. For an insular moment, she wonders why.

Then all at once, she remembers.

Sunil.

A rush of grief pins her down, heavy and fast. She hides her face with her hands, ashamed.

Sometime later, she resurfaces. Fills and empties her lungs slowly. Opens her repentant eyes. As she rubs the wet sleep away, she tries to summon up her dreams, but her memory is opaque. She went to bed wishing for dreams of him. She wanted to see his body move and hear his deep voice and touch him. She wanted to know: Was he okay?

Instead, she dreamed the same dream as she had since his disappearance. A dream full of motion but getting nowhere, like the futility of running on a treadmill. Always running, running, running through lifeless suburban streets she does not recognize, under the glare of an aggressive sun. Always panting, panting, panting in tandem with her heavy-heeled footsteps. Always searching for Sunil but never finding him.

But he has been found.

He is lying on a morgue slab somewhere in Montréal, with a coroner who is cutting and probing his decayed remains, identifying his body using dental records, and determining the cause of his death. Still, she dreamed of searching as if at some level she couldn't quite accept that it was time to stop. Perhaps her mind had gotten used to the way she and her parents had kept Sunil alive in their fictions. Hope is hard thing to give up.

Guilt pulls at her insides, as though an anchor hooked to her soul. She has never been so aware of gravity, never so dragged by an emotion.

"I'm sorry," she whispers to him. "I'm so sorry, my Bear."

Turning to look at the empty space beside her, she wonders where her husband is. Last night, she dropped into such a sleep, such a coma of exhaustion, she had not felt him leave the bed that morning.

Just then, she hears noise coming from the kitchen, the distant sound of muffled voices. She wants to stay in bed. Close her eyes and sleep, maybe forever. But there's work to do.

She finds her parents and Nirav sitting around the table in silence. Cups of ginger tea and barely nibbled toast in front of them. Balls of crumpled tissues scattered beside their plates like sad paper flowers.

"Morning," she says as she takes a seat beside Nirav. She stares at Sunil's empty chair across from her, the titanic vacancy in their lives now. Her breath hitches for a moment. She tries to untangle her expression.

"Fancy a brew, love?" asks Nirav.

"Please."

While he busies himself with the tea, she inspects her parents' faces. Have they lost weight while sleeping?

"Here we are." Nirav places a steaming cup in front of her. "A cuppa me best brew, strong and sweet, just the way you likes it, love," he says in the Cockney accent he uses when trying to coax a laugh out of her.

For his sake, she forces a smile, then wraps her hands around her sunflower-yellow mug Sunil gave her for her twenty-fifth birthday last year. In her mind, she hears his deep voice: *I saw the colour and thought of you. Yellow like sunshine.* Suddenly she has no taste for tea.

Although no one has voiced it yet, she knows they must be thinking it.

"We need to tell people," she says. "While we wait for the death certificate, we need to start making plans."

"I still can't believe it," her father says. "How can we tell people what doesn't seem real?"

"I don't know." A beat. "But we have to."

"He was supposed to scatter my ashes, not the other way around," says her mother. "What parent ever thinks about planning their child's funeral?"

"I know, Mom. I'm sorry. I can make the calls. Should I start with the temple?"

Her mother stares at the table, blank.

"Mom?"

"Back in India, a *pandit* once told me that people who take their lives are sent to the lowest level of hell. In their next lives, they have a lowly birth."

"It isn't true, Mom. You can't think of that now. It doesn't help."

"No *pandit*," her mother mutters. "And if we have to tell them something, we will say that he died in a car accident."

"But that isn't what happened."

"It's what we will tell them."

"But Mom—"

"It's nobody's business."

"If Sunil died of cancer we wouldn't be hiding it."

"No one judges people who die of cancer."

"People will understand."

"How do you know?"

Kavita pauses, briefly. "I guess I don't."

Her mother arches her eyebrows as if to say, *exactly*.

"What difference does it make what we tell them?" her

father interjects. "It won't bring back my boy." He holds his forehead. "My baby...."

Staring across the table, Kavita watches her parents, their slumped bodies and pained faces, aware of the broken pieces floating inside them, tearing at them with jagged edges, because her body holds the same broken pieces, too. "I'm sorry," she says. "I didn't mean to upset you." Leaning back on her chair, she rubs a line up and down her forehead, wishing for insight. "Whatever you want, that's what we'll do." It is her job to get them through this ordeal without causing any more harm than has been caused already.

"A private cremation," her mother continues as she dabs her cheeks. "The next day, we will have a memorial here. We will bring my *beta* home." Her chin quivers, uncontrollably. "He has been away from us for too long already." Her mother clamps her eyes shut, as she slowly shakes her head from side to side, in disbelief of their reality, and of the plans she has been forced to make, tear after tear dropping into her lap without a sound.

Kavita has witnessed her mother cry many times in the last ten days, and it is awful every time, but at least during the days of Sunil's disappearance, there was always hope to stop them. Now there is nothing but this awful reality to face. There is nothing but her mother's tears and the bleak knowledge that Kavita will never be able to make what has gone terribly wrong, right again. Helplessly, she tells them, "It's all right. Everything's going to be all right." But of course, it won't.

After compiling a list of people Kavita will have to call, her mother goes to lie down and her father goes to sit in the backyard, as though with Sunil's death the last stitch holding them together has snapped and at last they are free to fall away from each other. But Kavita can't think about her parents' failing marriage now. There's still too much work to do.

She scans her list again. Writes a note reminding herself to call the police inspector to find out when Sunil's body will be transported to Ottawa. Scribbles another reminder about calling her office to arrange bereavement leave for the rest of the week. After that, she will use up her sick days and unused vacation, which should buy her another month. Once that runs out, she will have to reassess. *What else?* she thinks. What does she know about funeral planning? Frustrated, she pushes the list away and decides to check on Nirav. She finds him in her bedroom, already dressed in work clothes, packing up his things.

"What's going on?" she asks.

"I'm going to work."

"I could use your help today. There are a lot of calls to make."

"I don't even know a quarter of the people on that list."

"Well, remember to call your family, okay?"

"What shall I tell them?"

"Please don't be like that, Niru."

"She's acting like she's ashamed."

"It isn't about shame. She just wants to keep him safe. You heard her story about that horrible *pandit*."

"Everyone's always saying we need to speak up about these sorts of things, isn't it?"

"Well, it's easy to be brave in a commercial." Real life was riskier. Real people, harder to predict. Not everyone was worthy of the personal truths entrusted to them. Whom you told was as important as telling.

Nirav slings his backpack over one shoulder and marches for the door.

"Niru?"

"I'll call you later."

Kavita slumps on the edge of the bed, too exhausted to convince her husband of why he should stay.

Kavita has always been a terrible actor. But if she hopes to make it through the long list of phone calls in front of her, she is going to need lines. Seated at her desk, she considers the two scripts scribbled on the notepad in front of her: the fiction and the truth.

First, she practices the fiction.

"I'm sorry to call you with bad news," she recites to her imaginary listener. "It's about Sunil. He passed away unexpectedly. It was a car accident. We're having a memorial soon. I'll have to get back to you with the date and time. Yes, of course, I'll tell them."

She blinks at her notes, equally unsatisfied with her material as with her performance. She clears her throat. Next, the truth.

"I'm sorry to call you with bad news. It's about Sunil." Her heart beats in her throat. "He passed away unexpectedly. He was very sick. He succumbed to his illness." But even this is only a partial truth. The whole truth is something she has voiced inside her head but has yet to say out loud. A steep drop plunges between the partial and whole truth—a freefall. Where is the bottom of this grief? Will her body bounce when she slams against it? Or will she just keep falling, and falling?

"He killed himself," she says, numb. It is the whole truth that sounds like fiction to her ears. It is the whole truth that is too unfathomable to be real. Kavita tears the scripts away from the notepad and squelches the stories in her fist.

Without thinking, she picks up her cell and dials her best friend, Chi. Back in grade nine, Chi had a crush on Sunil. Her nickname for him was Hot Chocolate, HC for short, not that she ever had the nerve to say it to his face.

Kavita bites her lower lip as she listens to the ring, three times.

"Kavs!" Chi booms at last. "She lives!"

"Hi, Chi," Kavita mumbles. She's unprepared for her friend's cheerfulness, as if suddenly remembering there is another world, intact, even joyful, which exists on the other end of the line. "Sorry it's been a while."

"I've been swamped, too. I don't have long to chat, though. Just on a smoke break before heading back to the clinic." Chi promised to quit smoking after her residency in emergency medicine.

"I can call you back later."

"You sound out of it. What's up?"

Kavita takes a bracing breath. Clenches her left fist. Stares at the crumpled script on her desk, wishing she hadn't crumpled it. "I don't know how to tell you this."

"Tell me what?"

She hoods her eyes. "It's about Sunil."

"Has HC gotten himself into trouble? He better not be engaged!"

Engaged, Kavita thinks. Something else he'll never do. The realization slams into her like a sandbag swinging on a rope. Kavita sees him dressed in wedding finery, taking the seven steps around the sacred fire with an unknown woman, promising the commitment of seven lifetimes. *Seven.* "Oh, Chi," she whimpers. Her heart pounds thickly in her ears. "He's gone."

"What do you mean?"

"He's gone," Kavita hears herself repeating.

"You mean he's missing?"

"No, not anymore."

"He *was* missing?"

"Yes," she says. "But not anymore."

"Kavita, I don't understand. If he's not missing anymore, then how can he be gone?"

"He's...he died." The words take everything Kavita has— blood, air, bones. She feels as if she might collapse into a sack of skin on her bedroom floor.

"Oh my God," Chi says, horrified. "What happened?"

As she stands at the precipice of the truth she has yet to voice, Kavita feels herself sway, her body preparing to surrender to the freefall. She swallows, saliva thick in her throat. There is no other way to tell Chi but plainly. "He was having a tough time, recently." Key moments of regret flash inside Kavita's head. "Things didn't go the way they were supposed to. He...."

She trails off. Even now, she can't bring herself to say it. "He's gone, Chi. He's just gone."

The silence stretches on long enough for Kavita to start wondering if her call has been dropped. Then, in the background, she hears the distant chatter of passers-by, the horn of a car, Chi pulling a drag and exhaling deeply.

"Chi?" she says, unable to bear the nothingness any longer. "Please, say something." *Please reach back.*

"A guy I went to school with in first year killed himself," Chi mutters, emotionless. "A janitor found him in one of the labs. It was right before an exam. One more bad grade and he was going to get kicked out of the program, or at least that's what he was afraid of. The pressure got to him, I guess. Classes were cancelled for a day. They brought in counsellors. All I could think was, sure we all want to be doctors, but it's not worth dying for. Nothing's that important."

"Well, it was different for Sunil."

Kavita waits, hopeful Chi might practice some of the bedside manner she has been honing. Instead, all Kavita hears is another puff of cigarette smoke. Suddenly she wants nothing more than to get off the phone. She feels so naked, waiting there for a morsel of kindness. "We're going to have a memorial soon. Will you come?" The way the conversation has gone, she can't be sure.

"I'll try."

"Thank you, Chi. Sunil always—"

"Listen, I hate to do this, but I've got to go."

"Okay. Sure."

Kavita listens to the nasal drone of the dial tone while she tries to figure out what just happened. She is learning people in crisis behave like exaggerated versions of themselves. Nirav is more reticent. Her parents are more divided. And Chi is more Chi.

Letting out a deep breath, she tells herself: *Shake it off.* There's work to do. Next, she calls Sunil's office.

"Hello, Patty speaking."

Was it Patty that Sunil said was the horrible HR gossip? "My name's Kavita Gupta. I'm Sunil's sister. I'm not sure if you're the one we met the other day?"

"When Sunil stopped by to fill out forms? No, unfortunately I was off sick that day. But Cathy told me about Sunil when I got back."

I'm sure she did, Kavita thinks.

"How's he feeling? You'll have to tell him we didn't win the lottery. Not even a free ticket since he's been away. He's our good luck charm."

"Actually, he's my reason for calling."

"Oh?"

Kavita hesitates. "He was very sick. He succumbed to his illness. He died of...." She is that far along in her head when she realizes she hasn't spoken yet.

"Hello?"

"A car accident," Kavita says, wooden. "He passed away unexpectedly. In a car accident."

Patty doesn't know what to say. She asks Kavita to please pass on her condolences. Kavita says of course she will. But there's more, Patty goes on: paperwork needs to be filled out by the executor of Sunil's estate. (Kavita.) He had a life insurance policy. There's a section that will have to be filled out by his doctor. As Patty prattles on about forms, Kavita wonders if Dr. Jones already knows about Sunil's death. Did the police tell him? And before that, did he ever wonder what might have happened to his distressed patient when Sunil didn't show up to his follow-up appointments with the social worker and psychiatrist?

Kavita tunes back into the conversation she is supposed to be having with the woman from HR. Patty is sorry about all the paperwork. It can be exhausting. One last thing, about the life insurance: Kavita is the beneficiary. Did she know?

No, Kavita replies, cold. She didn't know. The thought of

benefitting from their tragedy sickens her. Money has no value. It can't resurrect, or change the past, or answer the phone, or laugh until it hurts. If an insurance company is going to give her money, all it will ever do is remind Kavita of what she has lost, and more significantly, of what Sunil has lost because of her. Perhaps that is the money's true purpose.

Kavita feels a familiar weight, an unyielding downward pull, as she did when she first opened her eyes to this awful day. *Like an anchor*, she thinks.

"Kavita?"

She wonders if her brother named his torment, the way she has named hers. Or did he make the mistake of calling it Sunil?

"Hello?"

I don't want money.

"Are you still there?"

I want Sunil.

"Did she hang up?"

SunilSunilSunil….

Digging her nails deeply into her palm, Kavita focuses on the sharp pain, the captive heat burning in her flesh that won't know the release of broken skin. This pain she can handle. This pain she knows she deserves.

"I'll get the forms to you as soon as I can."

There is still so much to do. But Kavita can't think straight. A short break, she promises, as though a grief foreman is keeping time. She paces the room while kneading a knot in her lower back. Listening to Chi smoke over the phone has wakened a latent desire in her. She has been craving a menthol ever since. No, a whole pack. She quit smoking when she started dating Nirav, but he won't be home for hours. She will buy some gum, too.

Kavita pulls on a pair of jeans and a hoodie, and grabs Sunil's *rakhi* from her nightstand, stuffing it into her pocket. On her way out, she checks in on her mother. Her bedroom is dim. Kavita hears soft snoring. Grateful, she gingerly closes the door.

Outside, she finds her father sitting on a patio chair, staring at the hedge with a meditative gaze, his plastic chair a step beyond the umbrella's circle of shade. How odd it is to see him sitting in daylight, and darkness, at the same time.

"Hi, Dad."

"Hm?" her father says, drawing himself out from whatever inward place he has been.

"What are you doing out here?"

He blinks. "What is there to do?"

She presses her lips together. "I'm going out for a bit. Can I borrow the station wagon?" As she waits, she feels about seventeen years old. That was the year Sunil had taught her how to drive in the Zellers parking lot. That summer, she drove the family all the way to Wasaga Beach for their yearly vacation, with Sunil in the front seat, easing her through every highway merge and lane change, while their parents sat nervously in the backseat. There was nothing to worry about, he reassured them. A twinge to think of his confidence in her.

Her father turns away, resuming his yogic watch of the hedge.

"Did you want me to pick up anything? Maybe some of the cereal you like? Or those muffins with the...." Kavita stops. She knows she is talking to herself. "Okay then." She backs away. "I won't be long."

She waves him goodbye, not that he sees.

Menthols and gum on the dashboard, she drives. Half an hour later, she pulls into the marina parking lot. Turns off the ignition. Sits with her hands in her lap and looks around. On the green she sees a woman stretched out on a blanket, reading. A man playing tag with a toddler. A couple of guys tossing a football back and forth.

Now that she is there, having a smoke seems trivial. She senses something else has brought her to the marina. Could it be Sunil? Maybe there is an answer tucked under a pebble that can make sense of all the senselessness surrounding her now.

Squinting against the light of midday, she turns to face the harbour. A few sails are on the water. In the distance, she sees the lighthouse. Its magnetic pull moves her forward.

The breeze carries with it the fetid water of the river, thick today with the scent of earthworms. As she walks along the pier, her memories overlay the surroundings like an acetate transparency. She sees the old man fishing, the young family of four feeding fries to seagulls, the woman reading. Her feet move her no farther.

"We had fun, didn't we?" she asks Sunil. "There was at least something good about the last day we spent together, right?" She waits for a reply. Hears the squawk of seagulls. Grows impatient with his silence. "You could at least send me a sign, like, if a seagull shits on me, that mean 'no.' That sort of thing." The seagulls squawk and squawk. "Come on, Bear," she pleads, weakly. "Haunt me a little. I promise not to faint."

She starts walking again. At the lighthouse, she stands on the pebbled shore, watching as she and Sunil skip stones while nestled in an easy silence. She stuffs her hands into her pockets. Feels the smooth thread of the *rakhi,* and winces, as though it has transformed from an object of protection into an object of punishment. She drops her gaze to the rocks.

"I see everything so clearly now." She squeezes the *rakhi* tighter, wishing the barbs she imagines were real. "Can you forgive me?"

She holds her breath for a sign: a gust of wind, a rainbow, a thunderbolt. She would even settle for a milky splat of bird shit on the top of her head. Anything.

"Please, Sunil."

Anything at all.

"Please."

But he doesn't come to her.

Anchor pulls at her insides.

You know why he won't speak to you, it says in a flat, unwavering tone. *He blames you. You know this. You agree with him.*

I just—

You deserve this....

You deserve worse.

Kavita drops to her knees, the way she had yesterday, after the police left them with their fresh grief. The rocks beneath her shins hurt. She welcomes the hurt. She knows the hurt is all she deserves.

After a little while, she notices a dark blue stone to the right of her knees. Weathered smooth and oval, a natural worry stone. She picks up the striking pebble, and without thinking, starts rubbing it with her thumb.

"Dark blue," she mutters. Like the meaning of Sunil's name. She clutches the stone to her chest.

He might've touched this one. Her heart beats quicker with the thought.

Yes, she tells herself.

He did.

He touched this one.

She caresses the stone with reverence, pressing it to her lips, as if it still carries the memory of her brother's hand.

As she rises to her feet, she drops the stone into her pocket, where it slides next to the crimson thread.

4.

A WEEK AND A HALF LATER, Sunil's remains are transported from Montréal to Ottawa. In the meantime, Kavita met with a funeral director who guided her through the business of death with the gentle care of a grief counsellor. While he didn't know the circumstances of Sunil's death, he knew it was unusual enough to involve the police and coroner's office one province over, and was courteous enough not to pressure Kavita into elaborating any further. Most importantly, he knew how to handle bodies that had been found several days after the spirit had passed on. When Kavita asked if they could see Sunil's body once he was returned, the portly man told her, "In cases like these, the coffin is nailed shut." Until then, it hadn't occurred to Kavita how decomposed Sunil's body would have been by then. She had been so focused on getting her brother back, she hadn't stopped to consider that what she got back wouldn't resemble any brother she had ever known. For a few moments, as she sat stunned in the funeral director's office, she wondered what Sunil might look like now, then pushed the gruesome image out of her mind. Kavita decided then she wanted to remember Sunil as he was, full and unblemished. That was the image she would project into the nailed coffin.

"The coroner's office sent a bag of his clothes," the funeral director continued, shaking his head, "but I don't think you'll be able to save them. Perhaps the shoes?" The shoes. Which ones had he been wearing that day? The Nikes. His favourite pair of sneakers. The ones he used on their night runs. The ones that made no sound as he snuck out the door. No, she instructed, dispose it all.

Next, he handed her a large envelope heavy with death certificates. According to the thick-bond, official-looking document, her brother was dead. Because everything about his dying had happened beyond her view, and compounded by the fact she would never see his body, the proclamation seemed unreal. If Sunil had died an old man—as he was supposed to have died—there would have been a body for her to cleanse and honour according to the last rites. But there was no chance of that happening now.

On the certificate, no cause of death was listed, yet. The police had informed her the backlog for toxicology reports was about a year, if not more. If Sunil had died an old man— as he was supposed to have died—there would have been a cause of death listed on the certificate now. Something like, pneumonia or cardiac arrest or achingly-beautiful old age. Something natural.

There was no obituary in the paper. No memorial Facebook page. No announcement on the funeral home website with a section for family and friends to write messages of condolence. Their grief was silence, overwritten with fiction.

As they enter the stone building, the funeral director is waiting for them in the front lobby, dressed in a dark suit and tie. His wisps of grey hair are smoothed over his speckled rose scalp. His neck bulges over his collar.

He welcomes them with a slight bow and a thin smile. There is an enigmatic look in his eyes, some mysterious combination of pity and perplexity. He leads them through a set of French doors. The chapel is large, with high ceilings and maroon carpeting. Rows of wooden benches line the aisle, and at the end, rests a mahogany casket.

At first sight of it, Kavita's legs feel boneless. She gropes for Nirav's arm. They are told to take as long as they wish before the funeral director shuts them inside the dreadful room. If there is a moment when Kavita's heart breaks irreparably, it is then, as she witnesses her parents break right before her eyes.

Her mother runs her hands along the casket in a stupor, as though trying to see Sunil's body through the wood grain. At his feet, she pauses. Slowly drapes herself over the casket. Kisses his feet in an act of prostration, supplication. Her weeping echoes against the vaulted ceiling, echoes inside Kavita's hollow middle, the awful sound spreading cracks along her veins. Her skin is the only thing keeping her together.

Her father delicately lays flowers on the coffin lid above Sunil's heart, places one hand over his head, and gently strokes the mahogany, as though stroking Sunil's brow, like he did on the nights Sunil had trouble sleeping when he was a child. His shoulders begin to shake. "My baby," he whispers. "My boy."

There is cruelty in having Sunil back, less then a foot beneath their aching palms, and yet still so far away. If only they could see him, touch him. But the coffin shows them concretely what they have known abstractly for days. There is a barrier between them now, and there is only one way to cross it.

Oh Sunil, Kavita whispers as the first tears crest. *What have you done to yourself? My poor Bear. Look what you've done to yourself.*

Into the coffin, she sends a stream of regret. *You'll never marry the woman of your dreams. Or have children. Or teach them to skip stones. You'll never meet your nieces and nephews. Or hear them call you Sunil mama. And they'll never know their uncle….*

She stops. The coffin is too small to contain all the dreams that should have been, had he lived.

She imagines the moments after her death. Sees herself as an old woman—grey-haired, round, wrinkled—dressed in an ivory sari, surrounded by the white glow of the hereafter. A few steps away stands Sunil, young and beaming. As young as the day he died. She steps toward him. Cups her frail hands around his luminous face. Gazes deeply into his coffee-coloured eyes for an age. Wraps her arms around his broad shoulders. Pulls him close, and even closer still. Leans into the warmth of his body. "Life was the dream," she tells him. "Life was the dream."

She stands numbly for a while, until her parents' weeping has risen and fallen like ragged peaks, and Nirav holds her waist, telling her it is time to go.

Do they have to? They've only just gotten Sunil back. She doesn't want to leave him there in the unfamiliar place, with the hidden closet of fire. She doesn't want to leave him at all. Stop, she wants to cry. But since the nightmare first began, she hasn't been able to stop any of it.

At the French doors, Kavita pauses, glancing backward at the casket, knowing the next time she sees her brother, he will have changed again, in some unfathomable way she is not, and never will be, prepared to witness.

By dusk, it is time to collect the ashes. Kavita drives herself and Nirav to the chapel. When they arrive, the funeral director is waiting for them in the lobby with Sunil's urn.

As she takes hold of it, she is shocked by its lightness, and especially its warmth, the memory of fire still clinging to his remains. How can all six feet of him—all his breath and bones and beauty—be reduced to the ashes held inside the comparatively tiny urn? If she holds her ear to it, will she hear his big laugh trapped in there, like the ocean inside a shell?

They return home to find Kavita's mother waiting for them at the top of the stairs, reaching out with beggars' hands. Wordlessly, Kavita gives her what is left of Sunil. Her mother clutches the urn to her chest as she rushes to her bedroom. From the doorway, Kavita watches as she walls the vessel in with pillows, as though it is a slumbering infant in danger of rolling off the mattress, something she must have done countless times when Sunil was a baby.

"*Soja, mera beta*," her mother coos, as she strokes the balmy metal. "You're safe now. You're home. Sleep. Sleep."

Steeped in shadows, Kavita stands by the front window and gazes out onto the street dotted with tangerine light, while sipping ginger tea from her yellow mug.

The others have gone to bed. She tried to sleep too but her thoughts, loud and agitated, flit like a swarm of birds reacting to danger. Her mind keeps going places it shouldn't, wanting to know the things only Sunil can know for sure.

A small, still voice inside her warns her to stop. There are places in the mind that are unwise to travel, just as certain parts of the world. But she can't stop the flood of unknowns, or the hounding need to answer them. Stopping them would be like trying to dam a river with a net.

So, she surrenders to the flood. When was the precise moment Sunil died? Was it on the first night, when her pulsing gaze rarely left the street, as every part of her being focused on willing him home? Could it have been that soon? They waited for nine more days after that first night. Could he really have been gone while they prayed and searched and filled his voicemail with pleas?

When did he decide on the ski lodge? Had he chosen it weeks earlier? Had he been there before? Or had he simply driven past it and thought: *Good enough*.

Where did he buy the sleeping pills? At the Shoppers Drugmart a few blocks away, where they buy eco-friendly toilet paper and toothpaste and milk—life items? Did he visit more than one? How many boxes of pills did he buy? How many did he swallow?

What about the vodka? Sober Sunil buying vodka. Words that are too incongruous to make sense, like "Sunil killed himself." What kind was it? Smirnoff? Polar Ice? Did he splurge on something expensive, the way people toast special occasions with Champagne? Or did he see a cheap bottle of gut-thinner and think: *Good enough*.

Who was the last person to see him alive? A man or a woman? Old or young? Were they bored? Or—her chest tightens—were they rude? She prays they were kind. If they were kind, did it make him pause, and reconsider his plan? If they were awful, did it reinforce his resolve that the world was better off without him, and he was better off without the world?

Did he have any doubts during the long drive to the ski lodge? Did he think of turning back? Did he check his phone? Did he ever see *50 missed calls* reach for him with electric glare? Did he listen to the voicemails, their pleas, especially the last one that got cut short: "Hi, Bear. Just me aga—"

Her thoughts creep to the inside of his car, the inside of his mind during his last moments. She needs to know what he saw, what he felt, what he thought as he left the world. Was he scared to die alone? Was he relieved? The detective said they found the driver's chair reclined. Did he simply close his eyes and wait for poisonous sleep? Or did he lean his chair back, slip into a moonbeam, and star gaze one last time?

Did he listen to the radio? If so, what station? What CD? Or did he prefer the sounds of the night? Crickets chirp louder in the country, and stars shine brighter.

As tears slip down Kavita's cheeks, she wonders if he cried too before the end. If he mourned all the things he was about to leave. If he thought of her and their parents and Nirav as his eyes closed for the last time. If he missed them when he did.

Did he care about strangers finding him? Or was that part of the plan too? Was that why he drove so far from home, so they would be spared the sight of his destruction?

What about the man who found him, the ski lodge manager? And later, the police and paramedics. Who were they? What did they look like? What did their faces look like when they found him? What did they say? Did they handle him with care?

Did he really think they could live without him? Did he really misunderstand his importance so entirely?

Could death's quiet embrace really have been more comforting than the loving arms of their family?

Just then, a sky-blue car rolls by the window. Her neck jerks to follow its path.

A blue car.

Like Sunil's.

She dwells inside a second of pearlescent hope.

The yellow mug slips from her weak hands. She only glances at the broken pieces for a second, barely feels the warm wetness on her feet. She lifts her urgent gaze and finds the blue car again. It slows down as it approaches the stop sign on the corner.

Her reason catches up. A sky-blue car, yes. Sunil's sky-blue car, no. She remembers that the time for searching is over. The car disappears around the corner. When you lose your person, you never stop searching for them.

Kavita stares at the scattered shards and her naked feet soaked with sweet tea in a state of belated devastation. Squatting, she numbly gathers up the broken pieces of the last gift Sunil will ever give her.

5.

O N THE MORNING OF THE MEMORIAL, Chi texts, saying that something has come up and she won't be able to make it after all.

Sorry, Kavs. xo

The sorrier thing is that Kavita isn't entirely surprised.

Mourners start arriving around eleven o'clock. Along with condolences, most bring flowers and cards, although a few offer practical gifts of casseroles and soup.

Her parents sit on the couch in a half-comatose state to receive visitors, the way unconscious patients might from hospital beds. Kavita notices that they sit closer together than they would have in the absence of company.

The afternoon trudges on. She and Nirav tend to the guests. They weave in and out of conversations, freshen cups of tea, clear plates, offer consolation. Whenever someone asks how she's doing, she replies, "Fine, thank you," when all she wants to do is howl and howl.

Each time she recites the fiction about the car accident, she feels a bit thinner, as though deception is slowly corroding her. She finds herself having to answer an assault of questions she hasn't prepared for. Where did it happen? Was the other driver at fault? Did the other driver survive? Was alcohol involved? Were they thinking of pressing charges? Why wasn't there an obituary in the paper? A report on the news?

Somehow she fumbles through with short replies. It happened on his way to work. He collided with oncoming traffic while taking a left-hand turn. The other driver suffered minor injuries. Sunil died in the ambulance on the way to hospital. No, they weren't pressing charges. Everything happened so fast, they didn't think of an obituary.

"How tragic," says her neighbour, Janet. She is a short woman with a figure like a potbellied stove, a globe of permed chestnut locks, and pale grey eyes. She wears black, and in her hand, clutches a silver rosary. When they were younger, Janet occasionally babysat Sunil and Kavita after school. "The Lord giveth and the Lord taketh away," she proclaims, as she rubs her rosary beads.

Kavita strains for calm. She knows a sermon is on its way. Back when Janet used to babysit them, she once made Kavita stand in the corner of her living room with her nose to the wall for ten minutes for the highly punishable offense of muttering "Oh my God."

"He always takes the good ones young," Janet continues. "And who are we to question? After all, everything happens for a reason. And He never gives us more than we can handle. I know you miss your brother, dear, but don't weep for him. He's in a better place now."

Janet grabs Kavita's hand, closes her eyes, and mouths a soundless prayer. As Kavita watches the woman's lips move, ecstatic with liturgy, fibrillations flick under her skin in waves, hot and fizzy. Janet finishes with an audible "Amen," then kisses her rosary and opens her eyes, beaming.

"Thank you," says Kavita, flat on the outside, seething underneath. Pulling her hand away, she excuses herself.

Other mourners impart their grief wisdom upon her, words she knows are meant to comfort but instead stoke her anger like hot breath. When she can't tolerate any more, she slips out the back door, leans against the side of the house, and lights a cigarette. If one more person tells her "everything happens for a reason," she might have to kick every last one of them out of her house.

She pulls a deep drag. Her thoughts drift back to Janet, her words about God's faithfulness, God's plan, God never giving a person more than they can handle. How can she reconcile her brother's suicide with any of that?

Anger rises, hot and fast, like a line fire up her spine. No, not anger: rage. Like a blaze. She exhales smoke. It needs some direction, this inner fire, someplace to go, beyond her fleshy carapace. Somehow it needs to be released, before she is forced to go back inside, and get filled up again.

Without another thought, she flips the direction of the cigarette, opens her left hand, and presses the fiery end into the centre of her palm. It burns, sears, singes. She cloaks her eyes. Focuses on the pain, the sharp rise and taper like a bell curve. This pain she can manage. This pain she knows she deserves. Then she opens her eyes. Glances at the fresh scar with little interest. For now, the Blaze has been subdued.

Nirav will be wondering where she is. She stamps out the cigarette, kicks the butt into the cedars, and tucks her hand into the sleeve of her cardigan.

The last of the mourners finally depart a few hours later. Almost instantly, her parents disappear into their bedrooms; her mother, with Sunil's ashes tucked under her arm. Nirav helps with the clean-up, then goes downstairs to play video games.

Kavita flops on the couch, relishing the blessed solitude, and at last gives in to little weights that seem swept along her lashes. When she opens her eyes again, it is as dark in the living room as it is outside. She checks the time on her cell. Unbelievably, it tells her it's after seven.

She rubs at an ache in her neck, remembering the Band-Aid on her palm with a sharp wince. As she cradles her hand, she looks around the room lazily. Bouquets cover nearly every table surface in the living and dining rooms. The abundance of blooms is an unusual sight for their household. Sunil was allergic to flowers. Her mother, too. Her father would rather plant marigolds in the garden than pluck their lifeforce from the earth. The flowers, however well-meant, are clearly out of place in their home. Almost to the point of obscenity.

Kavita rises to her feet and fetches a garage bag from the kitchen. Something must be done about them. No one will mind, she tells herself. She hasn't even seen her parents stop to admire them. Probably because the flowers bother them as much as they do her. They will probably thank her for getting rid of them.

Looming over the dining table, she takes a passive inventory of the assortment of roses and lilies, Gerber daisies, and sun-flowers. She knows the flowers are supposed to make them feel better. Remind them that people care. That they are thought of in their time of hardship. But all they do is remind Kavita that Sunil is dead. Isn't that why the flowers are really there? Because her bother is gone. Well, she knows that already. And she doesn't need to be reminded by things that are so shamelessly joyful.

With a snap of her wrist, the garbage bag billows. Kavita reaches for the arrangement closest to her. It is an extravagant bouquet of Calla lilies sent from her co-workers. She drops them into the bag without sentiment. Next, she grabs the or-ange Gerber Daisies sent from Chi. Followed by the sunflowers from her in-laws in London. Then an assortment of carnations. A basket of lettuces and purple cabbage. An arrangement of chocolate-dipped fruit.

Kavita stops noticing what they are, as she tosses them into the bag, one after another, until the table is clear. The one thing she spares is the basket of sympathy cards, filled with sentiments too visceral to read, in case her parents may want to someday, although she doubts they ever will.

Once she declutters the side and coffee tables as well, Kavita pauses, taking note of the weight of the garbage bag, and its inverse relationship with the light feeling that has befallen her.

This is the most therapeutic thing she has done all day. The closest she has come to anything resembling closure.

She ties a knot in the garbage bag, hauls it to the garage, and stuffs it into the large black bin. Then she wheels the bin to the curb. In the morning, the flowers will be gone for good.

Back inside, Kavita locks the side door, rests her weary head against it, and whispers, "It's done."

PART II: CRAWL

A single person is missing for you, and the whole world is empty.
> —Joan Didion, *The Year of Magical Thinking*

6.

THE WEEK FOLLOWING Sunil's memorial, Kavita does little more than sleep. Occasionally, she wakes to check in on her parents or use the washroom or mindlessly eat a banana over the kitchen sink. Every other day or so, she somehow finds enough energy to shower and change into a fresh pair of pyjamas. Other than that, she prefers to drift in unconsciousness. What she hopes for every time she closes her eyes are dreams of Sunil, a message that he is all right wherever he is. What she dreams she can't remember.

Sometimes she awakens startled, as if the house phone has rung or the alarm on her cell has beeped. Her heart flutters like a hummingbird in a cage. Her breath is rapid and shallow. Her gut blares like a warning beacon. Its message: Danger is imminent. Be warned, be ready. And her first waking thoughts: *Mom and Dad. Where are Mom and Dad?* When this happens, she rushes out of bed and checks each of their bedrooms. Once she sees that they are safe in their beds, the maniacal panic tapers, but not completely—a pool of it remains like a pesky sip of pop that lingers at the bottom of a bottle, fizzing. Then, drained of the little energy she has acquired in sleep, she stumbles back to bed and hides inside a tent of covers.

Her parents keep to the same unstructured sleep regime; her mother in particular, like a newborn, tires herself out with weeping until her swollen eyelids finally shut. Her father has taken to staring at things—walls, hedges—with the same purposeless focus of a housecat, often leaving Kavita to wonder when she catches him, not only what he is staring at, but why? Nirav spends most of the time playing video games in the basement.

After about a week of living like this, Kavita's back aches and she knows it is time to leave her bed, if only long enough for the aches to stop their incessant moaning.

It is mid-afternoon—according to the cell phone—Sunday. She dresses in a forgotten pair of sweats she finds in her closet, then hobbles a path to the kitchen, hopeful they have run out of bananas.

The fridge shelves are stocked with leftovers and gifts of food from the memorial. From the top shelf, she grabs a Ziploc bag full of samosas and a jar of tamarind sauce. She bites off the pointy tip of the samosa. Her mother's samosas are better, and this one is a little stale, but neither of these facts stops her from taking another bite.

Out of nowhere, Anchor pulls at her insides.

Eat up, you pig, it says, cool and clipped.

With effort, she pushes down a swallow, a ball of glue and sand that scratches along her throat. At least while she slept she was spared the company of her unwelcome guests. Part of her had dared to hope they had gathered up their torment and left. Anchor, at least, shows no signs of leaving her in peace, yet.

"Look at me, stuffing my face," she frowns, sickened by the pleasing taste in her mouth. Sunil always loved samosas. "Sorry, Bear." She holds one hand over her navel, half-expecting the bites she took to revolt from her gut. When, after a few moments, this doesn't happen, she throws the rest of the samosa in the trash can under the sink.

"Who are you talking to, love?" says a voice from behind.

She jumps, the way their cat, Coal, does whenever he's surprised by the vacuum cleaner, the blender, the hairdryer.

"Niru, you scared me. I didn't hear you come upstairs."

"No, I don't suppose you did." He glances around the kitchen. "I heard voices and came up. Thought perhaps your folks were finally out of bed."

She blinks at the brown linoleum. "No, it's just me."

"Right, well, hello there." He steps forward and kisses her longingly on the cheek. "It's good to see you out and about."

She grins a millimetre.

"It's been terribly lonely round this place. I haven't played video games for this many days straight since uni. It'll be good to go home and sleep in our bed though, ay? Coal misses you like mad. I've been popping round every day to feed him and play with him for a bit."

She sits at the table and stares numbly at Sunil's vacant chair. "I didn't know you went anywhere."

He takes a seat across from her. "You've been dead to the world. But never mind all that. The point is, now that the fray is over, we should be getting on with it, shouldn't we?"

She reaches across the table with big eyes. Emotions weren't his thing, he used to tell her. In the beginning, it was a quality she admired. No drama. Not like her parents. Of course, that was before she realized how lonely life could be as the entire right brain of a relationship.

"I know what you're thinking," he continues. "But they're adults, Kavita. They can look after themselves."

"It's still too soon. I need to be here."

"You worry too much."

"I can't explain it. But I have this awful feeling that something bad is going to happen. Something else is going to fall apart. I know it."

"What do you reckon's going to happen?"

"I don't know." She holds her elbows. "It's just a feeling of unbearable dread. Like every cell in my body's been fixed with an alarm and I'm just waiting for them to go off. But I don't know when. So I can't ease up. I can't get comfortable like last time. I won't let myself fall into another false sense of security. Who knows what my parents will be like once their exhaustion wears off and they have to actually face a day rather than sleep through it."

"You're just stressed out. You need to go out for a stroll. Get some sun."

She stares at him with her lips slightly parted. Blaze churns, slow and thick. So, it hasn't left either. She hides her hands underneath the table and presses her thumb into the cigarette burn on her left palm that is covered up with a manky Band-Aid. Focuses on the pain. The scar has healed while she's been asleep. She presses harder and waits for the release.

"What about work?" he asks her.

"I'm not ready yet." The government job she slags off from time-to-time has its benefits, and extended leave, given the circumstances of her bereavement, is one of them.

"Well, I don't think that's a good idea. The sooner we get back to our old lives, the better."

Her eyes soften with pity for Nirav. He doesn't realize there is no old life to go back to anymore.

"I wish you wouldn't rush me through this, Niru." She wishes he would talk to her about what has happened, what is happening, rather than distract away from it. "You won't talk to me about Sunil. You won't even mention his name."

He scowls at the floor. "That's perhaps for the best."

"You know you can—"

"No, Kavita, I can't. And you wouldn't want me to either." He stands up. "Right, well, I can't take it anymore. It's too sad here, Kavita. I'll stay one more night but then I'm moving back to the condo. Tomorrow, I'm going back to work."

He storms out of the kitchen, tumbling down the stairs with noisy steps, she assumes, to resume his video game marathon.

She blinks at a Sunil's empty chair, wishing he was sitting across from her, like he had during every family meal. *How do I do it?* she wants to ask him. *How do I split myself into pieces and please them all?*

She agonized about how to save her relationship only once

before, at the end of Nirav's one-year exchange in university, the summer he went back to London. Back then, she had no desire to split herself in two, she wanted to follow him across the ocean, whole and devoted, all of herself with all of him, always. Even though she was young, twenty-one at the time, she knew he was different than the soppy sucks she usually attracted, and the accomplished assholes that attracted her. He was worth crossing the cold Atlantic for, because even in those early days, she knew she had met the man she was going marry, for love, not obligation, like her parents.

They met in Microbiology lab, arguably the least romantic of locales with its pungent scents of agar and microbial cultures oppressing the air, vapours sweet and mouldy. She arrived late for class after getting lost in the unfamiliar and winding halls of the newly constructed Biology building. By the time she tiptoed into the room, red-faced and hunched, and took a seat at the nearest unoccupied bench, the other students had already paired up. She was in the process of accepting that she would have to figure out the labs on her own, when she heard an intriguingly-exotic English voice say to her, "Pardon me, but you wouldn't be in the market for a laboratory partner, would you?" He beamed at her with a toothy smile that crinkled the corners of his hazel eyes. "I'm Nirav," he said. She noted his Indian name along with his fair complexion. It wasn't until their first date, after midterms, that he told her about his mixed heritage, an experience he described as not white enough for the English and not brown enough for the Asians. She eyed him, sceptical. A charming accent wasn't going to earn them nineties. Still, she needed a partner. "I'm Kavita," she grinned, not knowing at the time that such a small choice would change the course of her life.

When they weren't in class or at the library, they explored the city together. She assumed the role of tour guide and took him to the usual places—Parliament Hill, the Byward Market, various museums that had free admission on Thursday evenings.

During Winterlude, when the canal froze, she lent him a pair of Sunil's skates and taught him how to skate. She found it irresistibly cute every time he exclaimed, "I can't believe I'm actually skating on a river!" While inwardly she corrected his misnomer—*canal* not river—outwardly she could only smile. They shared their first kiss after an evening skate, in the orange glow of a Beavertails stand, the taste of cinnamon and sugar on their lips.

That kiss started everything. Sweet and innocent and plump with new love. It made her think they were different than her parents, they understood each other. Now, as she senses the growing distance between them, as cold and choppy as the ocean that once kept them apart, she wonders if this is how it happens, how people turn away from each other, one time, then another, and another, until all that is left of love are unspoken words crushed inside throats, and silence.

7.

THE NEXT MORNING, Kavita wakes up to an empty bed, except for the laptop that is beside her in Nirav's place. She must have fallen asleep watching episodes of *Buffy the Vampire Slayer*, again.

She reasons that Nirav probably left for work early that morning, except she doesn't remember him kissing her goodbye, something he never fails to do, even when they are fighting. Then it occurs to her, like a weight in her stomach, that she doesn't remember Nirav coming to bed at all last night. Slowly, she rolls out of bed, her body heavy and sore, her mind still thick with the mists of sleep. On the way to the washroom, she peers inside her mother's half-open door. It takes a few seconds for her to register that she is staring at a vacant bed. The mists part instantly as she scours the rest of the room. Sunil's urn is missing from her mother's nightstand, too. The warning beacon in Kavita's gut blares. Danger is imminent. She knew it was coming, and here it is. *Danger, danger, danger.*

She rushes down the hallway. Her first instinct is to check the driveway for the station wagon. *Please be there, please be there,* with every step. She pulls back the curtains, her eyes, large and pulsing. She releases the breath she has been holding. The car is parked where it should be. But then, where is her mother?

She backtracks toward the bedrooms. Her father's door is still closed but she knows her mother won't be in his room anyway. The rest of the floor is empty. She rushes outside to check the front lawn, garage, and backyard in case by some miracle her mother has decided to get a little fresh air, but she isn't in any of these places. Back inside, Kavita hurries downstairs, but no one is watching TV in the family room, or napping in the guest room for a change of scenery, or doing laundry to keep busy.

There is only one place left to look.

Sunil's door is ajar. "Mom?" she calls out. "Are you in there?"

As she presses her fingertips into her sore palm, she doesn't think she can do it, enter his private space, see his things. But she's wasting time. She knows better than to waste time. What if her mother is...? She squeezes a tighter fist and approaches the darkened threshold.

She finds her mother crouched on the floor, dressed in her lavender robe, with her head resting at the foot of Sunil's bed. She has walled his urn between two couch cushions. One of her hands rests upon it. The other loosely grips some tissues.

Kavita gently touches her mother's shoulder.

Her mother wakes, startled. Glances at Kavita, dismissively, and then closes her eyes again.

"Sorry," she says, gently. "I didn't mean to scare you. What are you doing down here? Why are you on the floor?"

"I didn't want to disturb anything," her mother answers. "You can still see where his head rested on the pillow."

Kavita can only glimpse at the indentation for a second. "Come on, Mom." She holds her mother by the shoulders. "Let me help you up."

"Leave me."

"I'll fix you some tea. Or maybe you'd like some—"

"I said leave me!" her mother shouts. "I feel him here."

Kavita kneels, placing a light hand on her mother's back. "Come on, let me fix you something. You have to keep your strength up."

"What does it matter?" Her mother strokes the urn. "I've already lost the most precious thing in my life."

Kavita contracts, pulling her hand away, as though protecting herself. Her mother's words replay inside her head: *...already lost the most precious thing....*

As Kavita kneels there mutely, waiting for the bite to stop throbbing, a gloom rolls over her, black and heavy, like leaded fog. Then it speaks. *She thinks the wrong child got sick*, it tells her. Its voice is cold confidence, so sure, so even, that what it says must be true. *She thinks the wrong child died.*

The weight of the fog holds her within its cave of dark thought. Kavita sits motionless, almost breathless, for some time, afraid to consider whether the Black Gloom is right.

Eventually, her throat to loosens, and she tries again. "Please, let's go upstairs," she manages to say. "You'll feel better with some food in your stomach. Then maybe you can take a shower and we can go for a walk? What do you think?"

"Just go," her mother mumbles. "Leave me alone."

Kavita releases a quiet, defeated sigh. She knows it's no use. She pushes herself up off her aching knees, reluctantly conceding to leave her mother in the hellish peace of Sunil's bedroom, as she wishes. At the doorway, she stalls, as she peers over her shoulder, with one last thing to say.

"I'm not going to leave you," she tells her mother. Perhaps for the moment, to respect her mother's wishes, but not in the greater sense. No matter how hard her mother shoves or bites her with words, Kavita won't leave, and she will never give up on her.

Kavita waits for her mother to acknowledge what she has said, waits for her mother to see her standing there, desperate to be seen. But today isn't the day her family comes back together after being blown apart. Today, they remain the pieces of what once was whole.

Without another word, Kavita carries the Gloom upstairs, its weight upon her shoulders like a cloak of stone.

After showering and changing into a pair of black jeans and a soft green sweater, she lets her hair air-dry as she sits on her bed and dials Chi.

"Chi's cell, here!" chimes the voicemail message after three rings. "I can't take your call right now, probably because I'm busy saving lives. Leave me a message and I'll get back to you stat!"

She hangs up the phone. She has left half a dozen messages for Chi already and leaving another feels too needy. *Is she that busy?* she wonders. Or is Chi avoiding her? An itchy paranoia makes Kavita want to redial Chi's number, but she supresses the impulse. The paranoia, however, remains. She considers creeping Chi's social media accounts to see what she's really been up to, but a second later feels ridiculous and juvenile, and blames her bout of insecurity on a lack of sleep. Sternly, Kavita orders herself to stop being ridiculous. Then she tosses her damp towel over her bedpost to dry, and starts combing her fingers through her hair, catching herself on a net of loose strands.

Beyond her bedroom walls, she hears her father's bedroom door whine open, followed by the creak of the floorboards as he thumps down the hall. She is grateful that he's at least moving around a little. Maybe she will have better luck convincing him to join her for a stroll around the block.

The clamour of cupboard doors slamming startles her, jerking her head in the direction of the living room. She rushes towards the clatter and finds her father sitting cross-legged in front of the walnut wall unit with family albums scattered around him on the carpet. "Dad?" she asks. "What are you doing?"

He seems too absorbed to hear her.

"Dad?"

"Pictures," he says. He is flipping through an old album she hasn't seen in years, made of shockingly-bright orange patent leather. "I'm looking for pictures."

"Which ones?" She kneels beside him. "Maybe I can help."

"All of them," he says as he turns another page. He scans the plastic sleeve with a pulsating sort of mania in his eyes. "I want to make an album of all his pictures from when he was a baby until…." He pauses. "I'm going back to the beginning. Back when everything was fine. Back when he was small and carefree. *Mera sunder beta.*" He caresses a grainy photo with his fingertips. "My sweet boy."

Kavita glances at the photo. It is a baby picture of Sunil. He is dressed in a cloth diaper and lying on his stomach on a maroon paisley comforter. His mouth is wide open in a toothless smile. He has a full head of black hair. A youthful version of her father—slimmer and smooth-skinned—is sitting on the edge of the bed beside him, his giant hand resting on Sunil's back. A look of gentle love softens her father's eyes as he gazes at his son, his sweet boy.

Anchor pulls. She diverts her eyes to the dusty rose carpet. "How old is he in this picture?"

"Maybe six months or so. Back then, I never dreamed something like this was even possible. How could my sweet boy grow up to be so troubled?"

"I don't know."

"When we first moved here, I felt depressed for a long time. We were far from home, far from our families and friends. Your mommy and I got along better back then. I guess we had no other choice. I remember being scared of everything. Not speaking the language well enough. Getting pulled over by the police. Not being able to pay our bills. Somehow, even after we became landed immigrants, I still felt like we could get kicked out and sent back to India."

Despite never having to apply in order to stay in Canada, Kavita has often felt a similar insecurity, as if belonging depended on how small she could make herself, how accommodating, how obedient. But wasn't this inherited self-doubt part of every first generation's experience? Her father couldn't blame himself for that.

"All I ever wanted to do was provide some safety and security for all of you," he continues. "My own father died when I was very young, before I started going to school. I saw how my mother suffered as a widow. I was always scared, even as a child, because we had to depend on the kindness of others, and they were not always as kind as they should have been. I wanted to give you all the good things in life. But in the end, I think the only thing I passed on was my fear."

"What do you mean?"

"I think he got it from me. The nervousness. The sadness. The worrying all the time about every little thing and every big thing. They say children are like little sponges. I should have done a better job of protecting him, of sheltering him from my worries, but I think he soaked them up and never squeezed them out." A beat. "I am to blame."

"No, Dad," she reassures him. "You're not. It's no one's fault."

"Look at this picture!" He lifts up the album close to her face. She turns away. "Look at how happy he is! Look how perfect!"

"Dad, please," she says. "Put it down."

Slowly, he lowers the album and lets it rest in the bowl formed by his crossed legs.

"I know we want answers," she continues after a short pause. "I know we want to understand where things went wrong. I'm just not sure we ever will. Blaming yourself isn't going to help."

Yes, the survivor in her agrees, its voice small and still. *Listen to yourself, Kavita.*

She keeps her eyes locked on her father's face, broken by loss. *Those words don't apply to me,* she tells it.

That's right, says Anchor. It pulls, pulls, pulls.

"I am his father. It was my job to protect him. I should have paid more attention."

"Well, I'm his sister, and I didn't do any better."

"We are both failures, then."

She might have challenged him with a look if she did not agree, at least as far as the matter concerned herself.

A silent minute passes.

"I need a new album," her father says at last.

"We can go together."

"*Challo*," he says, tilting his head to one side.

"Wait. What about Mom? We shouldn't leave her on her own."

"Where is she?"

"In Sunil's room."

He nods, tensing his mouth.

"Have you talked at all?"

He shakes his head. "Not since the memorial. Part of me thought this would bring us closer together. Maybe we would help each other, like in the old days before you kids were born. But she just ignores me now. So I leave her alone. What can I do?"

"Maybe she's waiting for you to make the first move." She clutches inside, the way she had as a girl whenever her parents would fight, which happened often enough to gnaw at her sense of safety. Back then, she moved between them like a needle and thread, desperate to mend the latest tear in their marriage.

"What can I do?" he shrugs. "She never listens to me anyway. I am glad you are here, *beti*. You have always been the peacemaker in this family. You should have been a therapist."

A flash of a frown, then she recomposes herself. "I'll go. I won't be long. Call my cell if you need anything."

"Okay, *beti*." He gazes at the album again. "Maybe buy two albums. Remember to ask for a receipt."

She grins at him and says, "I'll remember."

Squinting against the partial sun as though her eyes are no longer used to outdoor light, she walks with pace, trying to generate some lifelike heat within her sedentary skin. A wince as she walks through Sunil's empty parking space in the driveway, avoiding the oil patch that is all that remains of his sky-blue car. Another as she steps over the curb and glimpses herself and Nirav sitting to the right, news-punched, on the night the police came. Then she rolls over another memory as though tipping into a pothole. It surprises her, thrusts her off balance, makes her wobble.

"Remember that summer you made a skate ramp at the end of the driveway, Bear? You must've been about eleven or so. I guess I was about six? You made me watch for cars. I was so scared you were going to hurt yourself, but you were always taking risks like that. Your skateboard went flying and you landed on your ankle. I can still see you clutching your high-tops, rocking side-to-side. I could see the tears in your eyes, but you kept your voice calm and told me to go inside and get Mom. We got into so much trouble. And you got a *cast*. I was so proud to be the first to sign it."

Could that really have been almost twenty years ago? Do these pothole memories always wait here? How does her mind choose which memory is visible or felt?

Why the dip in the sidewalk across the street, in front of the Cyr's split level, where they played hacky sack while waiting for the school bus? Why the stop sign on the corner where the station wagon blew a tire and Sunil taught her how to change a flat in minus twenty degree weather, their hands pink and protesting, their throats sore with winter wind so cold that it seemed too bare to hold oxygen. Why the countless night runs they took through the streets of their neighbourhood, which were such a part of their summers until she moved away with Nirav, that she sees now like time-lapsed videos, the past superimposed over the present?

Will she always stumble into these dips, loose-ankled? Will the memory reel always through her off balance when she does?

Stuffing her hands into the pockets of her jean jacket, she rubs the *rakhi* with one hand, clutches the blue river stone with the other, and carries on to Zellers.

Half an hour later, she is back at home, fumbling for her keys, when she freezes. Muffled shouting pounds the front door. She hurries inside. At the top of the stairs, she finds her mother and father wrestling with the orange photo album as if it is a rope and they are playing a hostile game of tug-of-war.

"Let go!" her mother yells.

Kavita drops the plastic bag of albums and bounds upstairs, two at a time. They pause and stare at her. The anger drops from their faces, leaving behind only self-conscious surprise. She grabs the photo album and hugs it to her chest. "What's going on?" Her gaze darts between them.

"I came upstairs and I found *him* taking apart our family albums. I knew he was going to ruin them, the way he ruins everything. I had to stop him!"

"I was not going to ruin anything," her father says. "*Beti,* you know what I was doing. Explain it to her."

"He's just making an album of Sunil's pictures, Mom. It's a nice idea, don't you think?"

"No!" her mother cries. She gathers as many albums as she can carry. "He doesn't deserve to look at these pictures. He doesn't deserve any piece of my son!"

"Mom, please, don't say that."

"You lied to me! You said we would have a better life here. You took me away from my family! With family around us Sunil would have been happy. He would have had more people to talk to. More people looking out for him...."

"You could have left at anytime but you knew no one would take you back."

"Stop!" Kavita cries. "Please. You don't mean it. Everyone, just calm down." She lowers the album she has been clutching to her chest like a shield to the floor and reaches for her mother's forearm. With the other, she reaches for her father's hand.

"Please, don't fight. We're all we have left. We need to stick together. We *love* each other." Wide-eyed, she waits.

"I have never loved him," her mother says. She wriggles free of Kavita's grasp, fills her arms with albums, and rushes down the hallway.

Kavita lets go of her father's hand, disorientated, as she processes the melee. Her father disappears into his bedroom a few moments after her mother, shutting his door with a clack.

A few albums remain scattered on the carpet. Kavita leaves them where they lay and trudges down the front stairs to the foyer. She takes a seat, hunching on the second last step, and reaches for the plastic bag. She draws out one of the new albums and starts turning its empty sleeves.

"This is what we're like now," she says to Sunil.

Black Gloom spreads from her centre, outwards, like a drop of India ink in water.

They stayed together for Sunil, it tells her. *They loved him more.*

She swallows, hard.

You promised you would look after them. But you can't look after anyone. You didn't save him, and you won't save them either.

Kavita stares ahead at the dusty base boards until the heaviness subsides enough for her to resurface. The album is still in her hands. The empty album. The album that will remain empty because there is no family left to fill it with memories. No family because her parents won't try. No family because her parents can't see her needing them to stay together. Can't see her needing them to help clear the rubble instead of create more. Can't see her at all. She is hurting too, but it doesn't seem to matter. Not to them or Nirav or Chi.

It would have mattered to Sunil. But he's too far from her now. He's too far from her because she didn't keep her promise. The black voice is right. She didn't keep him safe. She failed him. She keeps failing.

Blaze awakens, begins to rise. Her hands feel hot and tight, her fingertips itchy and swollen, as quick waves of energy gather, build. Her heart beats strongly through her scar. It doesn't hurt enough. Not nearly enough.

She grips one of the album's glossy pages. Balls a fist around it. Rips it from the album's spine. Then another, and another, and another. Until there is nothing left to tear apart.

She blinks out of her stupor. Observes the mess around her feet, distantly, as if it was made by someone else. Sees a red smear at the crook of her right hand, the tender skin between her forefinger and thumb, torn and bleeding. When did that happen? She lifts the cut to her mouth and presses her tongue against it.

Then, with the taste of metal on her tongue, she calmly closes the pageless album, as if doing so is the most ordinary thing in the world.

8

ANOTHER DAY, ANOTHER WEEK, and another two more, all passing in restless sleeping at night, tired waking at dawn, and restless tiredness all through the day.

There were the crushing business-of-death appointments to confront—the reading of Sunil's will at Mr. Desjardins's office, "liquidating assets" at the bank, transferring car ownership, meeting with the accountant to file the last taxes, returning government-issued documents, applying for the callously named "death benefit" at City Hall, and on and on. Part of her felt relieved as she completed the tasks, and yet, their completion also left her feeling slightly paralyzed, as if Sunil were vanishing a little more every time she drew a line through another item on her list, the way an antacid tablet fizzed in a glass of water until it was gone, and she, like the water that overwhelms the tablet, was the one responsible for Sunil's dissolution. It was hard to reconcile the two: her duty, and this act of erasure.

After her parents' fight, silence resumed its noxious reign of the house. Each of them more or less kept to themselves. Kavita thought of them and herself as trapped in a kind of prison, each in solitary confinement, always using different rooms at different times, their paths almost never intersecting. When their paths did cross, they never crossed for long. If they talked, they never talked about what needed to be said.

The thinking side of her asserted that she should engage them, draw them out of their caves of sorrow, get them to eat more and talk more and move more. But the feeling side of her could not bear to be in the same room with them for longer than a few minutes at a time. They were bounded by grief but also torn apart by it. Every time she looked into their wounded eyes, she knew their pain, and it was more than she could stand.

Her mother kept to her routine of napping on the floor of Sunil's bedroom with his ashes tucked safely on his bed. Her father had finished his album project and moved on to checking out books on Buddhism from the library. Days earlier he even came home with a guide book about monastery tours in Dharamsala. Kavita didn't ask about it. If he was planning his Great Escape, she didn't want to know.

She cooked dal and rice or *kitchari* every few days or so in case her parents craved something other than toast and bananas and ginger tea. (Although she stocked those items too.) She herself never ate more than a few mouthfuls at a time. Got a strange sense of ecstasy from her hunger pangs, like a self-flagellating monk, because, just like the monk, she knew she deserved to suffer, that her suffering was an expression of love. With every hollow groan of her stomach it was as though she were paying off the debts that Anchor hissed in her ear, crumb by crumb, pound by pound. That week, she started cinching up her jeans with a belt.

To pass the time, she limped through long walks, smoked, texted Chi, brooded, denied her hunger pangs, emailed Chi, lost time in flashbacks, took scalding showers, ruminated, shopped for things she didn't need online, left voicemails for Chi, thought of every big and small fight she'd ever had with Sunil, lost time in weeping, read obsessively about suicide and bereavement and trauma, lost more time in weeping, occasionally hit herself to decompress, slept (except at night), watched more *Buffy* than was healthy (especially at night).

All the while, she kept an open line of one-way communication with Sunil.

The one advantage of Nirav's sparse visits was that she didn't have to pretend to be cheerful or functional for long intervals. Most of the time, she was free to be haunted.

She became numb to Nirav's excuses for not visiting more often. "I have an early meeting" was as popular as "I have to work late." Although because they involved work, she empathized with him, if only a speck. After all, she hadn't rejoined the world as a productive member of society, yet. The thought of going back to work was more insurmountable now that it had been weeks ago. Sometimes it felt as though she might never hold down a job again. All the steps involved in getting through a full day felt as long as a marathon to her. How had she ever done it before?

Other excuses, she had little sympathy for, like, "I have a footy match" or "I'm going to play Snooker with some mates" or "I'm too tired." Whenever he mumbled these excuses, she dismissed them, telling herself she didn't care, it didn't matter if he showed up or not, she was handling things well on her own, everything was fine, and, usually after a quick strike to the head, she more or less believed herself.

One day, the police inspector rang their doorbell. He was holding a white plastic bag. Her thoughts shot to the white plastic bag Sunil had given her, the one full of sleeping pills, the one she had gotten rid of. While rationally she knew that the white plastic bag in the inspector's hand was a different white plastic bag, knowing this didn't stop her insides from reacting with panic. "The rest of your brother's belongings," he told her. What he said after that, she couldn't remember.

Back in her room, she knelt by her bed and laid out his things with the care of an archivist handling lost treasures.

His wallet—curved, worn brown leather, a graduation present. Car and house keys held together on the plastic Taurus keychain she got him from a Hallmark store years ago. And his cell phone.

His cell phone. The repository of their pleas. She picked it up. It was off. Had it been off the whole time? Was the battery dead? Before turning it on, she hesitated. *It doesn't matter*, she thought. *It doesn't change anything. Stop torturing yourself.* But reasonable thoughts were easily overruled by her beastly need to know. She pressed the power button. It flickered to life. Which probably meant it had been off the whole time.

25 missed calls, she read, heart sinking.

5 new messages.

The glare of knowing began to sting her eyes.

This meant that while they were reaching out to him, Sunil had remained fixed on his plan. She had an answer now, and it proved her earlier assertion to be correct. The answer didn't matter, it didn't change anything, and it certainly didn't make her feel any closer to closure. All Kavita felt was torture at the hands of a past she couldn't alter.

She deleted the messages. They served no purpose anymore. She didn't need to hear their pleas, veiled with false cheer and calm, as they gently tried to ease Sunil home. She relived the futility of that helpless time enough as it is. She would never forget it.

Once the voicemail was empty, she dialled his number. The voicemail message was the only place the sound of his voice existed anymore. They weren't like other families who videotaped every event, momentous and mundane. The idea of spending money on a camcorder seemed like a frivolous waste to her frugal immigrant parents, who sacrificed everything—including trips back to India for births, wedding, and even funerals—to save for Sunil and Kavita's educations. Pushing down a violent surf of grief, she dilated her eardrums and listened, her heartbeat a slow throb in her throat. "This is Sunil," he said. "Leave me a message and have a good one."

His voice—easygoing, healthy, alive—vacuumed to her hollow centre, where spun against her insides, like a cold wind twisting against the walls of a cave, with nothing to break it, nowhere for it to escape.

Next came the beep and she hung up.

On Thanksgiving she drove up to Gatineau Park to see the hawks, one of their Thanksgiving traditions, a favourite of Sunil's. She followed the road that sliced through the hills surrounded by mixed forest on either side, so dense and lush it was almost possible to forget the fetters of urban life in the deep green of pine needles and the rose tone of cliffs. Every now and then, the trees would clear, revealing a small dark pond or cattail-hemmed marshland. At one point, she thought she spotted a beaver, but then again it might have been a deadhead bobbing in the water.

She parked in the grass alongside the road a few minutes away from Champlain Lookout. The trails were always frenzied during the holiday. Everywhere she looked there were families; small ones, big ones, some with dogs, others with strollers, others still with coolers and cameras, although considerably more with camera phones.

She wanted to hate them. Their togetherness and full bellies and smiles and laughter and posing for group photos and the fact that they had things to be thankful for. Since Anchor and Blaze and Black Gloom had colonized her insides, she could remember only distantly what gratitude felt like. Something like a long breath of relief exhaled skyward, the gentle sag into a loved one's arms, the happy idiot feeling of luck. She wanted to hate the other families for showing off.

But she couldn't. She knew they weren't to blame.

"You should be here watching the hawks," she said to Sunil.

But you were too slow, said Anchor as it pulled. *You let him down*. The sinking feeling spread.

Black Gloom slowly crushed her from crown to toe and she wondered how it was possible that she could be simultaneously sitting and flattened on the car mats.

Then she felt them all mixing together. Anchor and Blaze and Black Gloom, all at once, like a maelstrom—heavy, feverish, thick—churning under her skin. She couldn't hold them. She wanted them out.

She lit a cigarette, sucked in a long drag, and butted it out on her palm, pressing its molten tip into the place along her lifeline where everything had gone wrong. A yowl spurted up her throat like bile, sharp and scathing as her wound, but she stoppered it in her throat, where it shook. Guilty people didn't deserve to scream. They hadn't earned the right.

With a pulsing stare, she focused on the pain—hot, deep, sharp. That pain she could manage. That pain she knew she deserved.

Then she gagged the yowling welt with tissues and climbed out of the car. Hiked up to the crowded lookout point. Slipped into an opening along the curved stone wall and let the panoramic view calm her breath. To the right were the rolling hills of the Eardley Escarpment, which from a distance, resembled sleeping Vishnu covered in mosses. She admired the pines and cedars, as verdant as coriander chutney, and leafy trees, vibrant with shades of turmeric and saffron and paprika. Below, a steep drop gave way to farmland that marked the landscape like earth-toned Hippie patchwork cloth. Straight ahead in the distance, the Ottawa River trenched through the land, gleaming.

And above, the soaring hawks, like kites, only freer because they had no cords to bind them to the ground.

"That's why you loved them," she said to Sunil. He envied them. Maybe he even wanted to be one of them.

A dark-haired woman with a green Tilley hat beside her said, "*Pardonnez-moi*?"

Kavita glanced at her and left.

On Halloween, she kept the lights off, and paused her hunger strike for the evening, telling herself that she was eating the candies for Sunil. He always loved Halloween candies, especially mini chocolate bars. She sat outside his bedroom in the dark with a bag of them and ate her way through it until all that was left was a mess of wrappers littered around her like decaying leaves. While she gorged, they reminisced.

"Bear, do you remember the year you dressed up like a woman? I don't know if kids do that anymore. Mom gave you one of her old dresses and a bra. You stuffed it with cantaloupes, I think. Or was it grapefruits? And you let me put makeup on you! Every little sister's dream. What was I that year? The Karate Kid? I wore an old *gi* of yours, and you drew a beard on my face with Mom's eyeliner. She wasn't too pleased about that. We've got the pictures somewhere." Maybe one day she would have to will to look at them again.

She unwrapped a Coffee Crisp and ate the top wafer first, the way Sunil had taught her to do. As she nibbled, she felt the lightness she had momentarily enjoyed start to drain away as another memory surfaced. "Then there was the year I told you I wanted to go trick-or-treating with my friends. I must've been about eleven, I think. I can still see the wounded look in your eyes, like I'd rejected you." Why did the memory come back to her now? To punish her? To show her that she had always been careless with him?

A short while later, her stomach rejected the treats, heave by heave.

Are you surprised? Anchor said, as she rinsed the sweet and bitter tastes from her mouth. She held the counter against its drag. *You didn't deserve the chocolates in the first place. Sunil doesn't get to enjoy any. Why should you get a night off from remembering why?*

As she stood there, staring into the whiteness of the sink, it seemed to Kavita that Anchor was making more and more sense. She had let herself off too easily. Was she ever going to learn? Was she ever going to become a better person? The kind of person that did what needed to be done and said what needed to be said, at the right time, and the right place, when it mattered.

She pressed her thumb into her scar, breathing into its sting and screams.

One day, she finally forced herself to call Dr. Jones. Patty had been leaving polite yet insistent reminders on the answering machine about the life insurance paperwork and the report that needed to be filled our by Sunil's physician. Underneath some papers on her desk, she found one of Sunil's old appointment cards with the doctor's information. As she stared at the date and time written on the card, she remembered waiting for Sunil in the clinic parking lot with starved eyes, the fraying hope as the minutes ticked by without his arrival, the wordless shock of the long drive home without him.

Clenching the scar on her palm, which was healing but still ached, she dialled the doctor's number. After a few of minutes of being put on hold, he answered.

"This is Dr. Jones," he said, in the same clip voiced she remembered.

"Dr. Jones, my name is Kavita Gupta. My brother, Sunil, was one of your patients. Sunil Gupta."

"Yes, of course. I was sorry to hear about him."

For a few seconds, his words didn't make sense. "You know about what happened to him?"

"Yes, the police notified us."

The police. She forgot that they had requested the phone numbers of Sunil's dentist and doctor.

"Is there something I can do for you?"

Why had she called?

"Miss Gupta?"

The reason flooded back to her, and she detached, floating above the current of the things that didn't make sense—like Sunil's death, and insurance forms, and his doctor knowing about his suicide but never calling to make sure they were okay. She spoke numbly about the forms.

"You can mail them or drop them off at my office, if you prefer. I'll let my receptionist know to keep an eye out for them."

"Oh, okay," she said. The task she had agonized over for weeks was a matter of daily business for Dr. Jones.

"Is there anything else I can do for you?"

An entire unspoken conversation lay in the cradle of her partially-opened mouth, but she couldn't find her courage, nor the dexterity to unloop the stubborn knot in her tongue. "Uh-uh," she managed to grunt in reply.

"Well then, I apologize, but I have another patient waiting."

The electric drone of the dial tone resonated in her eardrum, packing it with sound. She hung up the phone and lowered it to the desk.

It was possible that this was simply how things were done. She wouldn't know. Even if that was the case, however, Kavita found herself asking whether it should be.

He didn't ask if we were okay. He didn't offer counselling. He didn't ask us to come in to discuss where the failure in your treatment occurred. Your family doctor. Yet here we are, your family, in pieces, and he's on to the next patient.

Blaze would have stirred then, but the chill of her shock was greater than even its fire. She crossed her arms over the cold balling in her stomach.

She had things to say to Dr. Jones. Things she had been working out over the past several weeks. Things she wanted to say on Sunil's behalf. Like: "You wrote the note." And, "You put it in his hands." And, "You wrote *completely debilitated* on a piece of paper and put that paper in a suicidal man's hand. He read your words, *completely debilitated*, and believed it. Yes, it's true, Sunil took his life. But you should know that you may have taken the last of his hope."

She wanted to say all of that. Yell it. Stand up for Sunil. But she didn't. When was she going to learn? When was she going to become a better person? The kind of person that did what needed to be done and said what needed to be said, at the right time, and the right place, when it mattered.

Anchor pulled, pulled, pulled.

Yes, she agreed with it. She was failing him, again.

Shortly after that, the weather grew damp and autumn quickly sloped from vibrant rhapsody to grim decay. As if synchronizing with the season, Kavita went into hibernation like the skeletal trees outside her bedroom window.

She stopped going for walks, or changing out of her pyjamas, she even stopped smoking. She lost interest in chasing Chi, and Nirav, and the world in general. Nothing seemed to matter outside the cave of sorrow that had domed around her, rock by rock.

She cooked but only because it was for someone else. Ate mouthfuls here and there but nothing substantial. Tried to read but couldn't focus. Attempted to ease the ache in her back with heating pads and Advil but found no relief. Napped to make up for her insomnia but grew too afraid of her nightmares.

She relived losing Sunil many times each day.

Beneath her mute exterior lurked tremors. Danger was imminent. She knew it in her quivering cells. With every car-alarm blare in her gut. Something bad was going to happen. She didn't know what or when. All she knew was that something else was about to blown up and scatter around them. Danger, danger, danger.

She needed to be ready. She would be ready this time, she told herself. Not like last time. Last time she was caught off guard and did all the wrong things and Sunil paid the price. But she wasn't going to fail again. She had made a promise to Sunil and this time she wouldn't break her promise. She would keep their parents safe. She would keep them alive. Sunil could trust her. Really, he could. She wasn't going to fail him. This time, she would be ready.

She kept all of this to herself, because like Anchor, Black Gloom was making more and more sense lately too. It told her that she was enough of a burden already, so she should keep quiet, and besides, she deserved whatever was happening to her, didn't she know that? Yes, she agreed, increasingly, she did.

9.

KAVITA LIES IN BED under the duvet with the cordless held up to her ear. For the several weeks, she and Nirav have ended their days this way, with a quick catch up. Already the ration of daylight is in decline. Although it's just after six o'clock, she switches on the lamp on the nightstand, which fills the room with milky, tapering light. Outside her window, dusk tints the surroundings in a deep grey-blue, revealing the first of the stars, opalescent and winking.

Lately, their conversations seem to follow a script. There are the usual warm-up questions to rely on: How was your day? How's the cat? What did you have for dinner? But once they exhaust these subjects, neither of them seems to know how to follow up, their chitchat encumbered by the questions that linger in their tense silences, both lacking the courage to ask them.

In the early days after Sunil's death, the early days of their separation, when Nirav moved back to the condo, they had put some effort into their nightly conversations, constructing elaborate replies to satisfy their need to hear the other's voice, as if the sound were a salve for their loneliness. Those conversations reminded her of the others they had endured during the arduous year they had spent apart, when they were dating long-distance.

Now, it seems as though they are facing a different kind of distance, an insidious, emotional type that has little to do with physical geography.

As she holds the receiver to her ear, she realizes that several moments have passed since either of them last spoke. The static sound of his breath brushes against the sensitive hairs of her inner ear. Just over a year ago, on their honeymoon in Jasper—a wedding present from Sunil—they soaked in the Miette hot springs with their limbs entwined and promised each other between ardent kisses to always tell each other everything without exception. She knew they would never suffer the taciturn plague that had turned her parents' mouths black and shrivelled their voices from lack of use. Back then, she would never have believed she and Nirav were capable of such prolonged silences—silences that seemed electrified with all they hesitated to say out loud. How long ago that dizzying utopian time feels from the reticent place they occupy now.

"Kavita?" he says. "Are you still there?"

"I'm here."

"Well?"

"I don't know." She gnaws on her thumbnail still unsure of how to circumvent his question.

"You're just being paranoid, Kavita."

"You only say that because you're never here."

Ten seconds tick by.

"I just want my wife back."

"You know where I am."

He clears his throat. This is as much as she has said about his absence in weeks. *He wants me to be his wife*, she thinks, *but where has my husband been*?

"We aren't like your family with aunties and uncles all over the place. It's a luxury. The only family we have here is each other. We have to stick together." Sticking together has always been a necessity, and now more than ever, it was a matter of survival.

"Your parents have each other."

"No, they don't." At least not in any romantic sense that might sustain a couple during hard times, the way fat reserves kick in during lean periods. No, their marriage, if you could call it that, was less than skin and bones. Until she started school, Kavita thought that all married people met the way her parents had, all marriages were arranged. Just like until her first sleepover, she thought that all married people slept in separate bedrooms. It was an awful burden to grow up knowing that the origin of one's birth was obligation, not love.

"The other day I went for a walk," she continues. "When I came back, I found them fighting in the living room. You know what Mom said? That she never loved Dad. You should've seen the look in her eyes, Nirav. I don't know what might've happened if I hadn't come home when I did. Don't you see? I'm here to keep them in their separate corners. To keep them civil. Just like Sunil and I always have."

"That's not your responsibility."

"But it is."

"Why?"

She shuts off the lamp on the nightstand. She has never learned how to talk about such things in the light.

"Because we're the reason they stayed together. We're the reason they're so miserable." It was an awful burden to grow up knowing that one's existence was the cause of so much unhappiness. "They've never asked me to touch their feet, but this is my way of doing it. This is how I repay them."

Sometimes she wonders if her parents' marriage would have worked out had they stayed in India. Maybe the success of arrangements like theirs was contingent on having ample buffers around, people to give advice, check behaviour, remind them that they were part of an ecosystem, that the integrity of the family web depended on cohesion.

"You need to live your own life."

"My family is my life, Nirav. Their pain is my pain. As long as we stay together, we'll survive this. I have to cling to that. It's the only thing keeping me sane."

He sighs. Pauses for a few moments. Then asks, "How are

you managing?" with a strained voice, as if frightened by his own question, as if already frightened by the answer, which is perhaps why he so rarely asks.

Silently, Kavita considers the excrescences of her new inner world.

How can she tell him about the nightmares where she sees Sunil's death but is powerless to stop it. And the way her heart sprints every time she sees a police cruiser. And the way she clutches inside when someone knocks on the door or calls, the warming beacon in her gut blaring: danger, danger, danger.

Or about how every time she hears the word *suicide* it triggers her memory, drawing her into her horrors, scenes replaying themselves without warning or consent.

Or how she stops breathing for a second every time she sees a sky-blue car roll by the house, losing herself in a moment of hope, believing Sunil has finally come home.

How does she tell her husband that between violent bouts of sobbing, she dips into numb periods of disbelief, as though her brain can't fully process or believe that Sunil killed himself, even now, months later.

She wonders if on his rare visits he has noticed the plum segments under her eyes, or the prominence of her ribs and pelvic bones when he holds her, or the Band Aid on her hand no one asks about.

How can she describe to him the waterlogged feeling of her limbs, the fuddled plodding of her mind, and the ache that has colonized every muscle in her body, maybe even every cell?

Then there are her guests.

How would Nirav react if she dared to tell him about Anchor's pull, or Blaze's heat, or Black Gloom's slowly crushing weight? What would he say if she told him about their distinct voices, which sound like her, and yet not.

No, she can't tell him.

He would send her away.

He would leave her.

And what about the other voice? The one she turns away from. Quiet and self-preserving, small and still, that tells her staying at her parents' house is slowly corroding her health with wrenching memories embedded in every room, piece of furniture, family portrait, even the air.

This is not your home anymore, it has been trying to convince her. *This place is a trigger zone. Staying here is making you sick.*

This is where I belong, she tells it.

No, Anchor says. *This is what you deserve.*

Is Anchor right? she wonders. When she looks at the armchair by the front window, does she *deserve* to get transported to the first night of Sunil's disappearance, to the place she waited all night, watching the street for his car, every part of her singularly focused on willing him home? When she gets the briefest glimpse of a family photograph, does she *deserve* to lose Sunil all over again?

Maybe.

Maybe Anchor is right.

In the cupboards, she finds Sunil's favourite cereal bowl, his favourite mug to drink tea, his favourite ketchup chips. In the fridge, she finds the jar of pickled onions he ate like olives. No one else likes them, and they're about to go off, but she doesn't have the strength to throw them out. All day, every day, she stumbles over these pieces of Sunil, and they disarm her, cause her memories of him to detonate inside her, and they are everywhere, these little bombs.

If only she knew how to stop the onslaught. The changing weather inside her. The hurricanes. The drag. The head talk. But how? She couldn't possibly ever have that power. These forces are bigger than her. And as their tall, tall shadows grow, she gets smaller and smaller beneath them.

"Kavita?"

She tries to swallow but can't. "I'm fine," she says.

Another pause.

"Have you heard from Chi?" he asks.

"No, not yet."

"Well, she wrote to me the other day."

"She wrote you?"

"Yes. She was concerned about you."

"I've been trying to get a hold of her for weeks. She's been ignoring me. Why would she write you instead?"

"I think you may have frightened her off."

"But I haven't even spoken to her. How could I have frightened her off?"

"Did you write her an e-mail recently?"

"A couple of days ago. How did you know?"

"She told me about it. She said you didn't sound like yourself."

It was strange to receive this external report, almost as if she were sitting through a performance evaluation at work. If she wasn't like herself, then who was she? Kavita didn't know anymore. Who was she in the wake of Sunil's death? It was too early, her grief still too fresh, for her to be able to claim resurrection like a Rose of Jericho, or transformation like an insect that emerges from its cocoon, winged, and more beautiful than before its seclusion. What she's becoming remains vague to her, a matter of process too close for her to see clearly, as though she is standing with her nose pressed up against a self-portrait, but she can't see her full likeness yet. "She told you that?"

"Mm hm."

The betrayal bites. "Did she tell you what I wrote?"

"No. Only that she was worried about you, and she thought I should know. I think she was hoping I would approach you and you would tell me yourself."

A few days earlier, after watching a talk show segment on the symptoms of depression, Kavita pushed her fears aside, and reached out to Chi, confiding in her that things weren't going well, and she thought she might be depressed. Kavita hoped Chi would be able to give her some advice or maybe even recommend one of her colleagues. At the very least, Kavita expected her to write back. Chi, her oldest friend, who was now treating her as if she was mildly toxic. "I don't know why she said that," Kavita tells him. "And I don't understand why she would go to you and not me."

"Maybe she doesn't know what to say."

Kavita knows the excuses. People didn't know what to say. They didn't want to say the wrong thing. She knows the excuses, and might have even thought they were acceptable at one time, but now, she sees how slanted they are. Saying nothing was worse than saying the wrong thing. So much worse.

"Maybe your frankness startled her."

Her lips part a sliver. She turns to the window, gazes at the smoky sickle moon that casts the barest light, and considers her husband's words. Considers how much she has kept bolted inside, mostly for his benefit, to save him from worry.

"Maybe you should try again."

But she has tried. To explain the changes occurring inside her that she doesn't understand. The foreign things that have no common language to express themselves, as if the distance between her pain and the world outside it is unbridgeable. If such a common language exists, she doesn't know how to speak it, yet.

Neither have those around her developed an ear to hear it. She has tried, taken risks, put herself out there, in her way, always at a cost, with Nirav and Chi and even Dr. Jones. These attempts have been failures. These failures have taught her it is best to keep quiet. There is no safety in jumping faithfully into a pair of dead arms. There is only rejection, and condemnation, to an even deeper silence, an even blacker gloom.

"I'm tired," she says.

"I suppose I should let you get some rest, then."

Once they say goodnight, Kavita sits up in bed, and reaches for the only person who seems to listen.

"What's wrong with me, Bear? I'm filled with such terrible dread. I know something bad is going to happen. I feel it in my gut. But I don't know what or when. I promise to be ready, though. I'm scared. But I'm ready."

Her chin starts to shake. "Being ready is wearing me out. I don't know how long I can keep this up. I can't seem to keep up, Sunil. But I'll try. I promise you, I'll try."

The first tear falls. "And I'll probably fail, like before. I can't stop thinking about how I failed you. I play it over and over in my head. I lose you, over and over. I don't know how long I can keep losing you, over and over."

She bows her heavy head. "I have no one to talk to, Sunil, only you. And you don't talk back, no matter how I beg. You were the person I talked to and you should be here now. And you would be, but I couldn't see the trouble underneath. I didn't know how bad it was. I didn't know any better."

She leans into the silence, waiting, receptive. Surely he knows she needs him more than ever. Surely he will come to her at last.

But all she finds is more silence. The silence that has poisoned her house. That is slowly claiming her marriage. That swallowed up Sunil.

She covers her face.

Then a voice cuts through, hard as stone. *No one's listening,* Black Gloom tells her.

No one can help.

You will always feel this way.

Searing tears rise. She lowers back onto the mattress. As she lies there, she sinks into an inward darkness that feels inescapable, ever-lasting. She is crouched at the bottom of a well. No moon shines silver hope above her.

"How do I get out?" she whispers. "Help me, Sunil. Please."

Toss her a rope. Send her a light.

10.

KAVITA DESCENDS into the church basement. She has the vague sense that she is back in high school. Something about the wide cement staircase, scent of cleaner, and relentless fluorescent lighting. She can't help but feel like she is trespassing. But this is nevertheless the place she is meant to be tonight.

She found the bereavement group online. They hold meetings on the first Thursday of every month. Newcomers are welcome. They offer support specific to the type of loss—parent, child, spouse, sibling, and, what caught Kavita's attention in particular, suicide survivors. It is a new term for her. That's what she is now, apparently. She didn't know there was a name for it. She hovers at the bottom of the stairs and peers through the double doors to her left. A pair of elderly women pass her on their way from the washroom and one of them gives her a smile. Inside the large room, by the entrance, she sees a young man, about her age, sitting at a table, doodling on a nametag with a blue Sharpie. His long brown hair is half up, he doesn't appear to shave very often, and he wears woollen socks inside his Birkenstocks.

Granola, she thinks.

The basement is lively with movement and chatter, which goes against the assumptions she has about bereavement groups. Aren't these meetings supposed to be sombre affairs filled with even more sombre people? She shoves her hands into her jean jacket, fumbles for Sunil's *rakhi*, and rubs it for comfort.

She hears voices approaching her from behind. Glancing over her shoulder, she sees a middle-aged couple slowing plodding down the stairs. She steps to one side.

"Sorry," says the man as they pass. The woman grins briefly at the tiled floor. Kavita follows their path to the table. The granola guy welcomes them with a broad smile. They chat for a bit and then he hands them each a paper to fill out. While they are hunched over, filling out forms, the granola guy keeps talking, pointing to different parts of the room. Kavita notices there are snacks laid out and a table of handouts. Lots of Kleenex. The couple stick the nametags onto their jackets and move somewhere beyond her sightline. It looks easy enough. But she still isn't sure if she's ready.

Just then, the granola guy looks right at her. He offers her the same wide smile her offered the couple and raises one hand in a wave.

"Hey," he mouths. He motions with his hand. "Come in."

Her insides seize. Her face must have too, because the granola guy's smile drops, as though he knows she is about to bolt back up the stairs. His dark eyes ask her to stay.

But she can't.

She sprints back up the two flights of stairs, nearly tripping on the last step, but finds her balance, and doesn't stop until she's outside in the cold night, panting visible breath, under a yellow dome of light. She stands off to one side to catch her breath. A family of three—a mother, father, and teenage daughter—approach the entrance from the parking lot. She avoids their gaze, although she can feel their eyes reaching for her, and senses they want to share a smile, a moment of understanding between the bereft. She keeps her eyes fixed on the lazy traffic rolling past the church.

Soon she is alone. Her shoulders relax a little. A sense of defeat drags her gaze to the cement. Coming here was a mistake. It was foolish to think she would have anything in common with these people. How could she tell them how badly she handled things with Sunil? If they found out, they would probably blame her for his death too. She has met the soft eyes of other mourners, and it is obvious that they can't help her, because she isn't like the rest of them. They haven't done anything wrong.

Sadness barrels into her.

No, she isn't like them at all.

She doesn't need to check her watch to know that the meeting should have started by now. She takes a deep breath. Watches the fog of her breath gather beyond her listless mouth.

It's okay, she coaches herself.

I'll get through this.

I can do this on my own.

Somewhere in the background, in the lampless corner she carries inside, she can sense the curling of lips, as Anchor and Gloom grin mockingly behind her back.

11.

A COUPLE OF FORGETTABLE WEEKS staggered into the past. One day, unexpectedly, her mother stopped napping in Sunil's room. She washed and dressed and had toast and tea in the living room. Afterward, Kavita accompanied her to Home Depot, where she picked up carpet samples and paint chips.

"The house needs a fresh start," her mother declared. So, she went about changing it. Perhaps if no one recognized it, the place might become liveable again.

Her father took to borrowing her laptop when she wasn't using it to search for meditations online. He made daily trips to the library and came back with more readings on Buddhism. On her laptop, she discovered that he had been visiting the website of a Buddhist abbey in Nova Scotia, the retreats page, specifically.

Meanwhile, Nirav grew more impatient. The pressure of separation had pushed him into a realm of his personality yet unknown to her. He gave her an ultimatum. "Move back in one week, Kavita, or I'm coming over to get you myself. Enough's enough."

She liked ultimatums as much as she liked the words *enough's enough*, something one might say to an impetuous child, rather than one's wife. Nevertheless, she felt the pressure to return home. The idea of losing her marriage on top of everything else was inconceivable. Without Nirav, what else would she have?

Nothing, Gloom told her as she considered what to do. *Except me.* The thought left her chilled as she glimpsed a future that hadn't happened yet, alone with it in the dark well, forever.

Today is moving day. After getting ready, she goes down to Sunil's room. When she reaches the threshold, she hesitates. Peeking inside, she sees that the curtains are split open an inch. In the partial shadows, his room feels peaceful, as if he might be taking one of his long, weekend naps. But there's no fooling herself into thinking his bed is anything but empty.

Holding her breath, she steps over the threshold, at last confronting his haunted belongings. With timid steps, she peers around. An eerie feeling rolls over her, as though she is in a museum. With airy brushes of her fingertips, she caresses the remnants of him in the reverent way elephants stroke the bones of their dead. Certain features stand out to her. The indentations on his pillow. (She bends to it and inhales deeply. A faint scent of him lingers on the pillowcase, earthy and oily.) The thick book on his nightstand. (She can see the pages he dog-eared, on the bottom of the pages, as was his habit) The green polar fleece hanging on the back of his desk chair. (She bends and inhales. It smells weakly of Bounce.) The pile of neatly folded work clothes on top of his desk, ready to be worn to the office.

Something in the trash bin beside his desk snags her attention. She recognizes the card she gave him on his last birthday, a few months before he disappeared. She leans forward and fishes it out.

"I got you this stupid gag card even though you didn't want any gifts this year. I thought that was strange at the time. But I figured you were just having your third-life crisis about turning thirty. I still remember the look on your face when I gave it to you. You shook your head as if to say, 'Kavita, why don't you ever listen?'"

Why didn't she? Listen, more closely. See the trouble in his eyes? They shone a message, but she didn't know what it was. There was a message in his actions too, in not wanting any presents, not even cards, but she didn't think that meant he wanted to die.

She places the birthday card on his desk, lets her gaze sweep over his things one last time, then drifts out of the room, mute as a ghost.

As the slanted autumnal rain falls, she waits for the bus at the corner of her street, regretful about not wearing something more waterproof than her jean jacket and scarf. She hoods the scarf around her head, but within a few minutes, it begins to droop soggily. She is about to risk fetching an umbrella from home when the red-and-white OC Transpo bus appears at the top of her street, like an ark. As she climbs aboard, she grins at the driver, sheepish. She chooses an empty seat in the middle of the bus, undrapes the drenched scarf from off her head, and gazes out the rain-spattered window, at the cars and bikes and people. It feels strange to be in the world again, around so much movement, that hasn't stopped for a moment since her own world experienced its apocalypse, and yet still not a part of it. She has felt Other when riding the bus before, the times when she's noticed she is the only brown person, the only woman. Now grief has made her Other in another way, but with this difference at least, she can hide and feel safe.

The automated voice—male and robotic—calls out each stop in English and French. "Vancouver Avenue. *Avenue Vancouver*." Intermittently, the stop bell dings. Soon she registers little as she peers out the window, slipping into the semi-coma that is so alluring about riding the bus.

About ten minutes later, the automated voice calls out the stop for the Sunnyside branch of the library. With a sharp inhale, she awakens from her half-sleep and pulls the yellow cord. A quick dash from the bus stop and she finds herself in the dry refuge of the stone building.

Now indoors, she seeks the refuge of books. Memoirs written by others who have lost their soul mate. Who have lost themselves to trauma. And yet have managed to remake themselves from the rubble into something whole again, albeit with cracks. In books, maybe she will be able to find a way to understand the strangeness of her new inner landscape. If someone else out there has felt the way she feels, has thought the things she thinks, has heard the dark whispers, then maybe she isn't so far gone after all, and there is still reason to hope.

Outside, she waits for another bus, in a mud-spattered shelter littered with cigarette butts and greying trampled gum. Within a few minutes, the bus arrives, and she squeezes in beside an elderly man with a shopping trolley. As the bus crawls up Bank Street, it cuts through the Glebe with its trendy high street storefronts: spa, florist, fair-trade-coffee shop, micro-brewery.

Once they pass under the Queensway, the street decays somewhat—gas station, pay-day loan office, Tim Horton's. Condo developments have sprouted in the minimal patches of concrete where the old neighbourhood was clear-cut.

As they near Parliament Hill, the surroundings gentrify again. The people in this area are polished, too, dressed in their office attire, marching this way and that, texting at stoplights. Whole blocks buzz with purpose and urgency.

She disembarks at Wellington, crosses the street, and stops to check the time on the Peace Tower, the city's grandfather clock. Even in the grey weather, the pointed copper roof stands out, green against grey. The Maple Leaf, though, hangs as limp as her sodden scarf. Squinting, she reads that it is a few minutes past noon. The rain has petered out to a fine fog-like mist. She decides to walk the rest of the way. Turning away from the Hill, she points herself westward, in the direction of her building. As she passes the National Archives, she admires the copper statue of the barefoot lovers sitting on a bench, the man grinning into the woman's hair as though pleased by its scent, and the woman staring straight ahead with a stoic expression, spirited away by her thoughts. *How lifelike*, Kavita thinks. *He doesn't even notice how far away she is.*

A short while later, she arrives at her building, twelve storeys of sandy-coloured brick and generous windows. The bored concierge gives her a nod as she enters. As the elevator rises to the tenth floor, her stomach begins to squirm.

She hears Coal's kitten-like mewling before she reaches their corner unit. She gently nudges the charcoal tabby aside with the door and catches him before he is able to dart past her into the hallway. He welcomes her with sandpaper licks on her nose and chin. She whispers *I love you* into the soft fur behind his ears and sets him down.

Nirav will be home in a couple of hours. She has at least some time to settle in on her own. She peels off her damp things and follows Coal along the short entryway to the kitchen, the daytime chill of the dark hardwood seeping through her thin socks. As she leans against the white waterfall island, she peers around the living space, that feels familiar yet foreign to her, after so many weeks away. But it's all still there, as she had left it: the paprika-red couch, the large cubby shelves, the wall-mounted flat-screen, the coffee table made of glass and a varnished tree stump.

She notices a couple of greeting cards on top of the cubby shelves and walks over to read them. The first is an anniversary card sent from Nirav's parents, congratulating them on their first year of marriage. The second is a *Raksha Bandan* card for Nirav sent from Maya. The *rakhi* is still taped inside. Kavita's fingers fumble around her pocket for Sunil's *rakhi*, where it is safe, and makes her wince as she touches it. As she places the card back on the shelf, she wonders why Nirav didn't ask her to tie the bracelet onto his wrist, as he normally would have, then reasons perhaps he didn't want to upset her. The lack of sympathy cards is puzzling, though. She might not have read them, then again she might have, but either way, reading the cards wasn't the point, the point was acknowledgment, a small gesture to make a lonely time less lonesome. It is possible that cards have been sent, and Nirav has placed them aside, for the same reason he failed to mention the *rakhi*. She will ask him about it later.

She is about to turn away when her gaze falls upon a wedding picture. Numbly, she reaches for the frame. The moment captured shows her and Sunil standing side by side, his arm slung comfortably around her shoulder, her painted nails peeking brightly out around his waist. She is dressed in a maroon *lengha*. Sunil is wearing a black Nehru-collared suit with a waistcoat that matches Kavita's dress. They are staring into the camera, nascent smiles suspended on their faces, as though they aren't sure when the photographer is going to take the photo. It is her favourite wedding picture of them because it is candid, imperfect, completely unlike the phony glamour shots in every Indian wedding magazine she has ever seen, which of course, is what makes the portrait perfect in her eyes.

Suddenly she can't stand to look at the photograph any longer. Its lost beauty burns her eyes as if backlit with fluorescence. She turns away. With blind fingers, she tries to place the frame back in its cubby, then hears it teeter and crash, but doesn't look at it again, not even to stand it upright, or check the glass for cracks.

Out on the terrace, the rain has stopped, but each gust of wind carries a lash. She feels her body contract as though retreating to warmer inward places. She makes a cave with her shoulders, lights her cigarette, and exhales slowly. The rattle of her nerves loses a bit of its shake as she shifts her gaze down to the street.

The sidewalk is tattooed with the umber pigments of decayed leaves. Usual traffic moves to and fro. Kavita watches a woman dressed in a camel trench coat walking a small white dog. The woman stoops over, picks up the dog's mess, and then they both trot on, somewhere, woman and dog alike seeming very hurried and purposeful in each step they take.

Just like all the people Kavita saw on the way home as she travelled to the condo. People on foot, people on bikes, people in cars, people on buses. People moving, moving, moving. People with somewhere to go, to be. Taking care of her parents had given her a purpose, but now, back in her own life, she feels aimless. Exhausted yet restless. A scribble in the margins. Watching the people. Wondering how she was ever part of them, and more bleakly, how she will ever be able find her way back.

As the wind gusts, Kavita gets a prickly feeling that she is being watched. Across the street, a couple of floors up, a man is leaning against his balcony railing, puffing too. When their eyes meet, he takes one more drag, flicks his cigarette butt over the railing, and goes back into his condo. She wonders about him. Why he's at home, like she is, at this time of day, when productive members of society found themselves in offices and shops and on wheels of some sort. Maybe he is sick. Or playing hooky. Or unemployed; unemployable. Or, she thinks, maybe he has lost somebody, like she has, and needs to withdraw from the forward motion of the world for a while, before surrendering again to its tow. She wants to ask him: Is he like her? But he's gone. Maybe she will get another chance tomorrow.

Her neighbour's terrace door unlocks with a click. Kavita buries her cigarette in the terracotta pot at her feet, the one that holds the twig-like remains of some forgotten annual. As her neighbour's door slides open, before she gets caught up in the polite lies of chitchat, she slips back inside.

Coal is curled up on the couch, twitching in dreams. She sits beside him, pulls out the library books from her bag, and selects *A Widow's Story*. As she considers the title, she realizes that there's no common name for what she is now—her new bereft identity—or possibly there is, but if so, she has never come across it. In the world, there are widows and widowers. One need only say "I am a widow" and somehow people understand with sympathetic *hmms* and *ahhs*. There is an understanding of the loss of one's "better half" "right hand" "life partner" "soul mate" but what about the loss of a soul brother? There is widowhood. There is an understanding of that lonely journey. Even divorcées have a label to communicate the challenges of their life state, despite the failure of their relationships.

What about the sibling bereft? What about her and Sunil's twenty-five year relationship, that should have been seventy-five years, eighty-five years? What about the promise of living together for most of their lives, side by side? Hasn't she lost a life partner too? Is her loss somehow lesser, her pain less devastating, because she is not a parent, a wife? What is her "—hood" or "—dom?"

I am brotherless, she thinks, the quiet pronouncement heavy and unmoving as a boulder as it sits at the centre of her mind. Can there be a lonelier state? Brotherless. Another way of saying she is cleaved. She is alone. She is like Yami crying a river of tears at the loss of Yama. But there is no common empathy, no common language, for her grief path, that endless black tunnel. It exists inside her, in perhaps the only place where it matters, or is seen.

Pinned by the boulder, Kavita sits, staring off into mid-space. Sometime later, Coal crosses her lap, padding her gently out of her stupor. Her dazed eyes follow his movements as he leaps off the couch and makes his way over to his food bowl. As he crunches satisfyingly on kibble, she remembers with the groan of her own stomach, Nirav will be home soon.

As she rinses romaine lettuce and chops red peppers, her stomach's earlier groan builds to a growl. She pours a glass of water into its hungry mouth, then flicks on the television to drown out its futile begging.

The evening news is on. She briefly considers changing the channel, to avoid anything triggering, but feels out of touch, so keeps it on for the sake of curiosity. She continues chopping the red pepper, semi-aware of the newscast in the background. The chopping is nearly done when she hears the top story. Hears the news anchor say the word *suicide* and feels her insides spasm as if speared. Letting go of the knife, she lifts her startled gaze to the screen.

A teenager has ended his life. He is the son of a local politician. He was loved by his friends and teachers. He was on the yearbook committee. Played trumpet in the school orchestra. Talked of studying animation after graduating next year. In the yearbook photo they show of him his hair is green, his braces shine, and his acne looks a rosy nuisance. The face of someone with so much life ahead of him, most of his whole life, and in this respect, not unlike Sunil.

Kavita springs for the remote control. Changes the channel. Flicks back. Changes the channel. Flicks back. Changes the channel.

She feels at war with the contrary push of needing to know how this could have happened to such a bright, young person, and the pull of wanting to remain ignorant. Her emotional side tells her: *Look away, protect yourself*. Her thinking side says: *Look*.

She flicks back to the newscast. The anchor explains that the boy's family have decided to share their story to help educate the public about teen mental health. A pre-recorded clip begins to play. Kavita can't pull her eyes away from the local politician, the boy's mother, as she stands at the podium and reads a statement from a piece of paper that quivers in her hands. Her husband stands by her side, his head bowed, his eyes pinned to the floor, his mouth a firm line. One of his hands remains pressed securely against the politician's lower back as if holding her upright.

She says they don't want their son's life, or death, to be in vain, which is why they have chosen to come forward, in the hopes of saving another child, another family, from the incredible pain and loss her family is experiencing now. Her voice quavers as she admits to not knowing about the bullying her son went through leading up to his death. Nor did she realize the toll it took on his mental health. She noticed recent a change in his mood, but like any mother of a teenage son, thought it must have been just another phase of adolescence. She was wrong.

If the stigma surrounding mental health didn't exist, their son might have been more open with them about his struggles. They have started a foundation in his name to collect donations for youth treatment programs at The Royal and encourage others to contribute if they can. She finishes by saying thank you for the messages of support they have received. They ask for prayers, for their son most of all. They thank the public for respecting their need for privacy at this difficult time.

The newscast flips to the next story. Kavita shuts off the television. The story rouses her turbulent grief, that storm beneath her skin. She feels it spinning and building. Crying to cut to the surface. Crying to be heard.

She has things in common with the politician's family, but their situations aren't the same. The politician's husband held her back the whole time she spoke, so she knew he was there, she wasn't alone. They were in pieces, yet unified. But crisis has fractured Kavita's family. The politician's family shared their story. But her family can't even talk to each other about what happened to Sunil. The politician's family want their son's life and death to mean something, to make a difference, to change things for the better. She wants the same thing for Sunil. Of course she does.

But how? She has no public persona. She has no platform. Lately, it doesn't even feel like she has much of a family anymore. She isn't important. She isn't a somebody. She is just a girl who loved her brother, and lost him, in the most inconceivable way. Why would anyone listen to her? Why would anyone care?

How can she change the world when she can barely stand the one she carries inside?

Heaviness pulls at her. She fills her lungs deeply in an effort to resist the drag. Still, it pulls. She knows what's about to happen next.

You're failing him again, Anchor tells her.

The weight settles upon her, heavier and heavier.

That's what you do, says Gloom. *Isn't it?*

Kavita remains there, at the centre of the living room, suspended in a stunned pause, as if locked inside a dark spell.

The metal twist of the front door unlocking shatters the iron shell encased around her. Kavita blinks back into the room and quickly sweeps away her tears. Sweeps away Anchor and Blaze and Gloom, for now, knowing they will be waiting to show themselves the moment she is alone again.

She shuffles back to the cutting board, picks up her knife in her nervous hand and continues chopping the red pepper. She forces her lips into what she hopes is a convincing smile.

"Hello-*oh*?" Nirav calls from the entryway.

"Hi," she calls back. Her voice sounds breathy and high, not her own.

He emerges from the hallway with Coal in one hand and a bottle of white wine in the other.

"Hello, love!" He is wearing a pair of black trousers, a blue dress shirt, and grey paisley tie. "I'm so pleased you're back." He kisses her warmly on the cheek. Coal wriggles from his grasp and pads off. "Look what I've got? Thought we could toast your homecoming with a bit of the ol' vino. What do you say?"

"Great." She forces a deeper grin. Then grabs the cutting board and slides the peppers into the saucepan on the stove, any excuse to turn away and hide for a moment. She hasn't swallowed a drop of alcohol since Sunil's disappearance. The small, still voice inside her continues to warn against the path of forgetting, but it is getting fainter and fainter all the time, taped over by the voices that strengthen in its place.

"It's Pinot Grigio—your favourite." He fetches a couple of stemless glasses, gives the cap a twist and pours. "Here you are, darling." As he holds out her glass, he glances at the Band-Aid on her palm, but doesn't ask about it.

"Generous pour," she says, as she takes hold of the glass.

"I reckon we've got loads to celebrate, don't you?"

She orders herself to smile again. It is what a normal person would do. A normal person would have reason to be happy right now. It doesn't matter that it isn't true. That is the part no one needs to know but her. They toast and she swallows an ample mouthful. She had forgotten how good it tastes, forgetting.

While Nirav showers and changes, she finishes making dinner. Tosses the salad. Plates the pasta and sauce. Mixes together some olive oil and balsamic vinegar in a finger bowl for dipping their bread. A feast compared to how she has been eating, or rather not eating, recently. Her stomach awakens. This time she drowns its complaints with another swig of Pinot.

Their evening progresses like any other, as though she hasn't spent weeks away. They eat dinner while seated across from each other at the island, balancing on ebony wooden stools. She picks at a small portion, pushing food around her plate more often than bringing her fork to her mouth. Nirav talks about a new project at work, but she can barely follow. They drink the rest of the wine. She likes how dull it makes her feel, less alert, less hyperaware. Another glass or two and she might even fall sleep before three a.m. without having to watch *Buffy*.

After supper, they move to the couch for tea and a couple of hours of television. Nirav wants to hold her in his arms. Wine makes him amorous. She loathes being touched but leans into his embrace regardless. It is what a normal person would do. A normal person would want to be close to their partner after spending weeks apart.

Before bed, she takes a scalding shower. Cries about the boy from the news, and Sunil, and her failures while the water burns tiny rivers over her skin. She welcomes the burn. She knows she deserves the burn. She knows she deserves worse.

Now, as she lies in bed at a chaste distance from Nirav, she has an urge to place a pillow between them, although hopes she won't have to. If the wine has done its job, he will be more sleepy than amorous.

The shallowness of his breath tells her that he is still awake, but it won't be much longer. She envies this about him, the way he sleeps like a child unfettered by worry. She wishes she could breathe in this magic like a lavender-filled pillow and drift away. She can't remember the last time she dipped effortlessly into sleep, nor the last time she closed her eyes without fearing the screech of her nightmares, nor the last time she was able to fall asleep without her laptop open, which is the only thing that seems to drown out her horrors, and stop them from shrieking in the night.

Nirav's lascivious grip around her waist jerks her away from her thoughts. She stiffens from crown to toe. A woman knows when she is being touched with expectation.

Pressing his weight against her, he kisses along her jutting collarbone and the taut muscle that bulges from her neck.

"I missed you," he whispers.

"I'm sorry," she says, turning her head to one side. "I can't right now."

Ignoring her, he continues to kiss his way up her cheek, across her eyes, down her other cheek, landing at last on her lips. He probes her mouth with his urgent tongue.

The thinking side of her says: *A good wife pays attention to her husband's needs. A good wife puts her husband's needs before her own. A good wife compromises.*

The feeling side of her shrinks away from his needy touch.

With effort, she frees herself from his deep kiss. "I don't feel well, I'm sorry."

He nuzzles her ear. "It might make you feel better."

Her body is too rigid to even flinch. "Nirav, I can't," she tells him, pleadingly.

He stops. "All right," he sighs, making no effort to mask his disappointment, as he rolls onto his side, his back like a barricade beside her, cold as moonlit stone.

Too rattled to move, she stares into the black nothingness in front of her, and breathes shallow breaths.

Anchor pulls her into the mattress.

You should feel lucky he still wants you, it says.

Yes, it seems that Anchor is right again. She wonders how long it will be before Nirav leaves her or has an affair. Maybe that would be for the best. Maybe he would be better off without her, happier with someone undamaged. He is young, he can start over, in a way that she knows she will never be able to. It isn't right to keep him from finding the happy life she knows she can't offer him anymore.

She blinks at the darkness and listens to the mute sound of late autumn, which is nothing more than the lifeless breath of a cold wind. Through the thin walls of their bedroom, she hears the muffled voices of the couple next door. A spirited laugh pops and fizzles. She envies her neighbour's pillow talk.

Soon, Nirav's breathing is deep and steady, as he navigates in dreams a plane of consciousness away from her. She pushes aside the comforter, climbs out of bed, and pads to the doorway, where she pauses to look over her shoulder, and admire his tranquil body.

She knows she has disappointed him tonight. That what she has given isn't enough. But it is all she has, and she has given it to him. Does he realize this? Did he taste it in the simple pasta dinner or see it in her false cheer or feel it as she reluctantly gave in to his embrace?

Can he tell that she is trying, by coming home early? Taking the blame a moment ago? And the things she does for him discreetly, like covering her scar with Band-Aids or remaining silent about her guests, to keep him from worry. All of this enduring, for him.

Does he notice any of these small sufferings of love? And if so, are they enough to make him stop and wonder what it costs her to carry on?

12.

AROUND THREE A.M., shortly after Kavita falls asleep in front of her laptop, the telephone rings, jolting her out of wavering sleep. The warning beacon in her gut blares, blares, blares. Danger is imminent. Her thoughts shoot to her parents as she hums with dread, vibrations high and quick in her chest. *What's happened?* No one calls with good news before sunrise.

Nirav answers. "Dad? What's the matter? It's the middle of the night."

Kavita rises from the couch and approaches the island. Nirav's expression, moment by moment, shifts from drowsy to alert, in the widening of eyes, the arching of eyebrows. On impulse, she holds one hand over her mouth to stop the scream that is slowly creeping up her throat.

"Oh God," he says.

What? she mouths at him.

He covers the receiver with one hand. "Nani passed away earlier this morning." Then he goes back to the call.

She silently gasps, *Oh no*, and holds her elbows and listens in on the call but can't make sense of the partial conversation she overhears. *I knew it*, she thinks to the hoof of the warning beacon. *I felt it in my gut. I knew something bad was going to happen, and it has.*

Gnawing at her thumbnail, she waits. This new grief stirs the still-fresh loss she has been holding, adding hail to the storm, raising water levels. Soon the flood overtakes her and tears slip down her cheeks. She wipes them away on the sleeve of her pyjamas before Nirav has a chance to see them.

When he hangs up the phone several minutes later, she approaches him carefully and wraps her arms around his torso, squeezing him tightly to shield him from the amputating pain of loss, the haemorrhaging. "I'm so sorry," she whispers.

"I knew it was going to happen sooner or later, you know?" he says, toneless. "We all knew she was terminal. But still, it's a shock, isn't it? It happened fast. Bloody hell, the last I'd heard, she was working a couple of days a week at the shop on Eling Road. She'd sit on a stool behind the register with her little oxygen tank beside her and chat with costumers."

Kavita loosens her embrace and takes a step back to see him better. "What happened?"

"Complications. She couldn't breathe. Her lungs finally gave out."

"I'm so sorry, Niru. What can I do?"

He stares at the floor for a long moment. "There's nothing anyone can do now. She should have stopped smoking decades ago. It's her own bloody fault."

She blinks. "You don't mean that."

"I do, actually. Filthy fucking habit. People need to take responsibility for their own lives. If you really want to do something, you just do it, don't you?"

Her eyes narrow on him. She suspects he has vaulted over shock to anger, knowing that anger is easier for him to manage than sadness. "Maybe she tried."

"Well, not nearly hard enough, obviously."

She presses her lips together and pauses for a second. "How's your mum handling things?"

"By the sound of it, she's pretty out of it, actually. She's sleeping now. Dad said she'll ring a bit later."

"Have they started making plans? Is there any news about the service?"

"The cremation's at the end of the week. They want me to make a speech."

"What an honour."

"Easy for you to say. You won't have to stand up and speak in front of two hundred people. I don't want to do it."

"I know it must feel overwhelming right now. But you'll probably feel differently once you're there. Trust me, Niru, you don't want to have any regrets about this." Kavita remembers the pantomime of Sunil's memorial service. "You only get one chance to do things right when it comes to saying goodbye."

"Regrets? Why should I have any? She's the one who got cancer and didn't fight hard enough to get better."

"Sometimes you try everything you can, Niru, and things still don't work out in the end." Kavita sees Sunil smiling softly to himself with the appointment cards in hand. Then staring darkly at the doctor's note. Then fixing his resolute gaze on the river and its current. She sees his eyes and the multitude of states between hope and dread they were conveying. She understands now what she didn't at the time, and it makes her wish she could gouge out her memory to stop hindsight's haunting. "It might have been like that for your grandmother. In any case, I think she deserves our compassion. Lung cancer, even self-inflicted, is an awful way die."

"If she'd taken better care of herself, she would still be here. The only people I feel sorry for are my mum and her brothers. All Nani's left them is a mess to clean up. Apparently, her will wasn't even in order, and she knew she was poorly. How selfish is that?" Nirav pours himself a glass of water and takes a gulp. "Last-minute tickets are going to cost a bloody fortune," he blurts before marching into the office.

Kavita follows a few steps behind him and leans against the doorjamb with her arms crossed, watching as he searches for flights.

"Don't worry about the money," she tells him, encouragingly. "This is the reason we save in the first place, right?"

He flashes her a black look.

She curls her chilled toes. "All I mean is you don't need to think about money right now. Just focus on your family. That's all that matters."

For a while, the only sound in the room is the clack of the keyboard. "You know," he says, eventually. "You don't have to come with me."

"What?"

He stops typing. "If you aren't ready to face my family, yet."

"What do you mean?"

He casts a side-eye. "If you're still embarrassed."

"About what?"

"...Your brother."

"Sunil?" she says, puzzled. "Why would I be embarrassed about him?" Kavita regards her husband's stony expression. "Unless you think I have something to be embarrassed about?"

The clack of the keyboard resumes with overcompensating fervour. "Forget I mentioned it," he tells her.

"How can I forget it?"

"Kavita, honestly, I don't have the energy for a row."

"Neither do I."

"Then can we just leave it, all right?" he snaps, raising his voice.

She stares at him, wide-eyed.

He collects himself with a sigh. "I think I just need some time on my own."

"Are you sure?" she asks. "I hate to leave you alone at a time like this."

"I'm sure."

As she considers him with a measuring stare, still confused about the direction their conversation has taken, doubt begins to burrow into her mind like a grub eating into the tender cork of a tree. Why wouldn't he look at her?

"Then I guess I'll leave you in peace. Let me know if you need anything."

He acknowledges her with a minute jut of his chin.

In the living room, she sits on the couch, covering herself with the ivory knitted throw. Coal swiftly occupies her lap and starts kneading her nervous stomach. Something wasn't right. She could feel it in her gut.

13.

THEY CATCH A RED-EYE FLIGHT two days later and taxi onto the runway at Heathrow just after ten a.m. local time.

As they exit the arrivals gate, rolling their suitcases behind them, they spot Nirav's father and sister, standing to the far right of the crowded rail, waving enthusiastically. They haven't seen each other since the wedding, almost a year and a half ago.

Maya rushes forward, flings her arms around Nirav, and buries her face in the curve of his neck.

"Isn't it horrid?" she says. "I haven't been able to eat a anything all day. I'm sure I'll faint soon. I've been surviving on tea and Hobnobs."

As Kavita waits for Maya to acknowledge her, she admires her sister-in-law's hairstyle (pink locks piled in a topknot reminiscent of samurai), makeup (bold cat eye in liquid liner and poppy red lipstick), and outfit (black leather tights and zebra-print faux fur coat), wondering how she managed to muster the energy for such an ensemble while surviving on a meagre diet of tea and Hobnobs. Self-conscious in her jean jacket, faded black cords, and concealer-free face, Kavita touches her hair, wishing it had occurred to her to do more than pull her air-dried waves into a ponytail.

Maya takes a step back and opens her coat. "What do you think?" she asks Nirav. She is wearing a purple T-shirt that says FUCK CANCER in bold pink letters.

"Subtle," he smirks.

"I'm having a bunch made for everyone. We've already donated to a few charities. Everyone's promised to run in the big cancer relay this year. It's going to be brill. Of course, you're going to miss it, like everything else."

"I'll wear mine to the funeral," he winks.

Kavita regards the slogan, impressed by the loudness of their grief, the way it testifies. It's so loud, it even has T-shirts.

As Nirav and Maya continue their conversation, she shifts her attention to her father-in-law. He looks more or less unchanged. Tall, broad, and alert. A man who has spent his career teaching high school History and Geography in a state of enduring disappointment, evident in his perma-frown. He is wearing a navy pea coat, khakis, saddle-coloured Oxfords, and what she considers a very British-looking newsboy cap, recalling a tirade he had gone on once about baseball caps and how appallingly "American" they were. His uncomfortably blue eyes gloss with rare emotion as he watches his children embrace, yet even now he emits a somewhat annoyed air. A moment later, he shifts his attention to Kavita. Walking toward her, he reaches out his hand. "Well hello, Kavita." As usual, he speaks without smiling. They shake hands. He isn't a hugger.

"Hi, Mr. Stone."

"How was the crossing, then?"

"What can you say? It's the red-eye." She scans her father-in-law's features. She suspects that the almost infected tint to his eyes speaks to how little he has slept in the past few days. "How are you managing?" she asks.

"Oh, you know, hanging in there. The missus is in a bit of haze, of course. But that's to be expected, isn't it? How's my lad?"

Kavita looks sidelong at Nirav. He is forehead-to-forehead with Maya, locked in conspiratorial chatter. "I'm not sure, to be honest. He keeps so much to himself. Sometimes I wish he'd have a good cry and let it out."

"Heavens, no. That wouldn't do at all. Kavita, you must understand, my dear, that the Stone men uphold a proud tradition of drinking in lieu of tears, and there's been a lot of that going on, I can assure you. Fortunately, my wife's family also partakes in this noble custom. It is perhaps one of the few similarities between our clans. In any case, I'm sure Maya will cry enough for all of us, isn't that right, my darling?"

"I can't help it," Maya pouts. "I'm sensitive." Locking arms with Nirav, she flashes Kavita a possessive look. "So lovely you could make it, Sis. You look absolutely brill, by the way. Lost a stone, have we?"

Nirav scans Kavita from neck to ankle, forehead wrinkling, as if noticing her weight loss for the first time.

Mr. Stone grins at his children. "Come along, then," he says, as he walks over to Nirav and grabs his suitcase. "Enough dilly-dallying. They're already fleecing us with the parking. Spit spot."

"All right, Mary Poppins," teases Nirav. "Don't swallow your umbrella."

Kavita follows a few steps behind them. The scratch of her suitcase wheels against the ground is the only sound she makes until they reach the car.

They drive from Heathrow to Harrow, where the rest of the Roy clan are gathered. As they drive along the narrow streets, on the opposite side of the road than she is accustomed to, Kavita observes the unfamiliar surroundings—the gloomy sky, the chilling drizzle, the tightly-packed Tudor-style houses, the frequent rotaries, the rundown high streets, the tube stations with their iconic emblem, the quaint pubs with even quainter names: The White Horse, The Castle, The Moon on the Hill.

They park along the street in front of Nirav's maternal grandmother's terraced, Tudor-style home, with beams painted periwinkle rather than the customary black or brown, and a front door that is a surprising shade of red. The front garden has been paved over with pink interlocking stones, where Nani's white Vauxhall is parked.

The cold vapours of the air leach into Kavita's bones in seconds as they approach the house. November in Ottawa is dreary, but this is another level of autumnal desolation.

A sepulchral chill crawls over Kavita as she expects to see Nani's thin, beaming face peeking through the doorway to greet them. She pictures her rusty hennaed roots and dark bindi like a beauty spot, and of course, her sari and cardigan uniform.

Nirav's mother answers the door a second before they are about to let themselves in. Nirav takes after his mother in the length of his limbs, warmth of his complexion, and darkness of his hair. Mrs. Stone is dressed in a navy chiffon sari and black cardigan. Her silver-streaked hair is pulled back into a ratty bun. Smudges of mascara blacken her eyes. Her lips are nude and shrivelled.

"There he is!" She lunges forward and locks Nirav in a constricting maternal embrace. "My boy!"

For a few moments, the air is grave-like around them. When Mrs. Stone finally loosens her embrace, she pulls back, and looks deeply into Nirav's eyes. "I can't believe Nani's gone, Niru. She's always been there for us. And now, in the blink of an eye, gone. What will we do without her? She held so much together. Now she's gone and we're falling apart already."

Staring at the stone steps, Kavita nods, solemn. She has heard the matriarch's fabled tale. Widowed at thirty when her husband was killed in a scooter accident, with one daughter and three sons to care for, Nani shook off the shackles of widowhood and used her savings to emigrate from Calcutta to London. For six years, she lived with her cousin and his family while she worked and saved enough money to open a small Asian supermarket on Eling Road. When she could finally afford the passage, she sent for her children.

"Oh, hello there, Kavita," Mrs. Stone says, at last. "Terribly sorry, dear. I didn't see you there. Quiet as a mouse, you are.

My, you look thin." A pause while Kavita is swept from ankle to crown. "Nani always liked you, you know. I think she
approved of you more than she approved of George, really.
Thought Nirav was going back to the culture when he married
you or some such. Oh, don't look at me like that, George!"

Mr. Stone flashes his wife a stern look, nudges his way through
the door, and marches across the foyer into the house. Maya
follows close behind him, her face pinched, and her nose slightly
lifted. "You would think it was their mother who died," Mrs.
Stone sighs. "Well now, don't stand out in the drizzle. Come
in, come in."

They crowd into the foyer. Shoes are scattered here and
there. Coats are piled onto hooks and the end of the banister.

Mrs. Stone wraps an arm around Nirav's shoulder and leads
him into the house. "Now," she continues, "the men are in the
back room. Niru, go and say hello. Kavita, come with me and
sit with the ladies," motioning to the front room.

Kavita peers inside. She recognizes a few of the aunties
seated on the floral sofa, sombre in their saris, talking in
hushed voices, but most of the other women gathered in the
sitting room she doesn't know. One of the unknown women
looks over at Kavita with a cool beam of judgement as only
an older Indian woman can give a younger. Kavita instantly
feels self-conscious and inappropriate in her faded cords and
jean jacket. She wishes she'd had some traditional clothes to
wear, but all of her Indian outfits were too offensively cheerful
to pack. "Is it all right if I join you in a bit?" she asks Mrs.
Stone. "I'd like to keep Nirav company for now."

"Fine, fine," Mrs. Stone says. "But don't be too long, dear.
We mustn't be rude in front of company." She gives Nirav one
last kiss on the cheek, then disappears into the front room.

Kavita finally tunes in to the low murmurs of the house. She
follows Nirav to the back room and stands in the doorway.
The men are seated in a circle, spread out among the black
leather sectional, club chairs, and a few kitchen chairs.

Mr. Stone is seated at one end of the couch, grim-faced, as he swigs scotch. Beside him are Nirav's three uncles, Dilip, Rajesh, and Sanjay. Tall and bald, Dilip mama, the second eldest, helps with the shop. Tall and round, Rajesh mama, the third eldest, runs a chippy. Tall and slim, Sanjay mama, the baby of the family, works as a clerk at NatWest. The other men Kavita hasn't met.

Despite the pre-lunch hour, a half-drunk bottle of dark liquor holds a place of honour at the centre of the coffee table, alongside an ice bucket, and a scattering of thick-bottomed tumblers. The din of the room swells excitedly with Nirav's shy arrival. The men rise to greet him with strong hugs and firm shoulder shakes.

As Kavita tiptoes into the room, the volume lulls, sharply. She feels like a character in an old Western, the stranger who walks into the saloon.

The surprise only lasts for a moment. The men quickly adapt. They sit up straighter, welcome her with timid hugs and dry pecks on the cheek, and clear a space for her on the couch beside Nirav. Before she has a chance to refuse it, one of the uncles pushes a scotch into her hand. And with that, her admittance into their fraternity appears complete.

She sips the caustic drink and catches fragments of the maudlin chatter.

I can't believe she's gone.

I spoke to her that morning.

The damp winter months were too hard on her lungs.

I'll miss her samosas and tamarind sauce.

I wonder what will happen to the shop now? Should we sell it? Should we keep it?

Heat rises from the drink into Kavita's cheeks. Sinking into the broken-in couch, she reflects on Nani, the closest thing she has ever had to a grandmother, having never met her own.

They would sit, drink tea, eat snacks—*bhajis* and tamarind sauce or fresh *dhokla* with coriander chutney. Nani would ask if they had good jobs, if they made enough money, when they were going to buy a house, when they were going to start a family. In turn, Kavita would ask: What was the sea voyage like from Bengal to South Hampton? Was it frightening to be a widow in a foreign place, or unexpectedly freeing? How had the community changed over the years? Nani would answer in her meandering singsong way, as though displaying a long-forgotten family quilt that had been packed away in a suitcase for safe keeping, each golden line of her story as rich as the finest zari work.

Kavita reaches for Nirav's hand, and squeezes.

"Are you all right?" he asks.

"I'm just thinking about Nani. She changed so many lives. You know, if she hadn't immigrated, you and I would never have met."

He smiles partway. "That's true, isn't it?"

Their reminiscing is interrupted when a man Kavita doesn't recognize enters the room. He is wearing a blue jacket and dark pants and looks to be middle-aged, as hinted at by his grizzled temples. Another family friend who has come to offer his condolences, Kavita assumes. She greets him, warmly.

As he passes, he flashes her an accusing glare. Points with his eyes to the whiskey in her hand, and sneers, "That better not be for you," then turns away from her in disgust.

The welcoming smile drops from Kavita's lips. A blink breaks her momentary paralysis. Puzzled, her eyes dart from the glass in her hand, to the stranger's hairless crown, and back to the glass again. *What did he just say?* she thinks. *Who is he?*

Sheepish, she places her scotch on the coffee table, and avoids the man's *pandit*-like gaze.

"Just ignore him," Nirav whispers.

"You heard what he said?"

"Just let it go, all right?" The next moment, Nirav's father introduces him to the strange man. Nirav stands, shakes hands, and tells him what a pleasure it is to meet him, with a wide grin.

Kavita sits in silence, unnamed, without being introduced.

She wonders if this her punishment for roguish behaviour, being out of place, disrupting their customary order of: women over here, men over there?

Quietly, she excuses herself and ventures next door to see if she can find better company among the women.

Maya sits hunched on a chair close to the doorway, frowning and texting on her mobile. Kavita leans on the wall beside her, clears her throat, and waits to see if any conversation might flow between them. Maya keeps her eyes fixed on the glowing screen in her hands, her thumbs moving with impressive speed.

"Kavita, dear," Mrs. Stone says from the opposite corner of the room. "Come and say hello to everyone."

Crossing the room, Kavita slowly makes her way along the line of women seated on the floral settee, folding her hands in *namaskar* and greeting them with a slight bow.

At the far end, she finally meets someone she knows, Nisha Auntie, Dilip mama's wife. She is a plump woman, with waist-length black hair, puffy from years of brushing out its disobedient curl, which she always wears in a long braid draped over one shoulder. She is wearing a purple cotton sari and grey cardigan. During their last visit, this same auntie pinned a charm into Kavita's sweater to help ward off the dreaded evil eye, a loving gesture as steeped in caring as it was village superstition. Kavita is happy to see her.

"How are you, Kavita?" Nisha Auntie asks, her grin warm and genuine.

"I'm fine, thank you, Auntie," Kavita replies. "And you?"

"As well as can be expected, *haan*?"

Kavita nods.

"Have you learned to speak Bengali yet?"

"No, Auntie, not yet."

"Ahh," Nisha Auntie nods, an expression of slight disappointment on her face. "And tell me, how are your parents? How is their health?"

"As well as can be expected," borrowing a line from Nisha Auntie.

"When will they be visiting us?"

The question comes as a slight shock. Kavita's parents are in no shape to make the journey and bear the exhaustion of visiting from house to house. Nevertheless she answers, "Maybe next year."

"And how about your brother?" Nisha Auntie goes on. "How is Sunil?"

Although Kavita hears the words, she doesn't understand their meaning, as though Nisha Auntie has suddenly switched to Bengali. She must have misheard.

"I'm sorry?"

"Your brother," Nisha Auntie repeats. "How is his health? Will he be marrying soon? I know some nice girls."

Before Kavita has a chance to respond, a hand claws her elbow and thrusts her out of the room. In the solitude of the foyer, Mrs. Stone whispers deeply into her ear, "No one knows about him."

Then she leaves.

14.

MINUTES PASS. The sounds of the house fall to the background of Kavita's shock. All she can hear are the senseless words spinning inside her head, over and over, and over and over.

What was happening? How could they not know about Sunil's passing? Why did Mrs. Stone rush off without explaining?

Part of her has an urgent need to tell Nirav what has happened. See his eyes bulge and the symmetry of his face screw with confusion. Hear him voice all the questions that are spinning inside her skull. But he is still anesthetising his feelings with the men, and after her shame-faced retreat, she can't bring herself to breach their clubhouse again.

The other part of her wants to hide.

"Kavita!" Mrs. Stone summons.

Oh no.

"Kavita?"

I can't go back in there.

"Ka-vi-ta!"

I need to get out of here.

15.

"Kavita!" There is no escape. "Don't just stand in the hallway, dear!"

Nor any confession of sin.

Her legs feel numb. How can she stumble back into that room and pretend something very wrong didn't just happen? What if someone else asks about Sunil? Is she supposed to tell them in passing that he died months ago? Or worse, pretend he is still alive? She doesn't know what to do. And there is nowhere else to go.

She suddenly realizes she is shaking. She balls her hands into fists to squeeze the quake into submission.

That is the moment she notices a deep emptiness, cold and spherical, like a hollow globe of ice, behind her navel, where she has been looted of something—something important. What was it? How does she get it back? What is the cold space that has replaced it, as frigid, lightless, and lonely as a den made of snow.

This can't be happening, she thinks. *None of this makes sense.*

The den of snow is limitless; its chill, endless.

She wraps her arms around her stomach.

She is alone with it.

Alone.

16

WHEN HER NAME IS CALLED again, Kavita knows there is no other choice but to go back into the room. She stabs her nails into the scar on her palm. *Forgive me, Bear*, she begs him, hoping he will understand.

Once in the front room, she leans against the wall beside Maya, which somehow feels like a less hostile place than it did earlier.

"Kavita," Mrs. Stone says. "There you are, dear. You wouldn't mind fixing us a brew, would you? Two sugars in mine, ta. Oh, and there's a box of cream teas on the counter."

"I take three sugars," Maya tells Kavita, eyes glued to her mobile.

Without a word, Kavita retreats to the safety of the kitchen. Through the thin wall, she hears the men chatting, toasting, clinking glasses. Mechanically, she goes about making tea.

When it's ready, she smooths out the creases of her face until she is blank, and carries out a tray of tea cups and cakes, bowing in front of the ladies as they help themselves. As she stoops in front of Mrs. Stone, the tray begins to rattle in her hands.

"Ah, bless," Mrs. Stone says. She slurps a sip. "Goodness, Kavita, are you all right? I must say, you do look a bit peeky, dear. Not coming down with flu, I hope. The last thing I need at the mo' is a sore throat to go with my runny nose, goodness me!"

After the tea is passed around, Kavita slips back into the

kitchen with the empty tray, until Mrs. Stone calls upon her again. She doesn't know how long she can maintain this state of shaky, forced calm, how long she can suppress the rumblings beneath her skin.

Back in the front room, she takes a seat beside Maya, who shifts ever-so-slightly in the opposite direction.

"My tea's too sweet," Maya says, flat.

Kavita sits, mutely, knifing her nails into the scar on her palm. While it doesn't hurt as much as she would like, as much as she knows she deserves, for now it will have to suffice.

Meanwhile, the words continue to funnel in her head, a bedlam she fights to contain within her statue of a body, as she trembles in ways no one else can see.

17.

HOURS LATER, they drive back to the Stone's. As soon as they enter the house, Kavita tries to pull Nirav aside and tell him what's happened, but he has to write his speech, and he is in a mood. It can wait a little longer, she tells herself.

Soiled with travel, she craves a shower, and the solitude of the washroom. She grabs a change of clothes and slips upstairs. As soon as she locks the washroom door, the words surge back to her with even more virulence, as if they have absorbed every bit of the force she used to push them down, and now they are pushing back—they are pushing her over.

No one knows about him.

No one knows about him.

No one knows about him....

She runs the shower, undresses, and steps into the bath with a shiver. She stands facing the stream, wanting the water to pour into the chill she has been holding in her belly, but even at full strength, the water isn't hot enough to melt away the frigid feeling.

As trickles trace her skin, she hugs her nakedness, and the words brim out of her in short, convulsive cries. Maybe if she lets them out this way, they will slip down the drain like dirty water and return to the rotten underground place where awful things belong.

But it doesn't work. No matter how she tries to empty herself, the words remain, as if they are a part of her now, like Anchor and Blaze and Gloom. And the nameless den of snow.

No one knows about him.

No one knows about him.

No one knows about him....

Gloom settles upon her back. Its weight curls her spine. She sinks to her knees and presses her palms against the tub, trying to resist its dark power, which feels heavy enough to crush her into the floor.

18

WHEN THE WATER FINALLY runs cold, she wakens, trembling. She lifts herself out of the bath and wraps herself in a towel that has been warming on the radiator. As she sits on the toilet, waiting for the quake in her flesh to still, she wonders, bleakly, what in the world she is going to do with herself while Nirav finishes his speech.

The feeling side of her wants to bury the incident in dreams within dreams.

The thinking side of her lectures she is overreacting. Why does she always have to be so *soft*? Doesn't she know her perspective is skewed by her emotions? Doesn't she know people who feel too much are usually wrong? No? Well, they are, it assures her. She has probably misunderstood the whole situation, so she should keep calm, and wait for a reasonable explanation. It repeats: be reasonable. Nirav will help her get to the bottom of things and then she will see how silly she has been. Everything is going to be fine. Now, it tells her, snap out of it, and get back out there, and for the love of God, be *useful*.

Wait for a reasonable explanation, she coaches herself. *Everything is going to be fine.*

Kavita finds Nirav seated at the oblong dining table, hunched over a spiral notepad with a pencil in his hand. He scribbles something, crosses it out, and then rubs his forehead, as if the friction might summon a muse. As she passes, she touches his shoulder. He keeps rubbing his forehead.

Mrs. Stone is seated in the living room watching a show on television. Kavita presumes that Nirav's father and sister are in their bedrooms.

As she looks at Mrs. Stone, Kavita feels the words resurge, the way they had in the shower, but quickly sandbags them with her reason-based mantra: *Wait for a reasonable explanation. Everything is going to be fine. Be pleasant and helpful and a good daughter-in-law.*

"Mrs. Stone," she says. "I was thinking about making dinner for us."

"Brilliant, brilliant," says Mrs. Stone without taking her eyes off the television. "And another brew when you've got a minute, dear, would be lovely. Ta."

Kavita lingers in case Mrs. Stone might add a please or a thank-you or perhaps the reasonable explanation she has been strenuously awaiting.

"Something else, dear?"

"N-no. The tea won't be long."

Kavita passes Nirav on the way to the kitchen.

"It's too bloody loud in here," he huffs, then marches off to his bedroom upstairs.

Kavita goes about making tea, concentrating on each step as a way of quietening her mind. She gets out cups, PG Tips, cubes of sugar, and pint-sized jug of milk. Meanwhile, she considers that perhaps it's a good thing Nirav went to his room. Maybe Mrs. Stone means to explain everything to her over a nice cup of tea.

Back in the living room, Kavita hands Mrs. Stone a steaming cup. "Ah, lovely." Mrs. Stone takes a loud slurp. "Really, really nice, dear. Much improved. I think you must have forgotten the sugar in mine last time. Never mind, never mind!"

Kavita sits and sips. Sips and waits. The mantra begins to fail her. She recites it again.

Wait for a reasonable explanation. Everything is going to be fine. She feels a bit calmer. *Now,* tells herself. *Be pleasant and helpful and a good daughter-in-law.*

"I guess I'll get dinner started."

"There's a Jamie Oliver cookbook on the counter if you need a dash of inspiration. He makes a lovely curry, you know."

As Kavita rises, the mantra fails her again. Blaze flashes like oil in a pan. *I don't need Jamie Oliver to teach me how to cook Indian food, thanks.*

Back in the kitchen, she scours the small fridge and the cupboards for ingredients. She is always surprised to see a washing machine under the sink, where she expects to find a dishwasher. By the end of her rummage, she has gathered together cauliflower, potatoes, onions, the necessary spices, and a pack of ready-made rotis.

First, she chops the onion. Blaze guides the knife. The pieces get smaller and smaller until they resemble grains of rice. Next, she moves on to the tomatoes. When Blaze is finished with them, they are jam.

She is about to start hacking the cauliflower, when Mrs. Stone enters the kitchen, the slap of her *chappals* announcing her arrival. *This is it*, Kavita thinks. She sets down the knife, orders herself to smile, and clasps her hands behind her back, an inviting pose.

Mrs. Stone places her empty cup in the sink. "Going up for a bit o' kip before dinner. See you in a bit, dear." The false smile drops from Kavita's lips, as she watches Mrs. Stone exit the kitchen and disappears upstairs, her blue sari swaying in time with her unhurried gait.

Kavita stares at the cauliflower. There is nothing more to do now other than finish cooking dinner. Mrs. Stone has been through a lot, she reminds herself. A nap will do her good. Maybe later she will have more energy to explain the mix-up. Yes, Kavita reasons, these conversations are best had when everyone is well-rested.

She grips the knife and attacks the cauliflower. That evening's *aloo gobi* will be more purée than *sabji*.

In the hot pan, she fries the onions and tomatoes. Adds salt, pepper, curry powder and cumin. Coaxes the masala to release its peppery perfume with a stir. Breathes in the warm and familiar bouquet. For the moment, she isn't in some unfamiliar neighbourhood in Greater London any longer. The aroma sails over the Atlantic, back home, where it is safe.

19

WHILE THE *SABJI* FINISHES in the pan, Kavita rinses basmati, grates cucumber for *raita*, and chops tomatoes, onions, and coriander salad. She even decides against serving the frozen rotis and rolls out pinches of dough instead. Then she sets the table, cleans the dishes, and lights a rose-scented incense stick that was already waiting for fire in a holder on the kitchen windowsill.

What else? she thinks, as she stands in the middle of the kitchen. What else can she do to maintain this state of forced calm. What else to distract away from the corkscrew of doubt twisting her gut, that whispers to her during the occasional lull in her chores: What if there is no reasonable explanation?

Chores, chores, chores. More of them. Now. She could take out the trash, or reorganize the cupboards, or clean out the fridge, or put a load of washing on. At home, she would have felt comfortable enough to lose herself among these mundane tasks. But she isn't at home. Home is supposed to be a safe place, but she doesn't feel safe here. Not safe enough to stop, and certainly not safe enough to be alone with her thoughts.

She wonders if Nirav has finished his speech by now and decides to check on him. Upstairs, she opens his bedroom door without a creak. She finds him hunched over a small desk. The room is dim apart from the desk lamp that offers a funnel of citrusy light over his pages. He lowers his pencil and glances over.

She grins and takes a seat on the end of his bed. "How's the speech coming?" she asks.

He leans back on his chair with a slight groan. "I'm rubbish at this sort of thing. I've never been comfortable speaking in front of crowds. Apparently loads of people are coming tomorrow. So many people knew Nani from the shop. I still don't know how I'm going to stand in front of them and say something that doesn't sound like a load of bollocks."

"Once your up there, things will start rolling, and it'll be over before you know it. You're going to do great. I know it."

"The thought of it makes me a bit ill, actually." He rubs soothing circles over his stomach. "You know me, love. I'd rather just keep my head down and keep to myself."

"Can I help at all?"

"No, it's all right. It's just taking a lot longer than I thought it would, is all." He scratches the stubble on his chin. "Anyway, how about you? What have you been up to?"

"I made dinner," she says. "Not much else." She hesitates. "I'm feeling a little stiff from the flight, actually. Do you feel like stretching your legs? The writing might come easier if you take a little break." Then she can tell him what happened, out in the open air, where it is safe.

"Sorry, love, but if I don't push through, I'll just give up."

"You're right," she says, crestfallen beneath her thin smile. "The speech is important. Of course, you should finish it."

"Hopefully it won't take much longer. Maybe we can go for a stroll after dinner, yeah?"

She gives him a faint parting smile, then leaves.

Back in the kitchen, she walks through a fine, rippling cloud of incense. Closing her eyes for a moment, she inhales the comforting aroma of smoky rose. As she exhales, she wonders what to do with herself.

She considers calling her parents, but they will be asleep by now because of the time difference. She craves a cigarette, but doesn't know where the nearest corner store is, nor does she trust her navigational skills in the warren roads of Nirav's old neighbourhood. She might have gotten some fresh air in the garden, if it weren't for the relentless drizzle, and patio chairs covered in unwelcoming puddles. She scolds herself for not packing one of her library books.

In the living room, she searches for something to read but only finds a copy of *The Sun* and a stack of *Hello!* magazines. Flopping on the couch, she reaches for the remote, and starts clicking.

Eventually, she comes across a rerun of *Friends*. "The smelly cat episode," she grins. "I love this one." She remembers watching this episode with Sunil, when it was first aired, back in the nineties. How he doubled over, his high-pitched, hyena of a laugh echoing through the basement as Phoebe strummed her guitar and sang in her nasal voice that was so charmingly out of key.

The fragile moment of nostalgia and the momentary joy it brought quickly fades. Something about the memory causes the words to surge back.

No one knows about him.

No one knows about him.

No one knows about him....

"I bloody love this episode," says a distant voice, pushing Kavita off her merry-go-round of thought. She looks to the right and finds Nirav's father standing there in a brown cardigan. As he lowers himself onto the adjacent loveseat by the window, he draws his black horn-rimmed glasses from his breast pocket, and makes himself comfortable. "This is the one when Rachel puts mince in the trifle, isn't it?"

Kavita blinks at the television, puzzled. The smelly cat episode had ended without her noticing.

By the end of the episode, the sun has nearly set. Nirav's father flicks on the lights. The room is suffused with soft pearly light. He peers over at the dining room. "I see you've made supper," He pats his stomach. "I'm famished. Shall we call the others?"

Kavita rises slowly to her feet, her head dull as if wakened from a heavy nap. "I'll get Nirav," she says.

Back upstairs, she peeks her head through Nirav's bedroom door and finds him in much the same hunched posture as earlier. "Dinner time," she grins. "Sorry for bothering you."

"It's no bother." He sets down his pencil on the notepad. "I just finished."

"Do you want to practice it in front of me?"

"I don't think so, love. If it's awful, I'd rather not know, if you get me." He winks at her.

She presses her lips together, wondering if now would be a good time to ask. "Niru," she says. "Now that you're finished your speech, can we talk about something after dinner?"

He gives her a cautious look. "Of course. What's it about?"

"Something that happened when we were at Nani's. I wanted to tell you about it when we got back, but I knew you needed to concentrate on your speech."

"I hope it's nothing serious?"

"That's what I'm hoping we'll be able to figure out." She hears people in the kitchen. "But it can wait till after dinner. Come on, everyone's waiting."

While the others gather around the table, she reheats the *sabji* and rice, gets the *raita* and salad out of the fridge, and rubs *ghee* on the rotis until they glisten.

Maya frowns. "My stomach's eating itself and there's nothing but veg on the table?"

Kavita approaches the table with a plate of rotis stacked high. "Aren't we supposed to eat vegetarian while we're in mourning?"

Maya rolls her eyes. "We aren't properly religious."

"Now, now, my darling," says Mrs. Stone. "I'm sure your blood sugar will balance out once you've had something to eat. Everyone gets a tad grouchy on an empty stomach, don't they?"

As Kavita takes her seat, Mrs. Stone holds out her plate, and says, "A little bit of everything for me, dear."

Kavita rises to her feet once more, takes Mrs. Stone's plate, who is seated across from her, and serves, then makes her way around the table, clockwise, and fills the plates of Mr. Stone, Maya, and Nirav. Lastly, she serves herself, a small portion, as usual.

No one speaks for the first few bites, appearing to enjoy the food, except for Maya, who pushes a curried cube of potato around her plate, her face drawn in a familiar dark sulk. Soon she abandons the potato and picks up her mobile. Kavita focuses on her plate and tears into a warm, glistening roti, admiring the simple pleasures of butter and bread.

"Kavita, dear," Mrs. Stone says over a partial mouthful. "I've been meaning to talk to you about something. I meant to bring it up earlier, actually, but it was so hectic at Nani's, it didn't feel like the right time."

Kavita lifts her gaze and peers across the table, wrists hovering over her plate.

Mrs. Stone gives her husband a serious sidelong look. "We need to confess something to you, don't we George?"

"Yes, that's right. We've left it too long already."

Kavita's heart beats quicker. "What is it?"

"Well, it's the kind of thing that's best discussed in person, really. It's so easy for misunderstandings about these sorts of things to take place. And we wouldn't want that, now would we? Anyway, you're here now. So we can speak about things openly, face to face. That's what families are meant to do. Families can talk about anything."

Kavita knew for a fact Nirav spoke to his family about precisely nothing, other than football scores and the trials of both English and Canadian weather, but she pushes this reality aside, nodding encouragingly for Mrs. Stone to edit the preamble and go on.

"Well dear, it's hard to talk about these things, of course. It's hard to find the right words. Stepping in it seems inevitable. What with the way things are. I suppose people of our generation have never really learned the proper way of approaching these matters. It's all very delicate, isn't it?"

With relief, Kavita senses what is coming. The explanation she has been faithfully awaiting since the moment after disbelief was hissed deeply into her ear.

"Right, well, out with it now," Mrs. Stone continues. "Kavita, Nirav: we think it's time the two of you started a family."

For a few beats, Kavita forgets to breath at all.

"I know, I know, you think we're out of bounds. But you've been married for over a year and the honeymoon can't last forever, you know. By the time we were your age, we already had both of our children." Mrs. Stone flicks a critical eye in the direction of Kavita's lap. "We trust everything's all right in that area, yes?"

"Hold up, yeah?" Maya interjects. "I'm too young to be an aunt. I only just started uni!"

Mrs. Stone gives Maya an indulgent smile. "This isn't about you, my darling." Then she fixes her eyes on Kavita again. "What this family needs is new life, Kavita. It's been a dreadful year, what with my mother passing so unexpectedly. A baby would surely sweep away all of our sorrows. One of the ladies who comes in to the shop regularly just had a grandchild. The other day, she brought in pictures of the little cherub, all snuggled in a pink blanket she had knitted herself. I was positively bursting with envy!"

"Stretch marks," Maya says, pulling a face. "*Rank.*"

"Oh, don't listen to her. It's all worth it in the end, isn't it? Stretch marks are a privilege! Just like motherhood. That's the problem with girls today. They care more about their careers and their figures that their duty to their families. It's all terribly selfish, isn't it?"

Maya snickers.

"But you know, dear," Mrs. Stone continues. "There are some serious things to consider. It may not seem immediate to you now, but the reality is you aren't getting any younger.

You'll never be healthier than you are now. Pregnancy only gets more difficult with age. And let's be honest, at this point, you don't even know if things will go smoothly in that department, if you read me. The truth is, you and Nirav aren't even really a family yet, not without children. Isn't that right, George?"

"Yes, quite right. Children are a family's *raison d'être*, isn't it?"

"We know you're resistant to changing your lives. You've grown accustomed to only thinking about yourselves. But trust me, children, you don't want have any regrets. I didn't want to have to mention it, but there's an elderly woman who comes into the shop nearly every day, a sad little thing, she is. Lives on her own in one of those fancy retirement residences, which I'm sure sounds like a luxurious old age, but let me tell you, despite all her money, she's as lonely as sin. It's absolutely heartbreaking. I suppose it's her own fault for being selfish and short-sighted, really. But, because I care, I wouldn't want that to happen to you." Mrs. Stone pauses, briefly, a thoughtful smile on face. "I can't wait to be called Dadi," she continues. "Dear me, I'm getting misty just thinking about it."

"The little nipper shall call me Grandpa Stone."

"What? Not G-Daddy?" Maya smirks, then she lets out a wistful sigh. "I suppose I could tolerate being called Auntie M. Oh no, will it have an horrible American accent and all?"

"*Canadian*, my darling."

"Uh, what's the difference?"

"Well, Kavita dear," Mrs. Stone says, leaning in. "Don't leave us in the lurch. Tell us about your plans."

"Yes," her father-in-law says, offering a rare smile. "Out with it, spit spot."

"Mary bloody Poppins," Maya mutters, thumbing at her mobile.

Kavita looks sidelong at Nirav. Somehow, miraculously, he hasn't lost his appetite amid the barrage. As he tears into a roti, she nudges his legs under the table.

"Wha?" he barks. She blinks at him. He's gone very London

all of a sudden, dropping the "t," which only happens when he's in a particularly surly mood.

She opens her eyes wide and begs him, wordlessly, for help.

"Bloody hell, can't we eat in peace for once?"

"Now, now, there's no need to get cross, darling."

"We haven't talked about having kids, all right?"

"Don't you want a family, Kavita?" her father-in-law asks. "You know, a woman isn't really a woman until she's given birth."

"Yes, exactly," Mrs. Stone agrees. "You're probably worried about losing your independence. But really, you won't be losing anything at all. You can't even imagine what you're going to gain."

"Yeah, like, three stone," Maya laughs.

The collective weight of their stares crush Kavita's voice. She glances at Nirav but he keeps his eye on his plate. "I need some more water," she manages to blurt beyond her shock, grabbing her already-full glass and escaping into the kitchen.

"*Wah-der*," Maya mimics behind her back.

Kavita runs the tap, rests her glass on the counter, and holds the rim of the sink. The chatter in the dinning room falls behind the roar of the torrent.

The rationalizing and scant hope and mantra have failed her completely. Instead of a reasonable explanation, she got what she was never expecting: unreasonable expectations. It has only been months since Sunil passed away. Do they really think she is in any shape for motherhood?

Before Sunil's passing, she and Nirav sometimes fantasized about having a child. They mused about what he or she might look like, the names they could live with and the ones they couldn't stand, how they wanted the baby to learn both Hindi and French.

Now, her fantasies are dyed a darker hue, and her thoughts about parenthood shoot to the worst possible scenario: What if mental illness is encoded in her genes? What if Gloom has always been inside of her like a spore waiting for ideal conditions to spread its suffocating taint, its black hypha branching through her like chocking vines until she is colonized? What if she has a child, and that child struggles like Sunil did? What if she has a child, and loves it, and cares for it, and makes it the centre of her world, and that child takes the life she gave it?

It could happen.

It happened to her parents. They wanted health and happiness and good fortune like anyone else. They had been blessed with those treasures for a while—been *lucky* as some might smugly boast as if the rest of the world were damned—but then those good things were plucked away, violently plucked away. What makes her think she is immune?

It could happen again.

If it happens again, she knows she won't survive it. Her bloody, broken heart can't be splintered into any smaller pieces, it simply isn't possible.

"Kavita?" Mrs. Stone calls out, puckering her ears against the trill. "Are you filling your glass or the Thames, dear?"

She shuts off the tap. She wants to excuse herself but there is no escape from the Roman arena that is their dining table. No, there is no safety in this place.

Kavita returns to her seat at the table. They have moved on to gossiping about the upcoming Royal wedding. Although she isn't hungry, she eats, if only to close herself off to conversation, her presence for the rest of the meal as slight as the sounds that she makes: tearing, scooping, swallowing with effort.

20.

AFTER DINNER, KAVITA SEQUESTERS Nirav in his bedroom at last. By the light of a single floor lamp, they sit on his bed, and she holds her hands in her lap to stop their mutinous quivering from betraying the saint-like air she is strenuously trying to exude, all openness and inner glow like a statue in a temple.

"That thing I wanted to talk to you about," she says in her softest manner. The baby shaming will have to wait its turn in the queue of inappropriate things have happened during this trip.

Nirav stifles a yawn. "Oh right. Go on, then."

"I don't know how to say this," she begins. "So, I'm just going to spit it out. When we were at Nani's, I went to say hi to the ladies, and Nisha Auntie asked me...." She trails off. She isn't sure she can go on.

"What?"

"She...Niru, she asked how Sunil was. If he was planning on getting married soon. As if he were still alive. As if she didn't know he had passed away."

Nirav doesn't react to what she has revealed, possibly because he is even more astonished than she is—or perhaps too embarrassed—so she carries on. "Then afterwards, your mom pulled me aside and told me that 'no one knows about him.' I'm not even sure what that means. Do you have any idea what's going on?"

Nirav says nothing and keeps his stare low. Kavita searches his face for an answer. She sees what she thinks is outrage slowly rippling underneath his placid exterior. She imagines its roar building in his long, introspective pause. Any moment now, it will burst through and shake the walls, validating her pain and confusion.

"The rest of the time we were there," she says. "I felt like I had to pretend Sunil was alive. Like I got roped into a terrible secret. I didn't know what else to do. I was so shell-shocked. I still don't know what it all means."

"Unbelievable," he says at last.

"I know," she agrees. "I still can't figure out why or what it all means."

Nirav looks up from the floor. She expected his amber eyes shine with anger, and yet also expected them to remain soft, at least while they rested upon her. But these eyes are hard, and they frighten her. "You're what's unbelievable, Kavita."

She blinks quickly as though his words have kicked dust into her eyes. "What did I do?"

"I can't believe how selfish you are."

He might as well have backhanded her with his steel wedding band. It would have left less of a bruise.

"I don't understand. Are you mad at me?"

"My grandmother just died, Kavita. I have to give a speech tomorrow that I don't want to give. We just had a really, really nice dinner with my family. But you have to go and spoil it, don't you?"

She stares at him, astonished. "I waited to tell you, Niru. I wanted you to finish your speech first. I've been so confused and hurt by this, but I waited, all day."

He leans forward, resting his forearms on his knees, and pushes a sigh past his flared nostrils.

"Don't you at least think it's odd?"

"Well, I don't know, do I?"

"Me neither. I was hoping we could figure it out together.

That's all. Was I not supposed to tell you?"

Wordlessly, he clenches his jaw, the muscles pulsing like a slow heartbeat.

"It's been really upsetting for me, Niru."

He rises from the bed and towers over her, blocking the lamp light with his long silhouette. "Not everything's about you, Kavita," he tells her, bluntly, before marching out of the room, and shutting her inside with only the yaw of her confusion for company.

21

*D*ID THAT JUST HAPPEN? she thinks, stunned. *Did he really call me selfish?*

    Her thinking self says it's her own fault for raising the subject at the wrong time. Nirav isn't himself right now. He has a short temper because he's grieving. She needs to give him time. Once the fog settles, he'll see things more objectively. Then he'll make things right. Her thinking self tells her she really should have waited.

Her feeling self careens as if shoved off balance. As it falls, this part of her knows that no reasonable explanation is coming. For whatever reason, Nirav's family has kept her brother's suicide a secret. *Families can talk about anything*, she remembers from the lecture at the dinner table. But not everything, apparently.

For a while, Kavita sits, holding her knees, still yet buzzing.

Then a sound breaks the cold silence of her mind. It is her mother's voice, monotone and frank: *No one judges people who die of cancer.*

Back then, when they had gathered around the kitchen table, on that first bleary morning after Sunil had been found, and struggled with how to plan his memorial, Kavita had criticized her mother for being paranoid about people's reactions. Now, she understands her mother's reasoning, perhaps in the only way children ever come to sympathize with their parents, in hindsight.

Her mother was right. People didn't judge. They pinned pink

ribbons on their jackets and wore t-shirts that shouted FUCK CANCER and ran in all-night relays and made record-breaking donations during celebrity-hosted telecasts.

Because no one asks for it. Because the ill fight courageous battles. The ones who make it are conquerors. The ones that don't are heroes. They deserve to be remembered.

Kavita's throat aches. *Well, it was the same for you, Bear. You wanted to get better too. You wanted to live as much as anyone. Living is all you ever wanted.*

With every tremulous moment, her hurt calcifies a little more, casting her like a splintered bone, until the only fluid part of her is her stark thoughts. The awful words surge back, and this time she has nothing left to stop them.

No one knows about him.

No one knows about him.

No one knows about him.

Selfish....

As the words spin and spin, they core her, they empty her. Cold spills into the vacant space where something important once lived. In its place, frigid emptiness.

At last, she knows what it is: Shame, cold and dark as a cellar.

They always say tell the truth. Tell someone. They never say be careful about who you tell. They never say the people you tell might be ignorant or awkward or unwilling to help you. Still, they say tell. Tell someone. Tell your dark truth. Even though the people you tell may use your truth against you.

22

THE STONES ARE IN THEIR BEDS. But Kavita is not. She is not a Stone. The combination of insomnia, jet lag, and the quiet rage that quakes her insides has kept her from finding any rest. Defiant, she invades her in-laws' well-stocked liquor cabinet and pours herself an inch of Glenfiddich—no water, no ice. Taking a generous gulp, she welcomes the sting at the back of her throat, which matches the blue heat cycling through her veins. Standing by the sliding doors that overlook the garden, she gazes up at the smoky night sky.

"Why am I here?" she asks Sunil. She hasn't spoken to him openly since she arrived in London. Now, they are alone at last. She knows it is safe enough. Leaning into the silence, she dilates her ears in the chance that he might finally answer her.

"All along, I've known something bad was going to happen. But I never dreamt of this."

The awful words unspool inside her head.

No one knows about him.

   No one knows about him.

      No one knows about him.

And mix with Nirav's words too.

I can't believe how selfish you are.

Not everything's about you, Kavita.

Is this her reward for pushing aside exhaustion and crossing the cold Atlantic? Smiling although she has lost her joy. Cooking even though the thought of finishing a meal repulses her.

Supporting them in their grief while they openly deny hers. Is this her reward for giving, and then, despite the inch of water left inside her meagre well, ladling out a little more?

She takes a deep sip, and another. Then she reaches for the bottle and pours the same again

Yes, she gave.

And it cost her.

Shame hollows her midsection—round, chilled, empty. A shiver rattles along her bones.

She forces down the drink with a few strained gulps, pushing through her gags for the promise of warmth shining at the bottom of her glass like an ice cube, an end to the unforgiving hoarfrost at her core. She relives the scene and its confusion, seeing all the things she should have said and done at the time. Why didn't she speak up? Why is she always too slow to act?

"I felt like I'd been kicked in the stomach," she explains to Sunil. "I didn't know how to react. I was in the middle of something I didn't understand and it stole my voice. This whole situation is inconceivable to me. How could I prepare for something I didn't think was even possible? Please understand, Bear." Her chest tightens. "I need you to understand." She wishes he was beside her, his arm wrapped around her shoulder, telling her of course he understands, he probably would have reacted the same way, so stop worrying, nothing has ever come between them, and this won't either. She longs for him to tell her that everything is going to be okay. He doesn't forgive her because there is nothing to forgive. But, as ever, the only sound that pours into her ears, is silence.

The skin of her face feels feverish. She holds the cool glass against her searing forehead, trying to slow her speeding thoughts, which race like frenetic molecules pinging off her inner skull. But there is no cooling their sickly motion. She finishes her drink and sets the glass aside. Even the power of whisky can't bolster her against Anchor's drag.

Despite all your promises, it tells her, *you're still failing him.*

You had a chance to do something, to set things right, but instead you did nothing, as usual.

As Anchor pulls, it gets harder to breathe, as if her guilt is water, and she is at risk of drowning in the open air.

The heaviness comes next, its shadow passing through her like a ghost, from her crown of her head, to the soles of her cemented feet.

Aren't you tired of these broken promises, says Gloom. *These thin apologies?*

You know he must be tired of them.

…You're an excuse for a sister.

A waste….

Anchor, Blaze, and Black Gloom all at once—subcutaneous, unsparing, swelling—moving in quick ripples, volatile fluids sliding together in an oily slick, a force that is building toward a burst, the want for release rising to need.

Moving mechanically, Kavita fetches a tea towel from the kitchen, retraces her way to the sliding door, and steps onto the wet patio stones, barefoot. After wrapping the tumbler in the towel, she places the bundle on the ground, hovers her foot above it for a second, then smashes it with her heel.

As she squats low, she unwraps the towel, and searches among the shards, choosing a piece that resembles a spearhead. Holding her breath, she presses the sharpest edge deeply into her palm, resurrecting her cigarette scar. Pain roars up into her throat where she gags on it. The rims of her eyes quiver with little vibrations that blur the edges of her vision.

She does not wince.

She knows she does not deserve to wince.

She does not scream.

She knows she does not deserve to scream.

As she closes her eyes, she dips into the pain—raw, bruised, slippery. This pain she can manage. This pain she knows she deserves.

When the roar of pain tapers to a whisper, Kavita slowly lets the night back into her eyes, and peers into her pitted palm, watching with detachment as blood pools and drips. Her throat aches. Her chin trembles. Hot tears slip down her cheeks.

She straightens her sore legs, pushing up from the squat, and lifts her tearful gaze to the smoky night sky. Sunil's face raises the silver topography of the moon. Is that where he has been? Watching them from on high? Shuddering at what he has witnessed since he's been gone? A charcoal puff of cloud slips across his eyes.

Shadows may obscure beams of moonlight, Kavita reasons, but the moon itself remains, waiting behind the veil for the darkness to move on. The moon is still the moon. It is always beautiful. Kavita thinks of Sunil, viewing from a distance the light masked by trouble, the silver beauty of his glow. That is what he deserves: To be remembered, with beauty.

The charcoal puff of a cloud drifts on. Moonbeams pour into her cold middle, filling it with silvery light. The empty space within her remains cold, but for now, not as lightless as before. She doesn't wish upon a star at that moment. Instead, she vows to the moon, promising to reclaim beauty for Sunil, somehow.

23.

KAVITA FUNCTIONED THROUGH the next few days with the rigid mechanics of something made of more metal than flesh. The only time she felt much of anything at all was when she stood over Nani's casket, but even then she was touched by greater disbelief than sadness, at the greying skin, the artificial plumpness of lips and cheeks, the husk without a soul to liven it, which left her thinking, *That isn't Nani. Nani isn't here*, and made Kavita realize she wasn't either. To live was to feel. Survival was doing what was necessary to get by.

Now they are at Heathrow, saying their goodbyes at the security gate. She lets them hug her and peck her on the cheek, but she doesn't feel any of it.

Normally, passing through security makes her anxious, especially in airports outside of Canada, where she somehow feels more conspicuously brown. Today, though, as she walks through the metal detector, and collects her things from the plastic bin, she breathes in ease, as if with every step she senses her humiliation shrink and shrink behind her. *It's over*, she thinks. Soon she will be home again. Soon she will be safe.

They stop at a newsagent for water, gum, and magazines. While they wait in line, Nirav says, "I know our reason for coming was horrible. But it was a lovely trip in the end, wasn't it?"

Dumbfounded, Kavita hides her shock by reaching for a copy

of *National Geographic* from the bottom shelf of the magazine stand. As they wait to pay, she considers how incongruent her husband's perception is from her own. How you can live a life with someone, and yet, not be living the same life at all.

On the way to the gate, Nirav tries to hold her hand, which she keeps hidden in her sleeve, and she lets out a faint whimper. When he asks her what's wrong, she tells him she accidentally cut herself while making sandwiches for the wake. Silly bean, he calls her. She needs to be more careful, doesn't she? He moves to the other side of her and takes hold of her good hand, thanking her for everything she did leading up to the service and after. She was his rock, he tells her. He couldn't have gotten through it without her. He doesn't bring up their fight, neither seeking an apology, nor offering one, as if whatever happened has been resolved in silence, as if by virtue of pardoning her, he himself has been pardoned.

At the gate, she flips through her copy of *National Geographic* and daydreams of jumping into the photos of exotic locales—bathing in the blue waters of Cuba, trekking on the sandy-coloured plains of the Savannah, and sailing the dunes of the Sahara. Of taking flight.

24

THE PLANE LANDS in the early afternoon. Without speaking, they disembark, wait in line at immigration, collect their bags from the carousel, and wait in another line for a taxi.

During the short ride to their condo, exhaustion begins to sink into her limbs as though her body is finally free to express the cost of the last few days. Leaning her head against the window, she gazes at the familiar surroundings, grateful for home and the cloudless sky. She craves the warm particulars of home—a scalding Epsom salt bath to ease the old-woman ache in her muscles, a strong cup of ginger tea, and Coal curled up on her lap purring in absolute bliss.

As they enter the condo, Coal welcomes them with urgent mews, brushing off his body against their legs as they pry off shoes and hang coats. Kavita picks him up, buries her face in his soft fur, and inhales his reassuring scent. They have a box of Marks and Spencer Scottish shortbread biscuits in her suitcase for her neighbour as a thank-you present for cat sitting.

Reluctantly, she sets him down, travels to the kitchen, and checks on his food and water bowls, while Nirav wheels their suitcases into the bedroom. She is about to top-up his kibbles, when the red blinker of the answering machine catches her eye: 5. 5. 5.

The warning beacon in her gut blares in tandem with the flashes. Danger is imminent. Something must have happened to her parents while she was away. She knows it. She can feel it. The bag of cat food slips from her hand with a bash. Coal's claws skitter across the hardwood as he bolts for cover. Kavita braces herself, then presses *play*.

"Kavita?" her father says. "It's Papa. I'm staying at a hotel. Call me when you get back. Bye."

What? she thinks. *Why is he at a hotel?*

The next message plays.

"It's Papa again. After I hung up, I realized I forgot to tell you where I'm staying. The hotel is called the Traveller's Lodge. The phone number is...have you got a pen? Okay, the number is...."

Kavita scrambles for the message pad beside the phone and scribbles out what she hears.

The third message begins.

"Hi, *beti*. Me again." For a few seconds, the message breaks, and all Kavita can hear is the static sound of her father's breath, its strain amplified through the receiver. "Your mother and I had a fight. She...." Another break in the recording, more heavy breathing. "...She blamed me. For his death. Said it was my fault. If I had been a better father, more attentive, then he wouldn't have...." Someone else might have filled the pause with their tears, but Kavita has still only ever seen her father cry at Sunil's cremation, the day he was brought back to them, and then taken away. "Remember when you caught us fighting in the living room? She said it then, too. But I didn't think she meant it. I thought she was just angry and needed to take it out on someone. Anyway, I hope you get home soon."

Before the fourth message plays, Kavita already knows who it will be.

"Kavita? It's Mom. I'm sure your father has called you by now. Don't listen to him. I didn't kick him out. He chose to leave. I'm sorry he dragged you into this. But please don't worry. It's nothing. I hope you had a good trip. Nirav's mother must have been so happy to see him." A pause that lasts a few beats too long. "Call me once you've settled in."

The last message on the machine is an automated recording is from the Canadian Diabetes Foundation notifying them about donation collection happening in their area next week.

Nirav enters the kitchen buttoning up a fresh shirt. "Anything for me?" he asks.

"We have to get Dad," she mutters past her shock.

"Get him from where?"

She holds up the message pad, stupefied.

Nirav reads her scribbles. "The Traveller's Lodge? What's all this about?"

"That's where he's staying. I think he's been there for days."

"Why isn't he at home?"

"They had a fight. The biggest one yet, by the sound of it. I think...." She can't quite bring herself to say it, swallows, tries again. "They're over, Niru."

"Over as in split up?"

"Didn't I tell you I can't leave them alone?"

"Surely it'll blow over like every other time."

"You can't take back the kind of things they've said to each other. Dad's blaming Mom. Mom's blaming Dad. Who am I supposed to believe? How am I supposed to choose sides? It's all falling apart. I didn't think things could get any worse, but they have."

"One thing at a time, yeah? Call your dad. Let him know we're on the way."

"He's allergic to cats."

"We'll arrange for him to stay in one of the guest rooms on the way out, all right? No one ever uses them."

Kavita knows she has to move; they're wasting precious time. Her brain tells her hand to pick up the phone and dial the number for the hotel, but her hand won't listen, as if she never had a hand to begin with.

"Kavita?" she hears Nirav say outside her shell. She feels his hands gently grip her shoulders. "Take a deep breath," he tells her. "That's it. And another. Good. We'll figure it out, okay? But first you need to call your dad."

He dials the number for her and places the receiver in her stiff hand. As she listens to the tireless ring of the bell, she gnaws on her bottom lip, anxious for her father to put an end to the noise, and her worries. At last, he answers.

"Dad?"

"Kavita," he says, a smile in his voice. "You're back."

"Are you okay?"

"I'm fine."

"We're coming to get you, okay?"

"You know how to get here?"

"Yes, it's not far."

"Did you listen to my messages?"

"Yes, Dad. Don't worry. Everything's going to be fine. Meet us in the lobby. We won't be long."

She hangs up and holds the counter for strength. Her body goes from feeling like it's been flash-frozen to flash-thawed. But there's no time to go limp and shiver. Her father needs rescuing.

When they arrive at the hotel, she finds him waiting in the lobby, standing stoically beside the navy Samsonite suitcase, hard plastic and combination locks, that he immigrated with over thirty years ago, as though despite the decades and determination, he has as little now as he did back then.

25

A FTER GETTING HIM SETTLED in the guest suite, they return to their condo to see if they can offer him something more substantial to eat than the McDonald's he has been subsisting on for days. Nirav excuses himself to take a shower, claiming the man who sat next to him on the flight must have had bloody whooping cough.

"There isn't much in the fridge," Kavita tells her father as she peruses its anorexic contents. "How about grilled cheese?"

"Fine," he shrugs.

From the fridge, she pulls out margarine, sourdough, and cheddar, and lays them out on the island, where he father is perched on a stool, looking as though he's eating at a diner counter. She starts buttering a slice of bread.

"So," she says at last. "You want to talk about it?"

"What is there to say? I've told you everything already."

"You haven't told me how you feel."

"What does that matter? It is what it is."

"It matters, Dad. You have to let these things out. Otherwise they can eat you up inside." She can appreciate how hypocritical she sounds.

Her father frowns into his glass of water.

"You've had blow-outs before, but you've never left." Leaving the home and the family that has been the centre of his existence for the past thirty years goes against everything she knows her father to be, everything he believes in, everything he has built. As a young man, he left his home once before, and if that kind of amputation had to be endured, once in a lifetime was enough.

"I can't go back there, not ever."

"But it's your home."

"Not anymore. Some things are unforgivable."

Kavita grills her father's sandwich in silence, recalling the London incident. She knows exactly what her father means. When the sandwich is perfectly brown and crispy, she slices it, and places it in front of him. He hands her one half, telling her that she has gotten too skinny, *khaana,* eat. Reluctantly, she takes the sandwich. They chew in silence for a while.

Once he is finished, he drinks half the water in his glass, and seems ready to talk. "When I started my own family," he tells her, "I promised myself I would provide my children with everything. A good home. A good education. The safety and security I never had. Every decision I've ever made, I made with you in mind."

Kavita knows this to be true. Generational and cultural indulgences like "me-time" or "man cave" or "mid-life crisis" were concepts as foreign to him as infidelity and divorce. He chose to work for the government because it was a good job if you wanted to raise a family. He was home every day by three o'clock, in time to make them after-school snacks. He never invested much in friendships or vied for promotions or conferences at work, because those things would take time away from his family. Kavita couldn't speak to how he was as a husband, but he was a good father.

"Look at how things have turned out," he continues. "I have devoted my life to my family, and now I have nothing."

Kavita stops, mid-chew. Looks at him with glossy pain in her eyes. Remembers the words her mother uttered weeks earlier: *I've already lost the most precious thing in my life.*

"You haven't lost everything, Dad," she says.

"I don't even have a place to live. I tried to make a place for myself in this country, this world, but it didn't work. Now I have to try something else."

"What are you talking about?"

"I have been reading about Buddhism, lately. Buddha understood suffering."

"Okay...."

"There's a monastery out east. They accept students. You can live there while you study."

Kavita remembers the day her father borrowed her laptop and the page he left open on the browser. She had been right back then. He had been planning his Great Escape. "Are you telling me you want to go there?"

"Yes."

"For how long?"

"As long as it takes for me to understand what has happened to my life, and what it all means."

"Dad, please don't go. Not now."

"Your mother doesn't want me around. My son is gone. You have your own life, Kavita. A husband to take care of. Life is pushing me in a new direction."

"I..." she stutters. "I don't know what to say."

"There is nothing to say. I have already contacted them. They have accepted my application and invited me to stay."

"When did you apply? While I was gone?"

He pauses. "No, before."

"So, even if you and Mom hadn't fought, you would have left us?"

"Our family is broken, Kavita," he says, as he peers deeply into her eyes. "There is nothing left to leave."

Kavita stares at him, moon-eyed, unsure of the man sitting across from her. *I don't have your magic*, she thinks to Sunil. *I can't make people stay.*

Suddenly she can't stand to be around her father any longer, as if the threat of his desertion has already thrust her away. She marches to the front door.

"Where are you going?" he calls out.

"To check on Mom." She pulls on her jean jacket and sneakers.

"While you're there, can you get a few things from my room?"

Blaze climbs. Up. Up. Up. She squeezes her fist, spearing her nails into her fresh scar.

"Kavita?"

Shuts her eyes tightly. Waits for the release.

"*Beti*?"

She squeezes harder and harder.

"Are you still there?"

But the pain isn't enough. It isn't enough to stifle Blaze. It burns, burns, burns. If she stays a moment longer, it will burn her alive.

She rushes out the door, its gusty thwack echoing along the hallway in a ripple of sound that chases and overtakes her, as if it were pain.

26.

THE SHORTER THE DISTANCE between her car and her parents' house, the saltier the puddle underneath her tongue. More than once she feels like pulling over and emptying her already void stomach. The warning beacon in her gut blares. Danger is imminent. She is vectoring right into it.

As she pulls up the driveway, she sees the *For Sale* sign on the front lawn, swaying back and forth with the breeze, over the curb where she sat with Nirav on the night the police came.

She tries to open the front door, jiggling the handle, even though she knows it is probably locked. Then she rings the doorbell. Waits. Rings again. Turns one ear towards the door but hears no one stirring inside. The warming beacon blares, blares, blares.

Does she have her house keys? She rummages through her purse. How is it they always find the darkest fold of her bag to hide in, this time wrapping themselves in an old ATM slip like and earwig inside a leaf. Her hands shake as she pushes into the house.

"Mom?" she calls out, bounding up the stairs, two by two. "Mom?" The living room is empty. So is the kitchen. And her mother's bedroom. Just then, she hears the toilet flush.

"Oh, for chrissake," she sighs. As she paces the hallway and waits for her mother to come out of the washroom, Kavita presses her hands over her stomach, attempting to muffle the warning beacon.

"Hello, *beti*," her mother says, calmly. "I heard the doorbell, but I was already in the washroom by then."

Kavita follows her mother into the kitchen.

"How was the trip?"

"Fine," eyeing her dubiously.

"And Nirav's mother? How is she managing?"

"She's okay."

"The poor woman. My heart goes out to her."

But would it, Kavita wonders, if her mother knew about how careless Mrs. Stone has been with Sunil?

She watches her mother fill the kettle, unsettled by her apparent calm. "Mom?" she asks. "Are you okay? You don't have to put on a brave face for me. Dad told me what happened."

Her mother sets the kettle on its base. "What can I say? Your father has always been a selfish man. He has abandoned us."

"He said you left him no other choice."

"Of course he would say that."

"You know I can't take sides."

"When have I ever asked you to?"

As her mother fetches cups from the cupboard, Kavita blinks at her in amazement. "The *For Sale* sign came as a surprise," she says. "That seems a bit rash."

"If your father can leave, then so can I. Honestly, I have never been happy in this country. I've called my brother in Dilli. He said I can stay with him."

"You're going to India?"

"Yes."

"For how long?"

"I'm moving back."

"Permanently?"

"I don't expect you to understand, Kavita. You've never been caged in a bad marriage. You've never lost a child."

Although Blaze settled during the car ride over, now it churns, an inner Coriolis effect of fire in her belly. She clenches her fist. Focuses on the pain. This pain she can manage.

"We all lost Sunil."

"It's not the same."

"We're all in pain. We all loved him."

"When you're a mother, you'll understand."

Kavita can't squeeze her fist any tighter. Blaze climbs. Up. Up. Up. She breathes its fire.

"When was the last time you went to India? Ten years ago? Now all of a sudden you want to live there again?"

"I've wanted to leave this country almost as soon as I arrived. I have never felt at home here. My family is in India. I belong in India."

"Aren't I your family?"

"You are married now, Kavita. Soon you will start a family of your own. You don't need me anymore."

"Of course I still need you. I'll always need you, Mom."

"Kavita, stop being childish."

"What about the renovations? You were so excited about them. Weren't you planning on remodelling the kitchen? Maybe once the house gets a little freshened up, you'll feel at home again. Like a fresh start. Isn't that what you called it?"

"Let the next owners worry about the kitchen. This isn't my home anymore."

"But it's Sunil's home. It's my home. We grew up here. We played in the yard and ate meals at this table and measured our heights on that wall," pointing to her left. "Do you really want to give all that away? "

"Those are just memories. I have to face reality. Sunil is gone. I have no one to taken care of me in my old age. I have to think about my own welfare."

"Mom, I'm right here. I haven't abandoned you. You can depend on me. I know our family isn't the same, and it never will be, but if we stick together, I know we can get through this. Please. I'm begging you. Stay. Take down the sign. Let some time pass."

While she awaits her mother's decree, Kavita feels as helpless as a girl again, at the mercy of her parents' moods and fights and vitriolic silences. The difference now is she doesn't have Sunil standing by her side, shoring her up.

"Kavita," her mother says. "Stop this. I'm tired. My mind is made up. I'm leaving. I've already booked my ticket."

"Then go," Kavita pleads, "but let me take care of the house. Please. I'm not ready to let it go, yet."

"If I didn't need the money I would burn this place to the ground." Her mother peers around the room with startled eyes. "It's haunted. I see him everywhere. I need to get away from here."

Kavita's legs begin to shake as if the very foundations of their house, their only home, is beginning to crumble. "What about Sunil's things?" she asks.

"You can take what you like. The house is being sold as furnished. The realtor will take care of everything while I'm gone. You might as well pack up your things while you're here. And take your father's junk too, or else I'll have it thrown out."

Kavita slackens her fist. The pain is not enough to smoother Blaze. It burns, burns, burns. If she stays much longer, it will burn her alive.

"There's only one thing I want," she says.

She strides down the hall into her mother's bedroom, where she finds Sunil's urn on the dresser. She hugs the cold metal snugly to her chest and canters to the front door. *I've got you, Bear,* she reassures him. *I'll protect you.*

"Kavita?" her mother cries out as she speeds past the kitchen. "What are you doing?"

Before her mother can stop her, she trundles down the stairs and out of the house.

I've got you. I've got you. I've got you—all the way to the car.

I'll protect you. I'll protect you. I'll protect you—all the way to the condo.

27

ABOUT A WEEK LATER, Kavita finally arranges to meet Chi for coffee. Perhaps Nirav was right. Perhaps Chi just needed time to figure out what to say. Now more than ever, Kavita needs an ally.

She rides the bus downtown, gazing passively out the slush-splattered window. The snow came early along with a push of cold weather that caught most people without their winter tires. Stories about black ice and collisions got nearly as much airtime on the CBC news last night as the usual headlines about war, natural disasters, and political scandals. She watches as pedestrians scurry along the sidewalk, buried in their winter garments. Soft snow begins to fall, light and stilling. *You always loved the winter*, she thinks to Sunil. She sees him snowshoeing along a trail in Gatineau Park, dressed in his navy winter gear. She went with him a few times. Remembers the Styrofoam sound of their shoes squeaking through slumbering trees, the awe she felt when it started snowing, the wood-smoke air in the warm-up cabin where they had lunch—peanut butter and chocolate chip sandwiches wrapped in aluminum foil, left to warm on one of the iron stoves. She can taste the first bite, gooey and sweet, a taste of childhood.

Just then, a man walking on the sidewalk in the opposite direction draws her eye. *Sunil?* she thinks, frozen in a breathless moment. His features stun her: his tall, broad frame; his deep complexion; his chocolate brown coat, black toque, and woollen mitts. All identical to Sunil's.

Blinded by impulse, she pulls the bell and leaps off the bus. Back-tracking at a trot, she weaves through the crowded side-walk, desperately trying to catch up with the doppelganger. While she's lost in the waking dream of it all, the man isn't a just double—he is Sunil.

"Sorry, sorry, sorry," she says to the other pedestrians. She rams into one man so hard he spills his coffee, a cappucci-no-coloured Rorschach blot all over the snowy sidewalk. She apologizes but doesn't stop her single-minded pursuit.

After another block, she relents, out of breath, the cold air burning her throat and lungs. She has lost track of the man. Only when a stranger nudges her in passing does she waken up from the spell, disoriented, as if drugged. Embarrassed, she shrinks into the anonymity of her hood, and marches to a bus stop farther down the street, a neutral spot, where no one has witnessed her temporary delirium.

She smokes a cigarette to hush her nerves. *He looked so much like you*, she tells Sunil. *I was convinced*. Or had she seen what she wanted? Will she ever stop looking for him? Ever stop expecting the nightmare to end?

She rides another bus to the coffee shop. Despite the unex-pected tangent, she still arrives on time. As she steps into the warm café, careful not to slip on the puddle on the tiles, she peers around. A few tables are still unoccupied. But there is no sign of Chi.

Kavita takes her place in line behind a few other patrons and reads the festive specials off the chalkboard hanging behind the register: *Spice up your life with a hot cider! Get into the ho-ho-holiday spirit with an eggnog latte!*

Is that all it takes? she wonders. She orders a gingerbread latte and settles into a coveted corner table by the front windows, a deep loveseat and armchair oriented for conversation. As she sips her saccharine drink, she observes a steady commotion of passersby through the snowflake-decaled window. Some people carry shopping bags with them, decorated in a variety of seasonal motifs—reindeer, snowflakes, Santa Claus. Somehow, Christmas is only a few weeks away. Where has the time gone? Where has she been?

She gazes inwardly, searching herself for an answer. But she doesn't know. Not where she has been, or where she is now, or where she is going. When she looks inside, all she finds are things she would rather not see.

Cupping her hands around her drink, she tries to pull away from her consuming inner world to observe the one that is unfolding around her with such sound and colour and motion. The din of the coffee shop—the competing conversations, the Christmas music, the keyboards tapping, the high-pitched squeal of the frother—fill her with too much sound, too many vibrations. All the activity feels alien, almost blasphemous, as though a personal affront to her devout state of mourning.

As Kavita blinks into her coffee, she knows nothing is wrong with her surroundings. The world is simply carrying on as it should, as it always has, without her noticing or questioning. She is what's different. She is what isn't quite right. She knows she has been spending too much time alone. Listening to the hoarse whispers of Anchor and Gloom. Watching home movie memories inside her head. Isolation is a precarious loop to be stuck in. At first, the intensity of her grief caused her to retreat into her cave of sorrow, for safety, containment. But now, it seems she has stayed in the cave too long, and it has mutated from haven to prison. Now the cave seems like the only place left on earth where she belongs.

She feels a strong impulse to leave. She wants to be back at home with Coal and her ivory throw and the anaesthesia of daytime television. She wants to be alone. When she's alone, she is safe.

Another part of her wants to stay. So much has happened on top of Sunil's passing. The incident in London, her parents' separation, the house being sold, and now the upcoming holidays to confront. Pain on top of pain, burying her layer by layer like wet snow, a slowly-mounting weight crushing against her chest.

If she can just talk to Chi, she knows it will help. If just one person can tell her they understand what she is going through, and why she is struggling, she knows it will make all the difference. The difference between being alone, and not.

Kavita loosens her throat with a warm swallow. *You always loved gingerbread lattes*, she thinks to Sunil. *And hanging out anonymously in coffee shops, reading your mystery novels. You probably would've ordered a biscotti too. No wait, a brownie. Should I get one for you? Place it by your urn?* Her mother has allowed her to keep Sunil's ashes, only because if she takes them with her to India, their relatives will pressure her to scatter them in the Ganges.

As Kavita debates whether or not to get Sunil a brownie, Chi finally arrives.

"Hey!" Chi swoops in for an awkward hug, patting Kavita on the shoulder a couple of times, the way one might hug a sick, distant relative, as if reluctant to touch her, as if her grief might be contagious. Chi has changed her hair, cropped it into a blunt bob, tinted plum. As she pulls off her grey woollen coat and black leather gloves, tossing them onto the loveseat across from Kavita, she apologizes for being late. "I came as soon as I could. Emerg is an absolute *zoo*. People are animals. Sick and injured people, especially."

"That's okay," Kavita grins. "I haven't been here long." Her hands dart involuntarily to the collar of her sweatshirt, then brush dust off her lap that isn't there, self-conscious and sloppy in her hoodie, jeans, and ratty braid.

"So, long time no see, hey?" Chi says, still standing. "You look great."

"I do?"

"Absolutely," Chi nods, unconvincing in her overenthusiasm.

"Wait, have you lost weight? Oh my God, you're so skinny!"

Kavita looks down at herself. "Not on purpose."

"I wish I could lose a few pounds without even trying. Oh, and I love that you're growing out your hair. Look how long your braid is!"

Kavita pulls her braid over her shoulder and plays with the elastic. "Thanks." The truth is she feels too awkward to make an appointment at the salon, weary of the inevitable chitchat. *How's life? How's work?* Questions that have no easy answers now. But it goes deeper than that. She feels too guilty to actually cut her hair, which she sees as a sign of moving on, accepting the passage of time. Growing her hair is simply a consequence of her resistance, the way her thinness is merely a consequence of her resistance to the life-giving sustenance of food. "I'm just going to grab a cappuccino. You want anything?"

"No thanks, I'm good"

"Back in two secs!"

Kavita watches her friend take her place in the short line. Meanwhile, she breathes, slow and full, to hush the busy chatter of her nerves. She craves a cigarette but doubts she will have time before Chi returns. Smoking in a rush only results in heightened edginess.

The St. John's Wort and valerian root she has been taking for the past week haven't offered any notable relief yet. The labels claimed the herbals were traditionally used to treat nervousness and insomnia. She imagines those conditions have mutated somewhat in modern times. So far, she hasn't even enjoyed the happy ignorance of a placebo effect.

Once, after reading an article in a magazine, she suggested Sunil consider switching to herbal remedies to treat his condition. She prattled on about the benefits of St. John's Wort and valerian, of fish oil and folic acid. Non-medicinal treatments, too, such as dark chocolate and yoga, nature walks and volunteering. Now, she clutches inside to think of his wordless expression, his eyes more sad than angry, the way one might look at a sheltered child. He knew she didn't know any better than to say stupid things.

Now she knows, though. Understands how far someone might go to make it stop. She feels that very need growing inside her every time she falls at the mercy of Anchor or Blaze or Gloom. After each assault, it is getting harder to pull herself back up. Harder to ignore their harsh reasoning.

While at the pharmacy the other day purchasing the herbals, as she turned down an aisle on the way to the cash registers, she found herself among a library of sleeping pills. She stood in front of them, dumb, expecting to feel repulsed, to want to sack the shelves. But she didn't. Instead, she reached for a box. Was this the brand Sunil chose? Or did he mix a few? What did it feel like to glide into forever sleep? Oh, to glide to sleep. To rest, unassailed by nightmares.

Sounds peaceful, said Gloom. *Doesn't it?*

She rushed from the aisle so quickly, she nearly forgot to pay for the St. John's Wort and valerian on her way to the exit.

Now, as she bounces her leg, she tells herself everything is going to be fine. She can trust Chi. She is her best and oldest friend, for goodness sake. She can be honest with her. She can tell her what's happened. All the nervousness she is feeling now will be worth it. When she reaches out to Chi this time, her friend will reach back, hold her tightly, and keep her from sliding any farther.

No matter how she tries to convince herself with studious repetition, her body never lies. Her stomach hoofs in unison with her brisk heartbeat. The warning beacon in her gut blares. Danger is imminent. She is vectoring right into it. No matter what lies her mind recites, her body always tells the truth.

Chi rejoins her at the table, setting down her coffee and an almond croissant. "So, tell me all about *toi*. What's new?"

"There isn't much to tell,"

"Don't give me that," Chi says, rolling her eyes, as she picks an almond slice free from her croissant. "It's been ages since we've had a good gab session. How's work?"

"I'm still on leave."

"Oh, right." Chi averts her gaze. "Well, it must be nice to have some time off, right? I haven't had a real vacation in years. But Tokyo this summer to visit the fam! I can't wait to get away. Emerg is like a war zone."

"I thought it was like a zoo?"

"That too."

"I'm just the opposite," Kavita goes on after a brief pause. "I wish I could work." The comforting structure of a routine. Wake, wash, dress. Ride the bus to work. Maybe grab a happy hour drink afterward. These mundane things she once did with robotic ease. Now, cut off in her cave of sorrow, she can't see a way back to them, as though the path has been swallowed by the dark presence in her life.

"Anyway," Chi says, groping for another topic. "How's Nirav? I haven't seen him in forever. I miss that guy!"

"He's fine. At least I think he's fine. It's hard to tell. Things have been pretty tense. We just got back from London. His grandmother passed away." Kavita hopes that speaking openly about one death might lead to them speaking openly about another.

"Oh God," Chi gasps. "Poor him."

"I know, it's sad. She was sick with cancer for a while, but it still came as a shock. He seems to be handling it well, though. Actually, I take that back. I don't know if he's handling it well at all. Whenever I ask about it, he says he's fine, and that's where the conversation ends. I guess he's dealing with it the same way he deals with everything. Honestly, I don't know where he puts things."

"Boys will be boys," Chi shrugs.

Was that how Sunil saw things too? Kavita wonders. Was that why he kept so much to himself? Because he thought showing vulnerability was inherently emasculating? Can the same be said of her anger? Does part of her think it's unfeminine, and therefore, inappropriate? A bleak thought. Both of them muzzled, without a common language to express their human pain.

Domed by the sounds of the coffee shop, they drop into silence, each sipping at her cup, unsure of what to say next, as if they are on bad first date. All that needs to happen next is for one of them to check her watch and make an excuse about leaving the stove on, and their failed interaction will be complete.

"Should I send flowers?" Chi asks at last.

"That's sweet. Only if you want to. I'll let him know you're thinking about him."

"That's okay, I'll write him an email."

Kavita's gaze hardens. She feels Blaze begin to simmer as she remembers how Chi ignored her emails, only to secretly correspond with her husband. Were they still writing each other? Were they still talking about her behind her back?

Part of her wants to let Blaze bubble over and finally confront Chi about being a shitty friend, but now is not the time. She needs an ally more than she needs an apology.

"By the way, did you get my thank-you card?"

"Mm hm," Chi nods, as she picks at her croissant.

"The flowers you sent were beautiful." Kavita omits their untimely toss into the garbage. "Thanks again. I'm sorry you couldn't make it to the memorial."

Chi flashes an insecure grin. "I'm sorry I couldn't make it. Emerg is like—"

"A refugee camp?"

They share a faint smile.

"It's okay," she says. "I understand." Kavita pushes onward despite the insistence of the warning beacon. "I'm sorry we haven't gotten together any sooner. I guess I've been in my own little world. It's great to see you, though. I've been bursting to vent with someone. So much has happened recently. To be honest, things have been really hard." There, she's done it. The hardest part. She's reached out. *Please Chi*, she thinks. *Reach back*.

"*Aw*," Chi says with a cloying half smile, half pout. Reaching across the table, she pats Kavita's hand a few times, then pulls away abruptly, as if suddenly remembering the grief germs. "Are you sure you don't want any of this croissant?" she asks. "I don't usually like coffee shop pastries, but this one isn't bad. Seriously, have some. You'd be doing me a favour!" Chi breaks into a plastic laugh.

Hope falls from her eyes. "No, thanks." She doesn't want a half-eaten croissant. Or to be distracted. What she wants is to talk openly about horror and hopelessness and shame. What she wants is for her friend to reach back.

With a level stare, she watches as Chi finishes the last triangle of her croissant, patiently awaiting something more, something solid to hold on to.

"Crazy story," Chi says, brushing off her fingertips. "So, I'm on rotation at the Civic. Well, a guy comes in with a thumb that's so infected it's turned *black*. I kid you not. The smell alone was enough to make me hurl. I mean, who even lets an infection get that bad? Honestly, if I were that stupid, I'd kill myself. "

As Kavita stares across the table, she wonders if it is possible to be both astonished, and not, at the same time.

Chi natters on about something else med-school related, but Kavita stops listening. She knows now that her friend isn't comfortable speaking openly about horror and hopelessness and shame. Her friend would rather pretend such things don't exist. And perhaps they don't in her world. At least not as they do for Kavita. It occurs to her, bleakly, she really is alone in this.

An unforgiving chill hollows her out. She hugs her stomach, cold, empty. These attempts at reaching out always have a cost.

She came today hoping for a hand to hold. What she didn't

expect was another dead limb. Another sign her problems aren't the world's. Another confirmation it is better—safer—not to speak about these things, with anyone.

28

KAVITA HUDDLES ON THE SOFA beneath her ivory throw with Coal curled on her lap, sipping a cup of ginger tea and watching the snow fall like shaved ice thickening the air. Daylight wanes. Soon the streetlights will flick on. She never accustoms to seeing their scalene triangles of orange light before five o'clock.

Before settling in with her cup, she had the impulse to call her home, only to remember there was no one left at home to call. Within the last couple of weeks, her parents have departed in search of their new lives, in a kind of reverse empty nest syndrome. Each of them called once to let her know they had arrived safely at their destinations. Her father told her not to expect to hear from him any time soon, he needed to cut his attachments to the outside world, and besides, talking at the abbey was frowned upon, it was a place of inner reflection, a sanctum. The few times Kavita tried reaching her mother, the connection was either terrible, or she was out visiting relatives.

Nirav will arrive home in another hour or so. She has already prepared dinner, vegetarian shepherd's pie—one of his favourite meals even without the mince—and left it to warm in the oven. The meal wasn't entirely innocent. Weeks have passed since their trip to London, with neither resurrecting the incident, but tonight she hopes they will finally talk, and if mashed potatoes and gravy can help soften him up, even a little, it will have been worth the effort. Anyway, she has to try. She vowed on the moon.

A few times she came close. She even made chicken parmesan once although the smell made her retch. She practised what to say, scribbling out lines and rehearsing them aloud in front of the washroom mirror until they felt natural. Despite all her preparations, in the end the words never made it beyond her tense lips.

She strokes the flat bridge of Coal's nose with one finger, thinking to herself, that she understands why people put things off. When you put things off, your mind is free to occupy itself with pleasant lies, that you are fine, your life is fine, your marriage is fine, everything is fine. The pleasant lies transform the unlivable into livable. They distract away from questions that have no easy answers, like: Will Nirav understand? Or will he brush her off? Tell her she's got it all wrong, she's overreacting. When she needs her husband the most, will he stand by her? Will he call her selfish, again?

She wonders if Nirav has been nauseating over similar worries. It is possible he hasn't wanted to upset her by raising the subject, but she fears his silence means something else.

What about her reticence? By not speaking up has she inadvertently communicated that what happened was acceptable? By waiting, has she lost her right to justice? Will her silence—a function of the time she needed to process the traumatic event—be used against her?

A grey image of Sunil seeps into her mind: deep frown, chin tucked, arms crossed.

He never let anyone even look at you the wrong way, says Anchor. *But now, when he needs you to defend him, because he can't defend himself, you're too scared to get the words out.*

No, no, she just needed a little time to catch her breath after what happened with her mother and father, and the house. She just—

Every time you whimper you only make things worse. "I'm

sorry, Sunil. I tried. I'm so sorry. Please forgive me." It's unbearable. *If you're going to do something, do it.*

She will.

Gloom sneers. *But you won't.*

This latest assault leaves her head buzzing as if struck, as if the tender flesh of her brain is ballooning against her skull. She thinks she might be sick. Her body goes limp and her chest sinks forward, as she folds into a position she has only ever seen on television when someone is hyperventilating. Coal springs out of the way with a high-pitched squeak. With her head between her knees, she tries to breathe.

Yet somehow this position is not lowly enough.

Rolling forward, she settles on the hardwood and hugs in her knees until she is curved like a C. Her body feels heavy against the floor, maybe as heavy as it has ever been. She looks out the terrace window at the thick snowfall, descending like a curtain, hiding her. She knows she will have to get up soon, and fake cheer and make conversation and function. But for now, as she lies pinned to the floor, she can be herself.

Black, black, black.

Gloom, gloom, gloom.

They are seated across from each other at the island. Kavita rolls a pea around her plate through a smear of mushroom gravy. She has already swallowed a few mouthfuls of shepherd's pie. Nirav is on his second portion.

"Want any more gravy?"

"No, no," he mumbles with his mouth full. "This is lovely, darling. Really, really nice."

"I'm glad you like it." She reaches for her glass of water and sips. They have already talked about their days. He had back-to-back meetings, tedious and over-long, but otherwise it was an ordinary workday in accounting. She lied about trekking through the snow and spending the afternoon at the library, and also about the chef's knife slipping as she was cubing potatoes for the shepherd's pie, when he had asked about her fresh bandage.

Soon the meal will be over, the mollifying powers of shepherd's pie all but gone, and she still hasn't found the courage or opportunity to raise the topic. Her legs starts to bounce on the footrest of her stool. She can't delay any longer. Purposeful, she clears her throat.

"Niru?"

"Hm?" he says, focused on his dinner.

"I was wondering if we could talk about something."

"Oh?" lifting his gaze.

"It's important."

He lowers his fork.

"I wanted to talk to you about what happened in London." She veils her eyes, partially. "I know I haven't brought it up since we got back, but it's been on my mind. I know you didn't want to talk about it before. And I understand why. It was a hard time for you, and I'm sorry. But some time has passed, and you seem like you're doing better, so I thought I should bring it up, before it festers any longer. I was hoping we could talk and figure out what we're going to do."

"What do you mean?"

"At the very least people need to be told Sunil that passed away. But equally, we need to know why they've kept it a secret. I have a million reasons spinning through my head. I just want to know the truth."

The corners of his mouth droop into a subtle frown. "Look," he says. "It's in the past. What's the sense in dredging it up again? "

"It isn't in the past for me, Niru."

"I don't want to row, Kavita."

"Neither do I. I just want to talk to you." She pauses. "I was so nervous to see your family for the first time since Sunil passed away. That would've been hard enough. But as it turned out, the hardest part wasn't facing their questions, or even their awkwardness at not knowing what to say to me, which was what I was expecting. The harder part was having to pretend. Getting caught up in an awful secret. Being blindsided and silenced. Can you even imagine what that was like?" She waits for an answer, but nothing comes. "Do you even care, Niru? You've never asked."

"I wasn't there."

"Don't you trust me?"

"We both know you're a bit off at the moment, don't we? Remember how you scared off Chi?"

"What does Chi have to do with this?"

"You're not seeing things straight."

"I'm grieving, Nirav. I haven't lost my mind. And I didn't make this up. It happened."

He stares at his lap.

"You obviously don't think anything wrong happened."

"I told you, I don't know what happened."

"What am I supposed to do now? Pretend that my brother's still alive every time we visit London?" A rhetorical question. She knows she is never going back there.

"Well, it's always something with your family, isn't it?"

"*Our* family, Nirav."

"No, not my family. *Your* family. We wouldn't be in this situation if it weren't for *your* family." His mouth screws with anger. "I hate being part of your family."

She can tell by the guilty look on his face he has let something slip that he meant to harbour in silence. God only knows how long he has been harbouring it. "You what?"

"Never mind."

"You *hate* my family?"

He shoots up from his stool, grabs his half-eaten plate, and lets it clatter in sink. "I didn't say that," he tells her.

"You said—"

"Just stop, all right? I haven't the patience for this tonight." He strides to the washroom and slams the door.

"You never have the patience," she mutters to herself. "And I never have the nerve."

Her cheeks burn. She crosses the room and steps onto the terrace in her slippers. The light evening wind carries with it the scent of snow, clean and metallic. She hugs the front panels of her cardigan close to her body, lifts her gaze, and stares fiercely at the pale grey sky.

"How can I speak up for you, Bear," she says, "when I still haven't figured out how to speak up for myself?" A braver, confident woman wouldn't have let Nirav escape. A woman with more self-esteem wouldn't have given up until she reached the resolution she knew she deserved. What kind of woman was she turning out to be? What kind of sister?

The rims of her eyes shiver. She wants to see beyond the ashen prairie of clouds, straight into Heaven, if it exists. See Sunil's pleasing half smile. Know what he thinks of them now, the people who have splintered so unutterably without him. Soft snow begins to fall, thick and wet, icy fairy footsteps tapping across her face.

29

A WEEK LATER, while she is scrolling through the library's DVD catalogue online, the phone rings. Her heart leaps in her chest, the way it always does whenever she is surprised by an unexpected sound. Maybe it is one of her parents calling to check on her, she thinks. Hopes.

"Hello?"

"Is that Kavita?"

Something inside her sinks. Not her mother's voice, or her father's.

"Mrs. Stone?" she says. "Nirav's not home at the moment. He won't be back from work for another couple of hours."

"I know," Mrs. Stone replies, curtly. "That's why I'm calling. I wanted to speak with you."

"Oh?"

"Listen, Kavita. Nirav called me the other day in quite a state. He said you were upset with me. Do we have anything to talk about?"

"I'm sorry?"

"I'm asking you, Kavita: Do you have anything you want to say to me?"

The bluntness of the question catches Kavita off guard. Nirav didn't mention he had spoken to his mother, or warn her that she might call. Now, the moment of confrontation Kavita has been awaiting is right in front of her, but thrust upon her in such a way, she can't think of what to say, as if Mrs. Stone has wiped her mind clean with her thumb, before pinning Kavita firmly under it.

"Because if you do," Mrs. Stone continues, "now is the time. Or I don't want to hear about it again."

Kavita doesn't know how to respond to this ultimatum, this limited time offer. This: speak now or forever hold your peace, or else.

"Well?" Mrs. Stone presses. "Was it our last conversation about the two of you having a child? That's the only thing I can think of."

Kavita opens her mouth, pulls in a tiny breath, and holds it.

"No? I didn't think so. No one can blame us for wanting to be grandparents, regardless." Mrs. Stone releases a frustrated breath into the phone. "Well, that settles it then. I've done my part. Tell Nirav I called, will you? And Kavita, that's the last I want to hear about it."

With the drone of the dial tone burrowing into her ear like confusion, Kavita blinks at the wall, wondering what just happened.

30

THAT EVENING, Kavita breaks the silence of their dinner.
"Your mother called today."

Nirav's eyes shine, alert. "She did?"

"You didn't know she was going to?"

"I never know what she's going to do."

"So, you spoke to her?"

"Isn't that what you wanted me to do?"

"Yes, but—"

"Well, I did. And you're still having a go at me. I can't do anything right, can I?"

"Calm down, Nirav. I just wasn't expecting it, that's all. I would've appreciated a little warning. When she called today, I was totally unprepared for it."

"Did you talk things out?"

"She thinks I'm upset about the baby stuff."

"Well, you set her straight, yeah?"

"Not exactly."

"Why not?"

"She caught me off guard and I didn't know what to say. The whole thing was over in about thirty seconds."

"Well, I'm not sure what to do. I talked to her like you wanted me to. At least she gave you the chance to speak your mind. It isn't her fault that you didn't, now is it?"

Kavita pauses, wide-eyed. "She didn't exactly give me the floor, Nirav. Now we can never talk about it again because she says so? Please tell me you see how slanted that is."

"Oh, Kavita, come on. Not every scenario is going to play out perfectly. Sometimes you just have to go with it."

"You still don't get it," she tells him. "It's hard for me to talk about. If I'd had time to prepare, things might have gone differently."

Nirav puffs his cheeks with a breath.

"You don't seem upset by how she spoke to me."

"At least she tried."

"Is that what she did?"

"Yes," he tells her. "And so have I. I'm not sure what more you want from us."

The explanation waits for breath behind her lips, like kites waiting for a breeze, but Kavita doesn't speak, out of weariness more than anger.

"Never mind," she tells him as she gathers her plate and carries it to the sink. Some things are meant to happen instinctually. She has many memories of Sunil, but not one of having to explain to him why she sometimes needed his support, when she was wronged or disrespected, he simply did so, as if by reflex. Some things are meant to happen naturally, out of love.

31

LYING IN THE BATH, Kavita gropes for the hot water tap with the dextrous toes of her left foot. A thick beeswax candle by the faucet offers warm, spare light and mildly honeys the air. Coal is crouched on the lid of the toilet, entranced by the vivid glow of the candle's occasional flit.

Nirav is out for the evening, attending his office's annual Christmas party held this year at a trendy wine bar in hipster-occupied Hintonburgh. Although he tried to entice her with promises of plentiful drink tickets, an open bar, gourmet poutine, and midnight karaoke, she didn't have the energy for chitchat and cheer.

Instead, she spent the evening watching episodes of *Family Ties* on DVD. Growing up, it was one of the shows she and Sunil rarely missed, like *The Facts of Life* and *The Cosby Show*. As she mixes the hot water in with the lukewarm, she softly hums the theme song. *I bet we've been together for a million years. And I bet we'll be together for a million more....* Compared to the Keatons, the Guptas are like one of those candleholders made of wood or marble, of a family linked arm in arm—a family circle—only with the arms lopped off. She hasn't heard from her father since he arrived at the abbey. He hasn't answered any of her messages. Her mother called once, but mostly they talked about the upcoming sale of the house, and if Kavita could forward her mail. She sinks a little deeper into the bath, the waterline skimming her lower lip, and closes her eyes. This year whenever she hears *I'll be Home for Christmas* the wound of losing Sunil splits its weak stitches. Christmas lights jar, cards are unreadable, setting up the tree—impossible.

So instead, she loses herself in memories of Christmas past, like Ebenezer Scrooge. Time condenses. It feels like mere weeks ago instead of almost a year.

On Christmas Eve, they watched *It's a Wonderful Life* (she'll never watch that movie again—where was Sunil's Clarence when he needed him?) and ate pizza in front of the fireplace. At midnight, their mother made cocoa that they sipped while opening one present each before bed. Thinking of the gift Sunil gave her weakens her stitches a little more. It was a blown-glass ornament made of red and white swirls with *Our First Christmas* written in gorgeous loops on one side. She pictures the ornament now, safely wrapped in green paper, among the others she has stored away in the closet, which she hasn't had the will to confront, let alone display. She brushes the slanted writing with her mind, knowing her brother meant the first Christmas of many, but now she doubts whether her marriage will survive another year. She went to bed that night with the feeling it really was a wonderful life, wasn't it? The tinny sound of a bell ringing made its way into her dreams. The next day, Sunil woke up first and cooked a breakfast of eggs and pancakes for breakfast. They ate hastily and then opened presents She had knitted him a blue scarf, her first ever, obvious from its raggedy edges. He wrapped it around his neck and told her it needed breaking in. They tried to recruit Nirav in joining their childlike regression, but he wasn't a fan of playing in the snow. They built a fort that could rival any they had made as kids, then had a snowball fight, and when their age finally caught up with them, collapsed in the snow and swept a pair of snow angels to life. Sunken in the drifts, she listened to the faint tap of snowfall against her hood, the ghostly trill of the north wind, and Sunil's breath, deep and constant, beside her.

Out of the tender memory, a heaviness descends upon her, like the heel of a god.

No more good times, says Anchor. *Every Christmas, and birthday, and milestone big and small, incomplete, like your family.*

...No more good times.

Because of you....

The heel crushes her even more, the heaviest weight yet, an unearthly gravity. Her body isn't built to endure its pressure. She grips the filmy rim of the tub to stop the sensation of plunging through the floor, as if she is being forced to the centre of the earth.

You never say or do the right things at the right time, says Gloom. *You never found the perfect words to make him stay. The perfect words to convince him everything was going to be all right. Now nothing is all right. Everything is broken. Everything is broken beyond repair.*

You tried to fix it. But you aren't him. You don't have the magic he had.

All you do is fail.

Although she has battled them for months, waited for them to sink back into the buried places from which they crawled, she can't deny their dark logic any longer. She has heard them for too long. She has seen too much of her life through their charcoal veil.

I know, she tells them. *I hate myself for it.*

Blaze slips through her veins like hot oil, lit by a spark of deep self-loathing, and spreads its wicked heat, a consumptive force she both fears and desires. Her body doesn't feel built for this force either, as if her skin is too thin to hold the molten energy searing against it.

She sits up in the bath. Pulls away the Band-Aid from her palm. Scrapes at the scab with her nails, digging them deeper into the wound. She focuses on the pain—torn, itchy, inflamed. This pain she can handle. This pain she knows she deserves.

But it isn't enough. Blaze burns, burns, burns. A few seconds and it will burn her alive.

This fire can only be met with fire. She reaches for the candle. Holds her breath and hovers her palm over the flame. Squeezes her eyes tightly as it bites into her lifeline. She doesn't wince.

She knows she doesn't deserve to wince.

She doesn't scream.

She knows she doesn't deserve to scream.

All she deserves is pain.

Blaze retreats somewhat, fire waiting within coals. She stares into her blistered palm. Her head is dizzy from the pain. Her sluggish thoughts reach for Sunil.

I know I failed you, Bear. And I'm sorry. I should have been a better sister to you. I should have watched over you more closely.

She cries.

I tried to keep things together here, look after everyone, but I failed at that too. Now nothing's the same. You wouldn't recognize us. Everything we were left with you. But I promise you I tried.

She weeps.

Losing you is the wound that never heals. It's bigger than me, Sunil. It's everywhere. It's everything. And this thing that's happening to me, whatever it is, it's bigger than me too. I'm sinking. I can feel it. But I don't know how to stop it.

She sobs.

I would have traded places with you.

…The wrong one got sick.

The wrong one died….

Violently, she sobs.

Enough.

I know I'm not enough.

But enough.

Please, dear God, enough.

After a little while, her sobbing peters to weeping, her weeping to crying, and her crying to staring at the tepid bathwater.

We will always be here to remind you, Gloom tells her. *You will always feel this way.*

Maybe she will hear them less underwater. Maybe she can drown them out. She takes a deep breath, and slips beneath the surface of the bathwater. Staring at the spackled the ceiling, she waits. All she hears is the muffled sound of air bubbles in her ears, like microphone static. No Anchor, no Gloom. She wonders how long she will be able to stay like this, in the quiet, the still.

Nothing else occupies her mind. Seconds tick by. Then, minutes. She ignores the protests of her body, its demands for air and life. Her vision swims. Her eyes cross and start to close.

Just then, Coal pads the bathwater, the way he sometimes swats at flies by the windowsill. *Thwap, thwap, thwap, thwap, thwap.* The ripples disturb her dark trance. *Thwap, thwap, thwap, thwap, thwap.* Her eyes pop open as if startled from a dream. *Thwap, thwap, thwap, thwap, thwap.*

Her lungs scream for air.

You deserve to sink, they tell her.

Inwardly, she sinks deeper and deeper, as if she is descending into a well.

Sink.

Dark walls grow around her.

Sink.

She lowers so deep, she drops out of the noise and into a quiet place inside.

The noise hangs over her like a snowy arctic wind tumbling over a deep ice-covered pool. It's still there, she can hear it, but in a detached way, as if standing behind glass. It isn't as loud as a moment ago. A moment ago, it nearly overwhelmed a deeper sound; a small, still voice she has heard before, that tells her: *Breathe.*

Minutely, she shakes her head, no.

Breathe, it repeats.

No, no, no.

Breathe, Kavita.

She resists.

Breathe, breathe, breathe.

The voice is so steady, wise, and true that she can't deny it any longer. She feels her resistance start to slip away like slowly unclenching eyes. She pushes her feet against the end of the tub and emerges, gasping. Her chest heaves. Her heart pounds. Her head throbs. She breathes, breathes, breathes.

Panting, she gazes at Coal with soft eyes. He is crouched on the toilet lid, hair bristled, ears perked, pupils wide and round. She reaches out to pet him, but he whines and rejects her. She is ashamed by how frightened he looks, how frightened she made him.

Then, feeling as exposed as if he is standing in the room, she remembers Sunil, and all he must have seen too. Slowly, she veils her eyes. "Don't look at me, Bear," she whispers to him. "Please."

No matter how she wants to hide in shame, she can't turn away from the parts of herself that have been revealed tonight. Or pretend she has been handling things well on her own, or that she isn't desperately lonely, or that she knows how help herself. As she hugs her knees, shaking, she prays the still, small voice won't abandon her. Maybe it knows a way out of the darkness. Maybe if she listens to it closely, she will be able to hear its whisper ahead of her, a sound like the soft glow of a candle, she can follow, up and out of this place.

PART III: RISE

You save yourself or you remain unsaved.
—Alice Sebold, *Lucky*

32

KAVITA'S BOOTS SQUEAK as she descends the stairs to the church basement. Yet again, she has the vague sense that she is back in high school, just as she had last fall when she had only made it as far as the bottom of the staircase.

She hovers to one side of the doorway and peers around. At the front of the large room, close to the stage, there are several rows of metal folding chairs arranged to face a TV and VCR that are set up on a trolley—yet another feature that reminds her of high school and watching outdated videos in Social Studies. A dozen or so people are scattered among the rows—couples, small groups, and some who are alone like she is. Adjacent to the seating there are a few long tables piled with reading material, photocopied sheets of white and blue and yellow, punctuated by several boxes of Kleenex. A couple of people peruse the literature.

At the back of the room there is a small kitchen where people are busy preparing snacks. Already, a juice station—a few cartons and a tower of clear plastic cups—has been set up along the service window. In front of the service window sits a small table with refreshments: a fruit tray, a cheese plate, a box of Ritz crackers, and what looks to be sliced pound cake.

"Can I help you, miss?" asks a cheerful voice. Kavita looks to her right. The woman seated behind the table appears to be in her late sixties. Or perhaps her seventies—it's hard to tell these days. Her short white hair is coiffed in soft curls.

She wears a peach sweater. "Come in, dear. We don't bite."

Kavita's stomach kicks, as though urging her to run back up the stairs, like last time. Squashing the impulse, she waits a beat, then approaches the table.

"Hi," she says with a dim smile.

"Well, hello there," says the woman. "I take it this is your first meeting?"

Kavita nods.

"I can always spot a newbie. They always have that deer-in-the-headlights look about them. No offence, dear. I'm sure I looked the same at my first meeting. But there's nothing to be nervous about. My name's Barbara, by the way. But everyone calls me Barbie." She reaches out a thin, wrinkled hand in greeting.

"I'm Kavita." She clasps the woman's fingers, a gentle shake.

"Oh now, what a lovely name. Very exotic. Now do me a favour, dear, and write it out on this sticker." Barbie winks, playful.

Grinning despite her nerves, Kavita grabs a blue Sharpie and does as instructed.

"When you're finished with that, I'll have you fill out your contact information on this sheet. Now, we keep everything confidential. Some people worry about their personal details being leaked or something like that. It's mostly for funding purposes. We need to show our that people actually come out to our little meetings."

"Not so little." Kavita peels away the rectangular sticker and pastes it on the outside of her coat over her heart. "Looks like a good turnout to me."

"We always expect a crowd before and after the holidays. It's a hard time of the year when you're nursing grief. Especially fresh grief. Fresh grief makes infants of us all."

"I used to love Christmastime. Now I'm just glad it's over," Kavita admits, surprised by her candour.

"Aren't we all, dear?" says Barbie with a knowing smile.

"It's never all bad, I suppose. But it's never quite the same either, is it?"

As Kavita fills in her contact information, Barbie explains that the meetings usually begin with a video about bereavement, followed by a ten-minute break. After the break, she continues, people split into groups specific to their loss. "It shouldn't be much longer," she says. "Feel free to help yourself to a glass of juice or any of the handouts while you wait. Or if you're like me, a fistful of Kleenex!" She smiles. "I know it might not seem like it yet, dear, but trust me, it's good that you're here. Welcome again."

Kavita smiles, insecure. Facing the room, she pauses, reluctant to abandon the safety of the sign-in table and Barbie, the only person she knows.

Cutting across the room, she marches over to the chairs. Her boots squeak with every step. So much for slipping in quietly. As she takes a seat in the back row, she hears an unexpected sound emerging from the kitchen, a sound that surprises her the way springtime birdsong does after a long, mute winter: laughter. Real laughter. The kind that pops from the belly without warning, loud and embarrassing. The kind that throws back heads. *Those must be the regulars*, she thinks, prickled by their light-heartedness, which to her, feels out of place. Then again, maybe she's the one who doesn't belong.

Glancing around, she notices that she is among the youngest of the mourners. While a few appear to be about her age, most are older, she guesses middle-aged or more.

A young man who is sitting at the end of her row draws her eye, maybe because he seems as out of place among the aged crowd as she does. He looks to be about Sunil's age, thirty-something. His longish, dark hair is half-up in a ponytail, and she guesses, he probably shaves slightly more often than he goes in for a trim. His outfit looks as if it has been pulled from a MEC catalogue: teal Gore-Tex jacket, cords, hiking boots. He is staring at a point on the floor, meditatively, with a gaze that is more inward than outward. She has an itchy sense that she knows him from somewhere, but she doesn't recall from where.

Her eyes must have lingered for a moment too long. He turns to look at her. As he grins widely—disarmingly—the outer edges of his dark eyes wrinkle. He has the artless look of someone who is always open to conversation, the kind of relaxed person who can talk without expectation in the shampoo aisle, at the bus stop, in line at the bank.

She looks away without smiling back. Out of the curve of her eye, she sees him return to his original position, his unaffected yogic-like pose.

What does he have to smile about? she wonders. What do any of them? She thought this was supposed to be a bereavement group, full of people missing parts, like her. What was with all the laughing and smiling and let's be friends pretense?

She takes a deep breath. Clearly, she isn't prepared for the openness of the place. She has habituated to people shutting her down. To secrecy and silence and judgment. Dealing with things alone. Now, she feels like her cave might fracture at the slightest kind gesture—a laugh, a smile. Then everything she has been trying to hold together will instantly crumble. Everything she has been trying to hold in will flood the church basement. She wonders if bears feel the same way after spending months in their winter dens. Do they grunt hello to the first bear they encounter in the bush, or simply growl, suspiciously?

After several uneasy minutes, a slender, auburn-haired woman walks up to the podium. She is dressed in a brown leather skirt, a cream-coloured turtleneck, and black leather knee boots. Her hair is twisted up in a clip. By now, nearly every chair has been filled, about forty people in all.

Smiling, the woman welcomes them. Her name is Brenda. She is the lead program coordinator of the bereavement group.

She thanks them for coming despite the snow, and is happy to see familiar faces in the crowd, as well as some new ones, too.

She offers a special welcome to the newcomers. It's never easy to come to a meeting, especially the first one, so they should pat themselves on the back, because they've done something really good for themselves tonight. She says they always joke that their group is the kind no one wants to be a part of but everybody joins, sooner or later. A light chuckle ripples through the crowd. If that doesn't seem funny yet, she goes on, hang in there, bereavement humour can take some time to get.

Her tone changes slightly, as does her expression. Although grief is a natural part of life, she explains, most people aren't prepared for it. The expectation is to put on a brave face and have the mettle to move on. People say life goes on. But it's never that simple.

Ten years ago, Brenda tells them, her mother passed away, unexpectedly. Suddenly, the world was a different place and she didn't know where she belonged anymore.

Fortunately, she smiles, she found this group and started coming to meetings every month. Little by little, she began processing her grief and understanding what grief actually was. By being among her peers, she learned that what she was going through, no matter how strange it seemed, was normal. She made friends and realized she wasn't alone. That was when she really started healing. When she reached out for support and found what she needed. When she opened up, shared, and also received.

The group had such a profound impact on her that after about a year of attending meetings, she started volunteering. Later, she decided to train as a grief counsellor. Now, she helps others the way she was helped.

The purpose of the group, she tells them, is to create a network for those living with grief, so they can learn from one another and support each other through this natural, yet challenging, part of life. She encourages them to view their time here as an opportunity to talk and laugh and cry, or even just listen. Whatever they need. They are in a safe place.

She goes on to tell them about the movie they are going to watch tonight. The people interviewed each represent a particular type of loss, so hopefully they will be able to find something to relate to in at least one of the grief stories. After the movie, they will take a quick break, no longer than ten minutes, please. Then they will split up into groups. She points as she speaks. In the back right corner, the loss of parent group. In the back left corner, the loss of spouse group. By the right of the stage, the loss of child and loss of sibling groups. And by the left of the stage, the loss by suicide group.

Kavita clutches inside when she hears the word. Her eyes dart among the rows, nervously, as she tries to read the reactions of the other mourners. Then she looks back at Brenda, who appears unfazed. There's no hint of shame in her demeanour, as if she has nothing to be ashamed about, and more incredibly to Kavita, she isn't afraid of what anyone might say or do.

Brenda finishes by saying she will be facilitating the loss by suicide group tonight, thanks them, and takes her seat in the front row.

Kavita stares at Brenda's twisted bun with wide eyes. She wonders if Brenda is a suicide survivor too. Although they are still strangers, and have yet to meet officially, Kavita can't deny she feels a kinship with the facilitator. This woman, Brenda, who has transformed her pain into so much good. Who lives a meaningful life. Is such a thing truly possible? Kavita dares to wonder. Even for her? The room goes dark and the video begins to play.

After the movie, the lights flick back on, and people start milling about. She goes to the washroom and considers spending the rest of the break in the stall, but there are only two, and a line-up is forming already.

Back in the room, she pours herself a glass of apple juice and tries to rehydrate.

Plastic cup in hand, she walks along the tables displaying bereavement literature and picks up a couple of handouts, pretending to read them, for the sake of appearing occupied.

"They definitely need to get some new videos," says a deep voice to her left. Surprised, she looks over with raised eyebrows. It is the young man with the half ponytail, smiling as widely—as disarmingly—as before. "I'm pretty sure I've seen that one."

"The puffy hairstyles and synthesizer were pretty funny," she offers.

"It's the mullets that really did it for me. But then again, I'm a sucker for a good mullet."

"True," she nods. "It's hard to deny a good mullet. If indeed such a thing exists."

"Oh, it does. Trust me. My Dad had one for most of my childhood." He pauses for a moment. "I wondered if I'd ever see you again."

She blinks at him. "I'm sorry?"

"Didn't you come to a meeting last fall?"

"Not really. I kind of lost my nerve at the last minute."

"I thought that was you. I was running the sign-in table that night. You're the one that got away."

"That's where I know you from." Her cheeks warm. "This is embarrassing."

"Don't worry about it. But I have to say, it's never happened to me before, or since, come to think of it. Usually I'm able to draw them in with my big brown eyes." He bats his lashes.

She can't help but smile.

"You know, I almost ran after you that night."

"You did?"

"I should warn you, I have a pretty substantial saviour complex to contend with, but I've been trying to tone it down. Anyway, if you wanted to leave, I figured you knew best. But I've looked for since then, hoping you'd come back someday. And here you are."

"Here I am."

"So, what changed your mind?"

She pauses. "I wasn't sure what else to do."

He nods, solemn for a moment. "I'm Hawthorn, by the way. But everyone calls me Hawk."

"I'm Kavita." After a brief pause, she says, "Why Hawk, if you don't mind my asking?"

"It's a nickname my twin, Sequoia, gave me. She always said I was a free spirit. I guess she pictured me soaring above the trees instead of being rooted in the ground."

Kavita thinks of Sunil and his favourite spot at Champlain Lookout where he would watch the hawks ride the thermals.

He pushes up his right sleeve, turns out his inner forearm, and says, "I got this tattoo a few months after Sequoia took her life."

Kavita's stomach spasms, the way it does whenever she encounters suicide, as though her whole self is howling: *No.* She remembers to breathe and tries to smooth out her startled expression, as she gazes at the tattoo, admiring the interconnected teardrops of the yin/yang drawn in black ink.

"Sequoia was always more yin than me," he goes on. "Quiet, private. I'm more yang, I guess. More of an extrovert. But we're parts of the same whole, if that makes sense."

"It's a lovely tribute." She swallows. "And I'm sorry about your sister."

"You look uncomfortable. Did I shock you?"

"I just wasn't expecting you to be so forthcoming. It isn't an easy thing to talk about, especially with a stranger."

"Actually, sometimes talking about it with strangers is easier than talking about it with people I know. I guess that's part of the appeal of group. At the beginning, you don't know anyone, and yet you have something so deep in common that draws you all together. It's the one place where I don't feel like I have to hide anything. But I guess coming to meetings for so long has turned me into a bit of an over-sharer. Sorry if I caught you off guard."

"There's nothing to be sorry about. Sharing's the point of being here. I'm just not used to it yet."

"Who did you lose?"

Kavita stalls, taking a sip of juice. She feels the impulse to clench her fist, to divert away from her emotional pain, to punish herself. But she resists reaction, lets the impulse build and taper. She has promised to let those wounds heal.

"My brother," she says at last. "His name was Sunil."

"Was he older or younger?"

"Older."

"Were the two of you close?"

"We were."

"How long has it been?"

"Six months." *Two weeks and five days.*

"That's not long at all."

"What about you?"

"Two years, just."

Kavita wonders what her grief might look like two years from now. Will she be as comfortable as Brenda and Hawthorn, able to talk about her loss with relative ease, as if it is an everyday topic?

"He must've been young."

"He was."

"My sister, too." Hawthorn eyes Kavita, closely. "So, I guess you'll be headed over to the sibling loss group." The way he says this is as much question as it is statement.

Wordlessly, she shakes her head, no.

A moment passes, and he says, "How about we grab a couple of chairs and start the circle. The loss by suicide group is over there tonight."

Kavita gazes up at him. His eyes are dark and soft and open. "I recognize the pain in your eyes," he says, anticipating her question. "I remember feeling the same way. Or at least my version of it, anyway. Survivors develop a kind of sixth sense about these things. Almost like we're able to pick up on a pattern most of the world can't see. It's hard to explain. You just know."

Kavita's eyes sting. She blinks quickly. She doesn't want to cry in front of a stranger, no matter how kind he is.

"Come on," he says. "It's okay."

Kavita grabs her chair and carries it alongside Hawthorn. Already she feels comfortable by his side. Something about him feels familiar. But how is that possible? She doesn't even know him.

Then she feels it. A subtle connection threaded between them, like a figure eight looping from his middle to hers. A connection through pain. Their loss, like no other, is what links them. Their pain is what makes them the same.

They set down their chairs and start the circle. Soon, others join. The room begins to quieten as everyone settles into their groups. Glancing around the circle, Kavita notices that she and Hawthorn are among the youngest. Apart from one other middle-aged man, Hawthorn is the only male. Kavita is the only person who isn't white.

Brenda takes a seat to Kavita's right, once removed. She starts by explaining how things are going to proceed. First, they will take turns introducing themselves. Then they will share the name of their loved one, when they died, how old they were, and how they died. This gives the session structure, but they shouldn't feel constricted by it. If other things come up, they can feel free to share them, bearing in mind everyone needs to be given a chance to speak by the end of the session.

"The more times we talk about our loss out loud, the more real it becomes. Sharing in a supportive environment also helps to combat shame. After all, shame can't survive when it's met with empathy." A few people nod in agreement. "I'll start things off. You heard a bit of my grief story earlier. What you didn't hear was that my mother completed suicide. She was bipolar for most of her life. But her bouts of depression were always more frequent and severe than her highs. Medication and therapy helped her cope, most of the time, but each time she sank into depression, she seemed to sink a little deeper. It would take her longer to come out of it. It would take more effort.

"Before she died, during another high spell, she stopped taking her meds, convinced that she didn't need them anymore. Shortly after that, her health started deteriorating. She went back on her meds, but they always took weeks to kick in. By then it was too late. She was convinced she would always feel as bad as she did in withdrawal. A few days before she died, we spent some time together, and she told me how worn out she was by it all. It was a red flag, although I didn't see it at the time. They found her car in a parking lot near Remic Rapids, along with a note on the dashboard that I wish I'd never read. Her body was never found. We had nothing to bury, other than some of her belongings. Her name was Anne. She was fifty-five. It's been ten years, but sometimes it feels like it happened this morning."

Brenda's story awakens the welter of emotion within Kavita. Her insides quake. She feels on the verge of breaking. She squeezes her arms around her midsection, tightly. As she tries to still herself, it occurs to Kavita, what shocks her almost as much as Brenda's story, is the counsellor's ability to speak about the nightmarish with ease, as if it is normal.

But that's what it is, she realizes, isn't it? For suicide survivors, the nightmarish is the norm. The nightmarish is what they wake to each morning, what they carry throughout the day, throughout their lives, unbeknownst to the world around them.

Brenda turns her attention to the woman sitting beside Kavita. The woman has long hair parted in the middle and it is dyed black. She is wearing a black leather jacket, black jeans, and sturdy black boots. She is biting her nails.

Brenda's eyes float across the woman's nametag. "Joan? Would you like to go next?"

The woman sits up straighter. As Joan shares, Kavita is too distracted by the rapid pace of her heartbeat to pay full attention, even though she wants to. Sparse words make it through:

"rifle" and "found him" and "forty-six" and "three children."

Kavita will have to share next. She doesn't know what to say, or how to say it to this circle of strangers, these people she has barely known ten minutes. How can she tell them more than she has told her husband, her best friend, her parents? How can she reveal parts of herself to these people who will carry her story with them from the church basement, to their homes, into their lives? How can she trust them?

She glances around the circle. Maybe because she has no other choice. She promised to find a better way, and this is where that promise has led her. These people her collective, the one she has been longing for since Sunil's death, the ones who understand as only they can.

Still, fear of speaking lights a fuse that travels from her heart, through her belly, to her feet. Why her feet? she wonders, as she becomes acutely aware of them inside her boots, the waves of energy buzzing from her heels, to her arches, to her toes, and back again, as if they are batteries charging up, as if her body is preparing to speed to the exit ahead of her thoughts.

"Kavita?" says Brenda, tilting her head to one side. "It's your turn to share, if you're ready. Although newcomers always get a free pass at their first meeting. It's fine if you just want to sit and listen this time."

The moment to speak has arrived, yet Kavita sits mutely. She thought her mind was made up before she descended into the church basement, but Brenda has offered her a way out, and with so many eyes upon her now, she can't ignore the appeal.

"I can go first," offers Hawthorn, as he peers at her sidelong.

All she has to do is utter one word—*pass*—and the discomfort will be over.

"If you want," he adds.

All she has to do is keep hiding the way she has been for months, without a voice, or a hope.

"Kavita?" Brenda asks.

Everyone in the circle is watching her. She can feel the weight of their stares. They are waiting for her to open her dry mouth, and make a choice.

"It's okay," she says to Hawthorn at last, then shifts her attention to the rest of the circle. "I'll go."

"Take your time," Brenda tells her.

Kavita clears a clot from her throat. As she stares at the middle of the circle, she suddenly knows that they have formed more than a shape with their chairs. They have formed a pit. A place to throw things. Their pain and sorrow and shame. The things inside them they have yet to name. The things they know too well and can't escape. The things the world either caused or rejected. The masks the world demands they wear everywhere, except here, in this safe place.

"My brother's name is Sunil," she begins. "He died six months ago. He used sleeping pills and vodka, at least that's what we think. We still don't have the toxicology report, so the exact cause of death is still unknown. He was thirty years old. I know he's gone, but it still doesn't seem real."

Kavita has no voice left. These short phrases have taken everything she has. A hand pats her shoulder. Although she doesn't lift her gaze, she offers Hawthorn a cheerless grin as thanks.

"I'm sorry," Brenda says. "Do you have any other siblings?"

Kavita shakes her head.

"Taking care of grieving parents can be a lot to bear alone. Do you have any other family you can lean on?"

"No," Kavita replies. "There's no one else close by. It's always just been the four of us."

"That must be difficult."

Kavita nods.

"In general, suicide survivors lack visibility, but among us, the silencing is usually even more pronounced for those that have lost a sibling. Sometimes the surviving sibling doesn't feel entitled to their grief. Sometimes their grief isn't acknowledged adequately by their families and friends because their loss is perceived as less severe than their parents'. All in all, it can be very invalidating, not to mention isolating." After a brief pause, Brenda asks if Kavita has anything else she would like to share. Kavita declines, Brenda thanks her for opening up, and moves on to Hawthorn.

"You did great," he whispers to her before addressing the group. "Hey everybody, I'm Hawk." He raises one hand in a wave. "Okay, here goes. My twin sister, Sequoia, died by suicide two years ago. We just got through the second anniversary. Two years, one week, and five days. Am I the only one who keeps track like that? Anyway, somehow I thought the second year would be easier than the first, but it wasn't. If the first year was about surviving, then the second year was about learning how to live my life without her. It finally hit me that she's gone. I guess shock protected me during the first year, but that's more or less worn off by now. I guess I had these expectations of what my life would look like down the road. I thought things would get easier. And they're different, that's for sure. Less raw, less intense. But I can't say things have gotten any easier, in a larger sense, is what I mean. I guess because what happened, losing Sequoia like we did, that won't ever change, it can't, so there's only so much better things can ever get. Sorry about the tangent. It's just been a lot to deal with, lately. So, about Sequoia. She lived with depression for most of her life. She medicated with alcohol mostly. She was on a waiting list for a treatment program. She lived out in Vancouver with her boyfriend. He found her. No note. She was twenty-eight. At the time, I was in Costa Rica taking a therapeutic yoga course that focused on treating depression and addictions. I was doing it for her. I spoke to her a couple of days before she died, and she sounded okay. Calm, which wasn't like her. I guess that must've been a sign but I didn't see it then. I feel guilty for being away when she needed me most. Maybe if I'd been closer she wouldn't have gone through with it." He falls silent and holds one hand over his tattoo.

Kavita wants to reach out and comfort him the way he comforted her, but doesn't feel familiar enough yet. Instead, she sends him a compassionate smile. He winks back, acknowledging.

"As survivors," Brenda says, "we often feel responsible for the death of our loved ones. We feel like we should've known what they were thinking. We blame ourselves for not seeing the signs, for not acting quickly enough. But we need to understand and accept that we did the best we could at the time. Hindsight is always twenty-twenty. But it's also hypothetical. The only real thing was the situation each of us faced. After all, no one here ever wanted their loved one to die." Brenda pauses, allowing time for the truth to sink in through the thick crust of hurt that covers each of them. "So," she continues, "the next time you feel the guilt and anger starting to creep up again, tell yourself that you did your best. You did all you could do at the time."

"That sounds good," Hawthorn says. "But the problem is, it wasn't enough."

Brenda grins at him, dimly, sympathetic, but doesn't say anything, because he is right, and there are no words she can offer to make that truth singe any less. It can only be borne like the other burdens that come with this loss.

"Hawk," Brenda says. "What you mentioned about your sister sounding better when you last spoke to her? That isn't unusual. For some people, once they've made up their mind, a kind of relief sets in, and for a while things can seem like they're improving."

"No more losing the war."

"Which of course only makes their deaths even more shocking to those of us left behind. Our guards were down. We blame ourselves for not being more vigilant."

Brenda thanks Hawk and moves on to the older woman sitting beside him, who tells the group about her grandson, Stephen, who passed away four weeks ago, and his struggles as a gay teen, and the medication he was put on despite the warnings.

The same medication Sunil was taking, Kavita notes. She's angry he was put on the medication to begin with. He wasn't sick, she insists. He was being bullied. They didn't do enough at the school to protect him. And there was bullying on the internet, too. What's wrong with children these days? How can they do these things to each other? He snuck out with the car, tied a pipe to the exhaust, and asphyxiated himself. He was seventeen. Not even graduated, yet. She doesn't know how to help her son through this loss. She buried her husband two years ago, but he was an old man, his death made sense. But this, burying the son of a son, it's too awful to comprehend. She's an old woman. How can life have turned out this way? She tried to get her son to join her tonight, but he won't talk, not to anyone, not even their pastor. Her family doctor told her about the group. That's why she came tonight. Also, she's started taking antidepressants, but hopefully not for long, just until things get better. Things will get better, won't they?

The middle-aged woman that shares next talks about her brother, Jeff, who was fifty-two, and his life with schizophrenia, and her frustrations with the system that isn't really a system at all, it's too disjointed to warrant such a name. How there's such an emphasis on youth, but youth grow up, and when they grow up, there isn't enough support to help them when they need it. She confesses his death has been harder for her to deal with than losing her husband to cancer. The cancer was awful, make no mistake, and losing her life partner is one of the hardest things she's ever been through, but the difference is her husband was given every resource. She can accept that, in the end, they did everything they could for him. But in her brother's case, it was like no one cared, no one acknowledged that his life was more acutely in danger than even her husband's had been at certain points. The healthcare professionals she met during his appointments acted as if they deserved awards for even the most mediocre care. She wants to sue the useless resident he saw at his last appointment. That fucking prick who downplayed her brother's symptoms and only cared about saving his own ass when she called him on it later. He was a carpenter. He loved working with wood. He fell on his table saw and bled to death. It's coming up on a year, and she's dreading the anniversary. Her parents have never looked so old. She feels helpless. There's nothing she can do to make things better for them.

The man after her chooses not to speak.

The next is a mother who has lost her son, Matthew, three months ago. He was thirty-six. She had never known him to struggle with mental illness, it doesn't run in their family, as far as she knows, so she can't say whether or not he was depressed. All she can think of is he was stressed at work. He had moved out to Calgary about a year ago for a new job and his boss had turned out to be a real piece of work. During their last conversation, he mentioned being worried about getting fired, and not being able to pay his mortgage. She downplayed it, as a way of calming him down, told him he was fretting over nothing. Over nothing. Those words still haunt her. A week later, he leapt from an overpass. He was her only child. And he didn't have any children. And she lives alone; she divorced his father when her son was still a boy. He was always a happy child, and an easy-going adult, her rock. No, he wasn't depressed. He wasn't sick. She hates it when people paint him with that brush. She misses him so much. Lately she's been wondering what she's living for. Brenda asks the woman to stay behind once the session has ended.

Another mother follows. Her son, Gabriel, was about to finish university. She knew him to be sensitive, but she didn't know he was depressed, if he was, it went undiagnosed. The only reason she can think of is that his long-time girlfriend broke up with him recently, and he took it hard. But even that doesn't seem like a good enough reason to do something so drastic. There must have been more to it, but she'll never really know. His roommate found him. He hung himself. She has a daughter too, a couple of years older than her son, but she's been hard to reach, she lives out east. Her husband won't talk about what's happened. Lately, he's been spending his evenings either at work, or at the Legion. They used to be a close family, but everything feels like it's coming apart. If things don't change, she thinks she's headed for a divorce. And she's worried about her daughter. What if it happens again? She never used to think like that, but the impossible happened, and now it's like a door's been opened, and she's worried about who else might walk through it. She can't sleep at night without the handful of pills her doctor prescribed. Does anyone else have nightmares? His twenty-third birthday is in two weeks. She doesn't know how she's going to face it. Later, the mothers exchange numbers.

A woman in her late-thirties speaks next. She lost her older sister, Stephanie, four years ago, but this is her first meeting. Her sister had struggled with eating disorders in the past, but had gotten treatment, and things seemed manageable, so she doesn't think that was the reason. Anyway, she was a dancer, so it was normal for her to be thinner than the average person. She lived in Toronto, where there were more auditions, and she taught dance, but she was about to turn forty and the big break she had been hoping for hadn't panned out. But she was happy, or at least seemed to be. She had a beautiful son, who was eight at the time, and a husband she adored. A good life. She came back to Ottawa for a week before she died, and while she seemed a little preoccupied, she was otherwise normal. They spent a lot of time together. She doted over her niece, who was only one at the time. They talked about meeting up in Toronto soon. The day after she got back home, her sister's husband found her in the bathtub. In the note she had left behind, she said she had made a deal with herself: she would live until forty and if things didn't get better by then, at least she would know she tried. The woman threw herself into motherhood as a way of coping with her grief. But now her daughter's in school and she has more time on her hands and suddenly everything's flooding back to her. She feels guilty for pushing it away like she did, not being there for her nephew and brother-in-law like she should have been, but she didn't know how else to handle everything at the time. What kind of sister is she? How could she not know her own sister was in trouble? There might have been signs, she keeps wracking her brain, but she was too wrapped up in herself and baby to notice. It's all so open-ended. Her sister was there, and now she isn't, and she can't make sense of any of it. What is she supposed to tell her daughter now that she's older?

By the time everyone in the circle has spoken, two hours have passed. The thread that runs through the stories is more than suicide. It's confusion, utter disbelief, even when there is a clear-cut reason for the loss of life, and devastatingly more so when there isn't. They are a circle of people, stunned, staring at each other from left to right, wondering what in God's name happened to their loved ones and their lives, how it could have happened, and always and forever, why?

Before the meeting concludes, Brenda challenges them to be good to themselves. They might not think they deserve it, but she assures them they do. So please, she implores, be kind. Be gentle.

The circle breaks, and people begin to disperse, folding up their chairs and stacking them against the wall. Kavita remains seated for a few extra moments, wrestling with Brenda's words about self-compassion.

"How do you feel?" Hawthorn asks as he folds his chair.

She rubs lines up and down her temples. "Like I've been snow-plowed."

"That sounds about right," he grins. "So, do you think you'll be back?"

Kavita considers. "I think so. Even though I feel exhausted right now, I also feel a bit...I don't know how to put it, exactly. I wouldn't say lighter. I guess like I've let something out." She wants to add that she feels alone but also not alone, which makes sense inside her tired mind, but probably not outside it, so she keeps that to herself.

"Do you want to know what I appreciate the most about group?"

"What's that?"

"Even if no one in my life understands what I'm going through, even if the rest of the world has forgotten about Sequoia, I know when I come here, I'm surrounded by people that get it. It helps."

She nods, yes. That's what she meant. Alone but not alone.

"Are you on your own tonight?"

"No, my husband's at home."

"He didn't come with you?"

"No," she says, not wanting to elaborate.

"Well, I hate to be the bearer of bad news, but expect a raging therapy hangover tomorrow."

"Something tells me I don't want to know what that is."

"Think, regular hangover, only without any of fun beforehand."

She touches her temples again. "I can feel it building already."

"Take it easy tonight. Maybe get your hub to get you some chocolate or Doritos or something."

"A fan of eating our feelings?"

"I have an unopened box of Jos Louis at home with my name on it."

She lets out a little laugh. "I'm not so good at the kindness thing." She rises her feet.

"Well," he says, reaching into his back pocket for his wallet. "If you're looking for something to do, why not pop by and take a class." He hands her a glossy green business card that reads: *Hawthorn Woods, Certified Yoga Instructor*.

She raises a playful eyebrow. "Yoga teachers have business cards now?"

"They come in handy every now and then."

"Promise to never say *na-mas-t*é to me and I'll overlook it."

"Deal," he laughs. "The schedule's online. I teach on Tuesdays and Fridays."

"I used to go to hot yoga, but I haven't exercised in months." She slips the card into the pocket of her jeans. "I'd never make it through a whole class."

"I only teach yin. But you know, even if you spend the whole time in Corpse Pose, it doesn't really matter. " He takes their chairs to the wall and stacks them with the others.

"No pressure," he adds. "But as a little extra encouragement, I have a book at the studio I think you'll like. It helped me a lot during my first year. Still does, actually."

"What book?"

"Ah, well," he says as starts walking backwards toward the exit. "That's for me to know. See you tomorrow?"

"Maybe," she shrugs.

"Maybe's better than no." He shakes his fist as if celebrating. "I'll take it!" Then he turns around and waves her goodbye.

She watches him exit the church basement and disappear up the stairs. A few moments later, she realizes she's still grinning.

She expects Anchor to pull, and Gloom to bully.

But they don't.

Not a bit.

33

KAVITA'S DREAMS THAT NIGHT are a living watercolour of images bleeding into one another, a haunting reel of gunshots, leapers, bloated corpses, hanging bodies, bloodied razors, empty caskets, car windows blackened out with soot and the choking smell of exhaust. Nightmares made all the more frightening by virtue of their truth, their belonging to the other survivors she had met at group and the people they have lost.

Now, as she lies in bed in the sallow morning light and wrestles with the throbbing ache of her first therapy hangover, she realizes something she has felt since Sunil's passing but hasn't been able to articulate: Suicide doesn't end suffering. It spreads it around. It's that time of January that is synonymous with semi-hibernation, thick sweaters, and peak vitamin D deprivation—a seasonal assault Kavita prefers to wait out within greenhouse-like warmth of her glass-walled condo. Today, however, for the second time in as many sunrises, she emerges from her cave, coaxed not by a change in the nostril-fusing weather, but rather by the possibility of at last finding another bear like her.

With the Styrofoam crunch of snow underfoot, Kavita trudges through shin-deep drifts along quiet residential streets of her neighbourhood, lined with ice-dipped trees, on her way to the yoga studio where Hawthorn teaches. Fat, wet flakes fall like albino moths and wreath her fur-trimmed hood in a sparkling halo. Occasionally, she pulls her gaze from the sidewalk to marvel at the deadly and beautiful icicles that hang from steep-roofed houses, some of them as tall as she is.

Her mat is slung over one shoulder. When she dug it out of the back of the closet earlier, it was covered in a fine layer of chalky dust, a testament to how sedentary she has become. As she turns down the correct street, she notices a green sandwich board a little ways ahead of her on the sidewalk, in front of the studio, that reads, *Lotus Yoga Centre*, in bold black letters. An elegant white stencil of a lotus bloom sits above the studio's name, and a picture of a woman balancing on her forearms, below.

Kavita's stomach seizes. She stops walking. Glances over her shoulder to make sure she isn't blocking the way. Anything to stall moving any farther. *It isn't too late to make a U-turn*, she thinks. She could buy herself a consolation peppermint hot chocolate on the way home and tell herself it's okay. She isn't ready yet. Last night was a big enough step. Hawthorn was just being nice to the new girl when he invited her. He doesn't actually expect her to show up. *It would be weird.* Seeing him out of context, outside of the church basement, in his real life.

But then, that's part of the draw. How does he do it? Go to group one night, and still have enough energy to wake up the next day, pert and ready, to teach a yoga class. How did he manage to get to such a healthy place, when she, in comparison, feels barely functional? She needs to see what recovery looks like up close. After all, she promised herself to find a better way.

She pushes onward, past the sign, up the stone walkway that leads to the converted red-brick century home, before she loses her nerve. A bell chimes as she passes through the first French door into a small closet-like foyer. As she glances at the community board to her left, she notices a poster of Hawthorn seated cross-legged with his hands folded in *namaskar*, advertising an upcoming karma class. She will have to ask him about it, she tells herself, as she passes through the second French door and enters the studio.

Pushing back her hood, she takes a moment to check out the space. The only place for coats and boots is a row of hooks above a bench to her left. The yoga room itself is large and open, with cork floors and high ceilings, and the usual collection of yoga paraphernalia available for use at the back of the room. A dozen or so people are milling around, fetching props, gabbing, limbering up on their mats, or simply lying still.

But there is no sign of Hawthorn.

She unzips her coat and tugs off her boots and wonders where he is. Is it possible she got her days mixed up when she checked the online schedule? She could have sworn he told her that he works on Tuesdays and Fridays, but to be honest, last night is a bit of a blur. Mid-way through the process of cramming her coat onto an overstuffed hook, she hears a familiar voice from behind.

"So, you decided to join the fun after all."

Glancing over her shoulder, she finds Hawthorn beaming a welcoming smile. He is dressed in grey shorts and a teal sleeved shirt. With his arms at his sides, she can see half of his memorial tattoo peaking out.

"Where were you hiding?" she asks.

"I was just signing in a student." He motions to the desk tucked around the corner. "I knew it was a long shot, but I was hoping you'd show up today."

"Well, I decided to take Brenda's advice and give this whole kindness thing a shot."

He rubs his stomach. "Much better for you than binging on a box of Jos Louis."

With a half grin, she reaches into her hoodie and hands him a folded paper. "Here you go."

"A real keener, eh?" he teases, taking the consent form. "We still have a few minutes before class, so I'll go ahead and put your name into the system. Grab a spot and settle in."

"But wait, I haven't paid."

"Consider it a friend's discount. Or what my therapist would call *good old-fashioned conditioning*. Work and reward. Besides," he shrugs, "I'm glad you came."

"Me too." A beat. "But I'm sure I'll regret it by the end of class."

He smirks.

"What?

"I knew it."

"Knew what?"

"That you were funny underneath all the sad."

She doesn't know what to say, can't remember the last time she brought joy to someone's life, or vice versa.

"I promise to go easy on you," he says as he starts walking back to the desk. "And hey, remind me to give you that book after class, okay?"

She watches him welcome another student with a hug, then looks for a spot, noting the slight cushion of the cork floor beneath the soles of her feet as she crosses the room. She unrolls her mat in the back corner, and settles into Child's Pose, focusing on the cool dot at the centre of her forehead as she surrenders the full weight of her head to the floor.

Her back feels stiff. Her ribs, tight. She focuses on her breath. Tries to deepen it. At first, it resists.

It takes a few cycles for her breath to find more room to move inside her lungs, her belly. Soon expansion replaces resistance. After a while, she is just breathing, and it happens, naturally.

After class, as she rests on her mat, splayed like a stickwoman, her body hums with gentle energy. A pleasant fog clouds her mind and slows her thinking. For the first time in a long time, she feels peaceful.

During the class, as she listened to Hawthorn's softly-spoken guidance, and settled into each pose, she discovered something more surprising than her body's lack of suppleness. It was a feeling. A feeling that undulated through her in waves, back and forth, back and forth, as if she could feel the very water that was such a part of her makeup moving through her. About halfway through the class, while she was in Cobbler's Pose, and her inner thighs finally stopped shrieking, a simple truth opened to her like the amber heart of a lotus bloom, and she finally knew what the feeling was: life. She was alive. Despite everything, still alive.

While the others busy themselves with putting props, and rushing off to their next commitments, she lingers on her mat, staring at the ceiling fans with her palms resting over her sunken stomach, reluctant to let go of the peaceful feeling. Mere days ago, she thought that everything about her, inside and outside, had been ruined by loss. That is what Anchor and Gloom have told her for months, like promises, like truth. That is what Blaze and her shame have burned and chilled into her marrow. And for months, she believed them.

Now, she isn't so sure.

By the time she rolls up her mat and limps over to the desk where Hawthorn is busying himself with boiling water for tea, the studio has emptied. On the floor in front of the large bay window overlooking the street, he has arranged a couple of bolsters for them to sit on and gathered a few woollen blankets, too.

"I have ginger lemon and blueberry green tea." He holds up a box of each. "Personally, I'm a fan of the ginger."

"I'll try that one, please." She lowers herself onto a bolster, sits cross-legged, and drapes one of the blankets over her legs. Then she peers through the window. The snowfall has tapered to a shimmery dusting.

"So," he asks. "How was the class?" He drops tea bags into a couple of green earthenware mugs. "Do you hate me?"

"A little bit," she grins as she kneads her fist into her lower back. "But really, it's not too bad. I expected to be a little sore. Otherwise, I feel good. Relaxed. You're a good teacher."

With a self-effacing grin, he hands her a steaming mug. She notices for the first time a comma-like dimple denting his left cheek. She wonders if Sequoia had the same feature, then remembers that fraternal twins don't share identical genetics. Still, she can't help but wonder what his sister looked like, this person who feels both known and unknown to her.

"Well," he says as he grabs a chunky green cardigan from the back of the desk chair and pulls it on. "If you're in the mood for more I'm teaching a karma class this Sunday afternoon." Mug in hand, he eases onto the bolster across from her and covers his legs with a blanket.

"I saw the poster when I came in."

"It's pay what you can. I'm raising money for the bereavement group."

"That's generous of you."

"I'm lucky to be able to give back." He takes a quiet slurp of tea, declares it's "Still too hot," and places the mug on the floor.

She bobs her tea bag up and down. "Teaching must be rewarding."

"It is most of the time. But teaching's nothing like taking a class. Sometimes I get a little burned out."

"At least you're helping people."

"Not as much as they help me. I'm hooked on that instant gratification you get from adjusting someone's pose or seeing them finally get quiet enough to sink into *Savasana*. It's awesome."

"I wish I had that kind of skill. All I seem to know how to do is write briefing notes. I'm a civil servant. Well, I used to be anyway. I'm not sure if I'm going back."

"What would you do instead?"

"I have no idea." She pauses. "Sometimes I feel like I'll never be able to hold down another job. It just seems so…enormous. I don't know how I ever did it before."

"That's just because you're a little overwhelmed right now. You won't always feel that way. But it takes some time. It's supposed to."

"Time heals all wounds?"

"Personally, I call bullshit on that one."

She laughs.

"The way I see it," he goes on. "All time ever gives you is an opportunity. It doesn't do any of the work. That's up to you. And it's the work that matters in the end. It's the work that'll save you."

"Well, that sounds exhausting."

This time, he laughs. "All I'm saying is when you're ready, all the things that feel impossible now will start to feel a little less impossible, and bit by bit, you'll start working towards whatever new goals you've decided on, and before you know it, you'll be a yoga teacher with a beard, who volunteers at a bereavement group once a month, and keeps an apiary on the roof of his apartment building."

She touches her chin in mock self-consciousness.

"But chances are, you aren't going to go climb Mount Everest or save the world tomorrow. And that's fine. You've got enough going on. Maybe the day after, though." He winks at her.

"The thing is, no one else in my life seems as messed up as I am. They've all been able to move on in some way. I don't know what's wrong with me. I've been so stuck lately."

"Well, sometimes getting stuck is necessary. Without it, most people wouldn't stop for long enough to really look at their lives. Everyone deals with loss differently. Just because you're struggling doesn't mean there's something wrong with you. Maybe you're the only person in your family who's actually paying attention to what's happening, instead of being in denial. Maybe you're the only one who's taking the time to deal with your shit."

"I wouldn't go that far." She thinks of the centre of her left palm, her scar. "I'm definitely not the poster child for good coping skills."

"Well, it's hard to wake up every morning and remember that your brother took his life. It's hard to face a life you didn't want. It takes a lot out of a person."

She stares into her cup.

"You aren't weak, Kavita. You just have more to carry than the average person. That's what you've been carrying: your brother." The invisible weight crushes against her, as it has since she found out Sunil took his life, the only difference being, for the first time since it settled upon her like a burden, it wasn't invisible, Hawthorn could see it, along with, she suspects, the shake of her joints. He could see her. "But you're doing it," he continues. "If that isn't strength—if that isn't *hopeful*—then frankly, they don't exist. So, do me a favour and stop being so hard on yourself, okay? You're being a real downer."

She grins, faintly. His eyes are dark and soft and open. She sees something in them she has been searching for in everyone else she knows, but she can't name it yet.

"I just wish it was over. I want to be on the other side of this. All figured out."

"Who wouldn't? But the thing is, you're healing, even if it doesn't seem like it. There's a ton of stuff happening under the surface. Soon enough you'll start to see little green shoots popping up from the dirt."

"Are you comparing my life to dirt?"

"Hey, that's where the story is, friend."

"I should've known you'd say something like that. You know when I first saw you, I nicknamed you Granola Guy."

"I like it."

"Of course you do."

They smile into their cups.

"You and Brenda impress me, though. You're both so motivated to do important things. Most of the time, I feel like an Olympian if I manage to take a shower and cook dinner. If I wasn't married, I probably wouldn't even bother."

"Want to know what I did my first year? Ate takeout, slept way too much, and watched every episode of *Star Trek* available on Netflix. *Twice.* I'm pretty sure going to group once a month was the only productive thing I did all year. Well, that, and I started seeing a therapist. Which is probably why I slept so much."

"It's hard for me to imagine you any other way than you are today."

"I didn't even practice yoga that year. I didn't give a shit about it. Not that I could even settle for long enough to meditate if I wanted to."

"How very un-yogi of you."

He smirks. "So, do you feel any better?"

"Maybe a little."

They drink tea for a while and watch the snow fall.

"Can you tell me about Sequoia?" she asks. He regards her, slightly taken aback by her directness. She notes the fullness of his eyebrows she doubts have ever been tweezed. The rusty tint of his brown eyes. The occasional hairless patch in his beard of week-old scruff.

He frees his hair from its half ponytail and shakes his head a few times. "That's a big question. What do you want to know?"

Kavita remembers something she was wondering about earlier. "Do you look alike?"

"Sort of. We're both tall and thin. Her eyes were a lighter shade of brown. She had short spiky hair and a gold lip ring. Her hair colour changed a lot. From pink to green to purple to platinum. When she died it was dark blue."

"What did she do?"

"She was a muralist. She liked riding her long-board around town and spotting new canvases. She loved the idea of beautifying urban spaces. Some of her work was commissioned by the city in Chinatown. Remember how I told you she was more yin than me, more of an introvert? Well, her murals were like her way of reaching out and connecting with people. I think maybe it came from being so lonely."

"I'd love to see them sometime. What did she like to paint?"

"She had a thing for koi fish and flowers. She painted a mural in my parents' yard along the back of our house. It's this psychedelic koi fish, kelp forest, botanical garden composition. Kind of hard to describe. But I'm glad we have it. Whenever I go home to visit my parents, it makes me feel like she's still around."

"I'd love to see that someday, too."

"Your turn," he asks, forcing a grin. "Tell me about Sunil."

Suddenly she can appreciate the enormity of the question. How to distill her brother into a few spare lines? How to express all he was, all he means to her, in words?

"Well, he was tall and handsome, but I'm biased. He worked with computers, although I never really understood what he did with them. Isn't that awful? He loved reading mystery novels. Val McDermid, Lee Child, Dean Koontz, that sort of thing. I saved a box of his books before my mom sold our house. I flipped through some of them the other day. He had a habit of underlining words, the ones he liked, or maybe didn't know and wanted to lookup. He dog-eared the bottom of pages, not the tops. Sometimes he scribbled his thoughts in the margins. There's something about seeing his handwriting that destroys me whenever I come across it now. I cherish it, but it destroys me. Maybe because I know it's finite. He'll never write another word. Whatever I find, that's it." She pauses. With anyone else, she would have ordered herself to smile. But with Hawthorn, she knows she doesn't have to pretend. "Where was I?" she says. "He liked ordering pizza on Fridays to celebrate the weekend. He loved the outdoors. Especially driving up to Gatineau Park and watching the hawks at Champlain Lookout. He was the funniest person I've ever known. We laughed a lot. I know things ended horribly, but we had good times in my family, too."

"He sounds like a great guy."

"He was," she says. "I've come to realize that he's probably the only person who ever really understood me or accepted me for what I am. I thought I understood him, too. But there's so much I didn't know. Sometimes I think I didn't really know him at all, and now it's too late."

"You knew him," Hawthorn tells her. "Don't torture yourself like that."

"Either way, our connection's gone, and I keep searching for it, but all I find is this awful silence." She looks up. "Sequoia was your twin. You two were close. It sounds like she was your person in the same way Sunil was mine. So, how do you manage it?"

"Manage what?"

"Living without your person?"

He releases a long exhale. "I don't have all the answers, friend. I'm all holes too."

For a while, they sit and listen to the sound of the thickening snow gently tap against the window. The warmth of the tea eases the strain in her throat and soon her tears recede like tideline.

"It feels good to sit and talk with you," she says. "I felt the same way after the meeting. I was so nervous before, though, I almost didn't go. But I'm glad I did."

"Now that you've had some time to digest it all, how did you find your first meeting?"

"It was intense. When we were in the circle, I was shaking. I felt so exposed. I was scared of being judged. I guess that's happened a lot lately. But after, when everyone was so receptive and kind, I felt relieved. This morning, though, I felt like crap. And I had terrible nightmares last night. Now I know what you mean by a therapy hangover."

"Consider your initiation complete." He pauses, thinking. "Group's complicated that way. You share your pain, which can be great, but you also open yourself up to the pain of others, and there's no telling what you're going to get or how it's going to affect you. I guess for those of us that stick with it, the benefits outweigh the costs. But it's not for everyone."

"I can see why."

He hesitates for a moment. "I noticed that your husband wasn't there last night. Do you think he'll come to the next one?"

"I tried to include him. I thought it might help us communicate. But he wasn't interested. Talking isn't really his thing. Lots of people are like that, though. It's not his fault. It's just how he was raised. I know because I was raised like that, too. He said he doesn't need group, but he supports me going."

"He just doesn't want to have to be there."

"Something like that."

"That sounds lonely."

"I suppose it is."

The awkwardness of this admission makes Kavita almost fidget. Thankfully, Hawthorn diffuses the tension by declaring, "I think these mugs could use a little warming up."

He pours hot water into their cups and sits back down. Then he pushes up the sleeve of his sweater, exposing the yin/yang tattoo underneath.

"I told you I got this about six months after Sequoia died." He extends his inner forearm toward her so she can get a closer look. "I remember lying on the couch watching a movie. I don't remember which one anymore. But I can still picture the scene that got to me. The characters were all dressed in black, standing around a grave. As they left the cemetery, it hit me that the tombstone was one of the only things that testified to the dead person's existence, and there it was, off to the side, in the cemetery. I realized I still had my whole life to live. I was going to meet new people and they would never get to know Sequoia. I couldn't stand that idea. She's a part of me. My other half. So, I got this tattoo. I think of it as a tombstone on my arm. It's my way of testifying to the world about Sequoia's life. It's how I stay true to my inner skin."

"Your inner skin? I'm not sure I understand."

"There's my outer skin, that the world sees, and knows about me. And then there's my inner skin, that only I see, and know about myself. That's where Sequoia lives now. That's where I keep her safe. The tattoo reminds me that I'm not moving on as I live my life, like every idiot says you should do, because moving on implies leaving her behind. I'll never do that. I might have lost my twin, but I'm moving *with* her. I'm carrying her along as I go. The tattoo helps my outer skin match my inner skin, at least a little."

Kavita traces the tattoo with her gaze, the curved teardrops joined at the middle, absorbing every curve, shade, and bit of negative space.

"Maybe you need to find your own way of testifying to Sunil's life, too."

"You mean get a tattoo? I'm afraid of needles."

"No ink, then." He chuckles. "What I mean is, maybe you need to find a way of inviting him back into your life. I was a lot less lonely once I started inviting Sequoia back into mine. My sister might be on the other side, but I still have a sister, if you get what I mean."

"Rediscovering our relationship sounds a little ambitious, considering I'm still mourning the one we lost."

"Your relationship's changed, but it isn't over."

"Yes, it is," she mutters. Anchor pulls. "It's gone. And it's my fault."

"That's just your broken heart talking." Hawthorn dunks his tea bag. "I remember that place. Thinking life was over. That I was a failure. That I'd failed Sequoia. I felt guilty about everything. I barely ate because Sequoia couldn't eat. I wouldn't see my friends because Sequoia couldn't see hers. For a while, I didn't even think it was right to laugh because she couldn't laugh anymore. I didn't realize it at the time, but I was slowly choking myself off. I was squeezing the life right out of myself, a little more each day."

"I can't even get a haircut."

"How do you think mine got so long?" he jokes. "But after a while, I finally understood that I wasn't honouring her memory, or showing her loyalty. I was punishing myself. I had decided, subconsciously, that if she couldn't live, then I wouldn't either. I would just get by until it was over."

Kavita blinks into her tea.

"How long is it going to last? Another year? Five? What's it going to take for you to stop punishing yourself?"

She looks up, unprepared for this question. "If I'm honest, I can't see an end to it."

"Forever's a long time, friend."

She peers into her tea, not seeing. Anchor pulls, pulls, pulls.

"It's not your fault, Kavita," he tells her, slow and deliberate, as if trying to convince her.

"Look, I know what you're trying to do. You're trying to make me feel better. But I don't want to feel better about this. Okay? I don't deserve to feel better about this. I messed up. And it cost my brother his life. That's the truth. I have to live with it."

"I felt the same way for a long time. But it's like Brenda said last night. We did the best we could at the time. If we could have saved our siblings, we would have. We didn't want them to die."

"Don't you feel like you're letting yourself off the hook?"

"Maybe," he shrugs. "Mostly, though, I've accepted my limitations. I can't go back in time. I can't read minds. I couldn't take Sequoia's illness onto myself. I couldn't save her. I wanted to more than anything. Even now, it's what I want more than *anything*. It always will be. But all my love and good intentions and regret don't change a thing. There's no way to undo this. Not the damage she did to herself or the damage she unknowingly did to us. So, in order to live my life, and face all the decades ahead of me, I've had to accept the choice she made. That doesn't mean I agree with it even remotely. It doesn't lessen the pain whenever I think about her and how she died. It doesn't change the fact that I wish she'd believed in her resilience as much as I did, and made a different choice. It just means I accept that I can't change what happened. She made a choice from a place of pain, hoping the pain would end, but it didn't. I don't have the power to change any of that."

"Well, that's a lot to accept."

"People always talk about acceptance like it's the thing that'll set you free. To me, it's been the thing that's humbled me. At one point, it almost broke me." He wets his lips. "Listen Kavita, I understand how much you're hurting. Or at least I know my version of it. If I've learned anything from Sequoia, it's that nothing can grow in that place."

"Isn't it wrong to move on without them?"

"We're not moving on without them." He places a hand over his tattoo. "With them, right? If our siblings have taught us anything, it's that we need light."

"And what if I don't deserve any?"

"What would your brother say to that?"

"Sometimes I think he's disappointed in me for not keeping it together. I imagine him looking down on me and all I see is disgust in his eyes. I'm such a mess now." She rubs her forehead. "He's never seen me like this. He doesn't know this person." She presses her fingers into her sternum. "I'm not sure he'd want to know this person. I'm not sure even I do."

"He'd know better than anyone what suffering looks like. If he's looking down on you with anything in his eyes, it's compassion."

Kavita peers into Hawthorn's eyes. They are dark and soft and open. Wells of empathy.

"I hear what you're saying. And I'm not trying to be resistant. You obviously know what you're talking about. You're further along than I am. But I can't see things the way you do. I'm not sure I ever will."

"You're broken-hearted. I get it. I am too. The thing about broken hearts is they're still open. Wide open. Almost more than they can take. But, still open. It might not seem like it now, but trust me, life slowly starts seeping back in through the cracks. Then one day, you'll be doing something, and you'll suddenly realize your life's taken a new shape. Like it was always meant to."

"I'm a long way from where I was meant to be. It feels like starting over. I don't know if I can."

"Sure. But, I mean, you're here, aren't you?" He nudges her knee. "Making a new friend." His smile is infectiously broad.

"Just like in kindergarten."

"I'll remember to bring the Play-Doh next time."

Pausing, she tucks the blanket underneath her ankles, which ache from resting on the floor for too long. Then she gazes out the window at the snowfall that floats and settles on the front bushes wrapped in burlap. The snowfall transports her back to her childhood, to the forts, the snowball fights, the snow angels, the tobogganing. Sunil always loved winter. Anchor pulls. She feels the impulse. Resists the urge to squeeze. Looks at the Band-Aids covering the scar on her palm.

"Can I show you something?" she asks.

"You bet." He pulls down the sleeve of his sweater and covers his tattoo.

"Promise not to freak out?"

He raises his hands. "Yogis never freak out."

"I haven't shown this to anyone."

He nods, encouraging her to go on.

She pulls away the Band-Aids. The scab is bark-like and itchy and outlined with pink.

The grin slips from Hawthorn's lips. "Cooking accident?" He holds her in a steady gaze.

She shakes her head. Feels the unforgiving chill. Observes it. Waits for it to pass. Then she starts replacing the Band-Aids.

"No, don't," he says.

He reaches for her hand and gently lifts her palm, holding it with a leaf-light touch. His fingertips are warm from cradling his tea cup. He draws her hand close to his face as he reads the patterns on her skin, those lines that run like roads, and the sinkhole at their centre that breaks them. His warm breath sweeps across her skin.

"So," he says.

"...So."

"A glimpse of the hurt."

"Something like that."

He lets go of her hand and she lowers it onto her lap.

"You know what they say about scars, don't you?"

She shakes her head.

"They only form on the living. They mean you survived."

She resticks her Band-Aids.

"I'm sorry," he says.

"What for?"

"I'm just sorry, that's all."

"I don't want your pity. That's not why I showed you."

"I wasn't offering pity."

"I showed you because in a way this is what led me to group. After what happened, I promised myself to find a better way of coping."

He grins. "And of course, you have me now, too."

"I told you I'm not looking for pity."

"And I told you about my saviour complex."

"We barely know each other."

"But in some ways we probably know each other better than our family and friends do."

He wasn't wrong.

"My cell number's on my card. I told you they come in handy."

A minute or so passes in silence and tea sipping and window gazing. "You know how earlier you talked about life taking shape again?"

He nods.

"I think someday I'd like to find a way of helping people, the way you and Brenda do. I'm not sure how yet. But it would be comforting to know something good's come out of all this pain."

"I've thought about it, and in the end, I think all this pain goes back to love. We grieve the deepest for the ones we've loved the most. In a sense, grief isn't possible without love.

And love isn't possible without grief. They're like fraternal twins of a different kind, I guess."

Like Yama and Yami. "I've never thought about it like that."

"I guess it's a matter of perspective. Which reminds me, I owe you a book." He rises and approaches the antique bookcase beside the desk. "Here it is," he says, as he frees a slim volume from its place on the shelf. Once he finds the page he's looking for, he hands the book over to her.

"The *Gita*," she says, surprised. They have a copy just like the one she is holding at home, or at least they used to.

He sits back down. "I had to study it during yoga teachers' training. But I found myself going back to certain parts when I was grieving and searching for answers. I've marked off some of the passages that spoke to me."

Kavita sets her eyes on the first passage and starts reading aloud. "'Our bodies are known to end, but the embodied self is enduring, indestructible, and immeasurable. Therefore Arjuna, fight the battle.'"

She flips to the next passage.

"'As man discards worn-out clothes to put on new and different ones, so the embodied self discards its worn-out bodies to take on new ones. Weapons do not cut it. Fire does not burn it. Waters do not wet it. Wind does not wither it. It cannot be cut or burned. It cannot be wet or withered. It is enduring, all-pervasive, fixed, immovable, and timeless. It is called unmanifest, inconceivable, and immutable. Since you know that to be so, you should not grieve. If you think of its birth and death as ever-recurring, then too, Great Warrior, you have no cause to grieve. Death is certain for anyone born, and birth is certain for the dead. Since the cycle is inevitable, you have no cause to grieve. Creatures are unmanifest in origin, manifest in the midst of life, and unmanifest again in the end. Since this is so, why do you lament?'"

Falling silent, she lets the words seep in, still unsure of how she feels about them.

"Like I said, it's is a matter of perspective," he says. "Of course, that doesn't make fighting the battle any easier. To physicists, those verses are law. Isn't that wild? Like it's written into the universe."

"I think I'll read the rest later."

"We can talk about it next time, if you want. Oh, and don't forget about the inscription."

On the front page, she finds a neatly printed paragraph in green ink. "Did you write this?"

He nods, a touch embarrassed.

"A little guru Hawthorn wisdom, is it?"

"No teasing," he says, "or I'll banish you from the cult."

She indulges her grin for another second, then tries to act more serious. "Thank you for lending me the book. But are you sure you don't need it?"

"I'm sure," he says. "Besides, I'll sleep easier knowing you have it close by."

34

THROUGHOUT THE WINTER, Kavita's days began reshaping themselves as her friend foretold. Once a month, she went to group and met Hawthorn there. Although she asked Nirav to come to the meetings too, he would tell her, "I don't need therapy, but you go, it'll be good for you," and stayed home instead.

At group, the faces in the circle revolved like diners at a bistro, survivors drawn by a deeper hunger to understand the senseless. She practised opening up, sharing, and receiving. With the other survivors, among the safety net of hands that caught her when she was sinking, she learned how to speak openly about things long shamed.

They talked about the physical and psychological ravages of grief. The weighty guilt and fiery anger that were often at the heart of a suicide survivor's grief. They talked about triggers, how to recognize them, how to manage them. They talked about the ripple effects of suicide, the collateral damage. They talked about ways of coping with all these challenges, ways of surviving them. They talked about the slow and steady path back to living. Little by little, Kavita honoured her promise to herself. She was finding a better way.

In the circle, it was true that she encountered the nightmarish, at the centre of the pit where it was tossed, where it churned and settled, and later, got swept away by the janitor. But that wasn't all. Around the circle, within the brick of people that made its protective wall, she discovered resilience, as primal and resolute as spring, as inured as ancient forces of resurrection. At last, in the church basement, she found a place to belong, and to believe, again.

At home, the distance between herself and Nirav expanded, as if every breath that should have been used for talking went to filling a balloon that was slowly pushing them apart, and on the verge of bursting with things unsaid. The closer she drew to her grief, the further apart they drifted. He started working late almost every night. When they were together, they spent most of their time either in separate rooms or watching television. It seemed like they had wordlessly decided if they wouldn't talk about what needed to be said, then there was no point in talking at all.

When alone, she studied the little book of verses Hawthorn had loaned her, letting its wisdom seep into her core, into that quiet place she had discovered inside, that dwelling of truth and self. Somehow, the words felt familiar, as if the small, still voice were narrating them, as if they already belonged to her, but she had misplaced them.

Words such as: *You grieve for those beyond grief. And you speak words of insight. But learned men do not grieve for the dead or the living.*

And: *Never have I not existed, nor you, nor these kings. And never in the future shall we cease to exist.*

And: *The self embodied in the body of every being is indestructible.*

Indestructible.

She found herself visiting with Hawthorn's inscription no less than the verses. The survivor wisdom he had learned himself, expressed in his own words, that she wished she could inscribe onto her insides, so she would always know them, too.

The mountain never changes, he wrote. *But my ability to scale its jagged sides does. Some days, I'm young. Some days, I'm an old man. Some days, my boots are thick like tires. On others, they're iron shackles made of everything that's gone wrong. Even so, I've learned to move forward, if only an infinitesimal amount, known only to me. The breath in my lungs is infused with the same hope of green things, persistent, and ever-seeking even the finest dusting of sunlight. Tenacious as a seed that splits asphalt with its shoots, I will find the light, and grow, another word for: live. This is my destiny. Not suffering.*

On Tuesdays and Fridays, she trudged through the snow to attend Hawthorn's yoga classes. Afterward, they fell into the habit of sitting on bolsters by the expansive bay window, sipping tea and talking. Every week, he revealed a little more of his story.

He had a double Major in Philosophy and Psychology from UBC. Sequoia had studied Fine Arts at Emily Carr. During undergrad, they shared an apartment above an Asian grocery store. During the summer, they earned their tuition by tree planting in the backcountry of northern BC.

He wrote his Honours thesis on the efficacy of art therapy in the treatment of depression and addictions, a project inspired by Sequoia. In truth, it was his way of coaxing her to paint again during a period of rehabilitation she had taken between her third and forth year. When he visited her on the weekends, she taught him about the colour wheel, composition, and the importance of negative space. Over the course of the eight weeks she was in treatment, he noticed her paintings start to shift from dark abstract swirls to saffron-coloured koi fish, symbols of good fortune and prosperity. When her treatment was finished, she enrolled in an out-patient program, moved back in with Hawthorn, and spent the rest of the year exploring new subjects, and taking qualifying courses.

He graduated summa cum laude. Some of his friends were taking a gap year to travel. He wanted to join them but he was worried about leaving Sequoia behind. He asked her to go with him. She wanted to stay and finish her studies.

"Fly little Hawk, fly," she told him.

Reluctant, he agreed to go without her, although only if her boyfriend—another outpatient—moved into his old room. At the airport, they hugged each, teary-eyed. Until then, other than the time she had spent in rehab, they had never been apart.

He "woofed" his way across parts of Europe—Italy, Greece, Spain—although France turned out to be his favourite. He got into yoga while working at an organic winery in the Burgundy region of France. Every morning, the childless couple he worked for practised and meditated for an hour before breakfast. In the beginning, he could barely sit still for ten minutes. Soon, though, he got hooked on the stillness, amazed that it was a state he could access all on his own. He thought of Sequoia. Although she wasn't into granola trends, he hoped it might help her manage her condition.

He returned in time to watch her cross the stage in her cap and gown. Her gaunt and worn appearance—as though there were only the barest of flesh between her skin and her bones—startled him. His parents let him know she had relapsed a week before her final project was due. The stress triggered her old patterns. She hadn't told him during their weekly phone calls because she didn't want to ruin his trip. Instantly, he knew it was his fault for leaving her behind.

They moved back to Ottawa and lived with their parents for a while. They got Sequoia on another treatment program waiting list. He started attending yoga classes and researched teacher training courses. She started experimenting with new media—stencils, airbrushes, brick walls. That summer, she painted the mural in their parents' yard. Its composition burst with meaning as bright as its colours. The kelp forest because of her love of BC. The koi fish because they symbolized good fortune and prosperity, her hopes for the future. Flowers because they were beautiful and carefree and made her smile. At last, she seemed to find her artistic voice, the media and subject matter that made her soul happy. Hawthorn seemed to find his calling, too, in teaching yoga.

For a time, life seemed to slowly spiral upward rather than down. But there were always breaks, times of stopping and shifting, descending and ascending like an Escherian staircase. He had been away again for her last descent, when she let go of the railing altogether. In that instance too, he knew it was his fault for leaving, even though he had gone to the workshop in Costa Rica for her, to learn therapeutic yoga that might have helped her. Part of him knew they weren't meant to be apart, that together they formed a balanced entity, like the symbol for yin and yang.

Now it is spring. The month of their thirtieth birthday, which coincides with the fragrant bloom of magnolia trees, flowers that, like Sequoia, blossom first and lose their petals too soon.

Hawthorn invited Kavita to his family home to help him with a task he didn't disclose beforehand.

Sequoia's mural is the main feature of the yard, filling a large rectangle along the back of the house, above the deck. When she first set eyes on it, Kavita couldn't pull away from the painting, taken by its colours and movement. It was so much more captivating than she had imagined. Although it clung to a brick wall, it rippled and looped, began and ended, in waves of giant koi that tangled with kelp, kelp that burst with blooms like those tossed at weddings, blooms that transformed into tail fins. While Kavita didn't know what Sequoia looked like yet, after seeing her work, she got a sense of her likeness. Kavita knew Hawthorn's sister was beautiful.

Now, as she kneels in the grass, by the edge of Hawthorn's minor excavation project, Kavita feels dampness seep into her jeans. The air is thick with the fresh scent of mud, that nostril-opening smell of spring. A shower hangs over them in a field of grey clouds that have been gathering raindrops like seeds. They threaten to shed their weight in a distant rumble.

Hawthorn digs into the ground with a trowel. The hole is one foot across and one foot deep. Peering inside, Kavita sees the pink ribbed flesh of a partially excavated earthworm and a few disoriented ants scurrying along the ragged sides of the hole. Shivering, she feels them crawl all over her skin.

"Are you sure this is the right spot?" she asks.

"Positive," he replies. With a grunt, he loosens another shovel full of earth and rocks. "I can't imagine we dug much deeper than this."

Just then, his trowel strikes something hard with a *thunk*.

"I think I've got it," he says, cautious.

He spears his trowel against the object again. Kavita hears the distinct metallic tap: *thunk, thunk*.

"Sounds like a tackle box to me," she smiles.

A bit more digging unearths the handle. Heaving, Hawthorn frees the time capsule from its grave of twenty years. He rests the mint green box on the grass and brushes off most of the dirt.

"Look at this old thing," he marvels. "It used to be Dad's. He stored lures in it."

"Aren't you going to open it?"

He knits his hands together on his lap. "I know this is why I dragged you here today. But now that we've found it, I'm a bit nervous, actually."

"We can always bury it again if you've changed your mind."

He presses his lips together and nods, debating.

"We made this time capsule when we were ten. We promised each other to wait until we turned thirty to open it. Now that day's come, but Sequoia isn't here. I'm not sure I want to look back without her."

"Ten years old, eh? The world looked so different back then, didn't it?"

"Do you remember what you wanted to be?"

"A veterinarian. But only to whales." She lets out a tiny embarrassed laugh. "I don't know why."

"What about Sunil?"

"When he was ten, he was obsessed with skateboarding. This one time, he broke his ankle after flying off a ramp at the end of our driveway. He loved basketball, too, though. I remember him saying he would either skateboard professionally or make it in the NBA. Get a scholarship and everything."

"Did he?"

"No, he outgrew skateboarding. But he did play basketball in high school. Then he got into computers and studied programming. Nothing ever turns out the way we think, I guess. How about you and Sequoia?"

"She always loved to draw. I think she wanted to be a teacher like our parents. I was always changing my mind. But I remember wanting to travel and see the world. I guess that hasn't changed."

Kavita shifts off her knees and sits cross-legged and listens to the call and response of chickadees. Somewhere behind them, she hears another faint and distant rumble in the sky, the low rattling of raindrops. As she stares at the tackle box, she wonders about its contents. Maybe a mixed tape? A She-Ra doll? A copy of MAD magazine?

"Enough of this stalling," he says as he wrenches open the rusted latch. Slowly, he lifts the lid, which screeches with old age.

Kavita keeps her eyes fixed on the clover patch. Somehow looking into the box feels voyeuristic, as though she is about to steel a glimpse of Sequoia's diary.

"Look at this old stuff." He pulls out a concert ticket. "About a month before we buried the capsule, Sequoia dragged me to see Corey Hart. I remember hating every minute of it. But it was our first concert."

Kavita blinks at the ticket stub. She remembers wanting to go to that same concert but being too young. "Sunglasses at Night" plays in her head.

Sensing it's all right to look, Kavita peers inside the capsule. She sees a Rubik's cube, a cassette tape, a red egg of Silly Putty, hockey cards, and the white edge of a Polaroid picture. The photograph reminds her of the one Hawthorn asked her to bring of Sunil, if she wanted to, which she has tucked away in the pocket of her jean jacket. As Hawthorn shifts the contents of the box around, she sees two blue envelopes, and winces. *Letters*, she thinks.

"I'm surprised everything's so well preserved," she says, watching his expression. She knows he must have seen the letters by now, too. "That box must've been airtight."

"No water damage," he mutters. He reaches for the envelopes. "We didn't write letters to ourselves. We wrote letters to each other."

She rests one hand on his knee and squeezes.

"I'm not sure I can do this."

"You don't have to."

He hands her one of the letters. "Can you?" His eyes are dark and soft and open. "Please?"

"Are you sure you don't want to be the one to read it? It seems like a private thing."

"You reading it is like me reading it."

She takes the letter and pauses for a breath. Then she unseals the envelope, little by little, cringing with every tiny tear. Her heart hurts to see Sequoia's childhood penmanship and the doodles tucked into the corners and along the margin; daisies and swirls and what Kavita presumes is a hawk beside Hawthorn's name. A bittersweet grin lifts the corners of her mouth.

"'Dear Hawk,'" she reads aloud, feeling odd for using the nickname she feels is reserved for Sequoia. "'Happy thirtieth birthday, little brother.'" Three exclamation marks punctuate the end of the sentence, but Kavita can't find any cheer to liven her tone. "'By now I bet we both have families and our kids are best friends, just like you and me. I'm a world famous artist and spend half the year in Paris living the life. I bet by now you've seen at least half the world. And you're a famous karate master. And an Olympian. We rock.'"

"Oh my God," he interrupts. "I was obsessed with *The Karate Kid* back then. I can't believe I forgot about that. Sorry, go on."

After a moment, she finds her place again. "'If we haven't been to California yet to see the redwoods, please take me there for my birthday present this year. If you do, I promise to take you to Disneyland. Love, your big sister, Sequoia.'" Beside her signature, a drawing of a tree. Lowering the letter, Kavita remains silent, as she gently chews the side of her tongue and waits for Hawthorn to speak.

"I forgot about the redwoods. They're her namesake."

"Did she ever get to see them?"

"We always meant to go. We were so close, too, when we lived out in BC for all those years. But we never found the right time."

She hands him the letter and envelope. "I'm sorry."

"It's not your fault." He slips the letter back into its envelope. "It's no one's fault. It just makes me sad."

She tucks her hands into the pocket of her jean jacket and touches Sunil's picture. "Do you think you'll ever go someday?"

"Maybe." He taps the edge of the envelope with one finger. "If you come with me."

She smiles at him, not taking him seriously.

"We could hike deep into the woods and scatter her ashes at the roots of a two-thousand-year-old redwood. I like the idea of her ashes filtering into the soil with the rain. Getting sucked up by the roots. Then travelling all the way to the canopy. I like the idea of her being able to see all the way to the ocean."

"That does sound beautiful."

"Then don't make me go alone."

As Kavita watches him behold the objects of his lost youth, she knows she is witnessing a rare moment of frailty in her friend. Normally, she is accustomed to him so sure of himself, so sage. In the end, they aren't so different. Watching as his chin dips toward his chest, she knows that they are the same, haunted and incomplete, without their other halves.

He reaches into the box and lifts out the Polaroid. The first sight of Sequoia and Hawthorn as children stalls Kavita's breath. They share the same dark hair and fair complexion, the same penetrating brown eyes and tempting smile. Sequoia's hair is styled in a side ponytail. She is dressed an oversized fuchsia Roots sweatshirt and tapered acid-wash jeans. Hawthorn is wearing an identical outfit, although his sweatshirt is teal and his jeans a lighter wash. His hair is cut short. It feels strange to see him without his trademark half-up ponytail. She notices the comma-like dimple denting his left cheek. Something about seeing the two of them standing side by side, smiling, completely unaware of the future that would tear them apart, weakens her

"Tell me about this picture," she asks.

"Well," he says, gazing, "we'd just finished digging the hole. Instead of including a newspaper like most people do, we wanted to include a picture of us. Mom took it. Dad was right next to her, joking around, trying to get us to crack up. God, look how young we are."

"She's beautiful," Kavita manages to say despite the tears gathering in her throat. "You're beautiful together."

Hawthorn can't take his eyes off of his sister's childhood image. "You know, it's impossible to encompass everything she was. Even if I talked about her for a year straight, it still wouldn't be enough. I wanted you to be here today because I wanted you to get to know her the way I knew her. But it's impossible. You can't get to know someone from a few random objects in an old tackle box."

Kavita pulls the picture of Sunil out of her pocket. "Or from a photograph."

His eyes widen with awe. "You brought it."

He holds the picture carefully. In it, Sunil is standing beside her in their dining room with his arm around her shoulder. He is at least a head taller than her. He is wearing a grey sweatshirt and a black Nike cap. Her hair is in two braids, and she is dressed in a canary yellow Bart Simpson t-shirt. On the table is a round ice-cream cake decorated with pink sugar flowers.

"Is that a hospital bracelet on your wrist?" he asks.

She nods. "I spent a few days in the hospital after getting

my tonsils out. I must've been about seven or eight, I think, so he was about twelve or thirteen. When he visited me at the hospital, he brought a bunch of games: Operation, Connect Four, a deck of cards. Before I knew it, visiting hours were over. I started to panic. I didn't want to be left behind in a strange place. So, he asked our parents if he could spend the night. The nurse said it was fine. He could sleep in the bed beside mine as long as they didn't need it for another patient. You know how hospitals are never quite dark or quiet enough at night? Well, I kept falling back in and out of sleep. But every time I got startled awake, I would look over at Sunil, and I felt safe again. Like I was home."

Although he doesn't say so, Kavita knows Hawthorn understands exactly what she means by home.

"When I found out he was struggling, I thought to myself, finally Kavita, here's your chance to save him for a change. I honestly thought I could." Anchor pulls. "The truth is, Sunil was close to turning things around, but he couldn't see it. He had his appointments. He'd taken the first steps towards recovery. If he'd held on a little longer, he would've been able to see it for himself, one day. That's one of the hardest things to accept. We almost made it." The centre of her palm pulses like a heartbeat, and she recalls all the pain that gathered in her tortured flesh. She wants to squeeze her nails into her scar, but breathes shallowly instead, waiting for the feeling to pass, as she knows it will, given time.

Hawthorn hands her back the photo. Frowning, he gazes more deeply at the picture of Sequoia, as though searching for details that he had missed.

"The guilt that gets me is that I'm the healthy twin, and I don't know why. We shared almost everything. But I couldn't share the loneliness of her illness. It kills me that she went through it alone."

"When does it go away?" she asks.

He looks at her sideways. "What?"

Anchor pulls, pulls, pulls. "The guilt."

He tosses the Polaroid into the box. "I'll let you know."

They sit for a while, nestled in quiet, as though even the birds dare not sing. Kavita slides the photograph back into her pocket.

"Thanks for being here," he says. "I think I'll open the other letter later." He slips the letters back into the tackle box and shuts the lid. "Are you coming inside for cake? My parents can't wait to meet the friend from group I keep talking about."

"I'm a sucker for cake," she grins. "But look at my jeans. I'm all dirty."

"They won't care. To be honest, I think they miss having a girl around, on days like today especially."

"Are you sure I won't be intruding?"

"Yogis never lie." He gives her a shallow bow.

"We talked about that."

"I didn't say *namaste*."

She smiles and pulls at the clover. "It would be nice to celebrate a birthday. I didn't do anything for mine this year." She pushes out a sad laugh. "Didn't even get a card from my parents."

"Still lost at sea, are they?"

She nods. "I miss them."

"Didn't your hub do anything for you?"

"He asked if I wanted to do something but I wasn't up for it. I hate the idea of getting older without Sunil. I keep aging but he'll always be thirty. In a few years, I'll be as old as he was when he died. Then I'll be older than him. Older than my older brother. It doesn't make sense."

"In that case, I'll make sure we stick a candle in your slice."

"I wouldn't want to steal your moment." She knows he is just being kind, as always.

"Honestly, it would feel good to share it with someone again."

Kavita searches his face for pity. She knows by his dark, soft eyes that he's being more than kind, he is telling the truth. "Well, when you put it like that."

A broad smile spreads across his face, squeezing his dimple, the sight of which always causes a smile to spread across Kavita's face, too. He rises to his feet and leans over for the tackle box. With his free hand, he reaches out to her and helps her to her feet. Neither of them lets go as they walk toward the house, and the daring beauty of Sequoia's mural, with water on their lips, as a warm spring shower comes swinging in.

35

THE HIGH-PITCHED *PING* of the singing bowl signals the end of class. The unexpected ring startles Kavita as she sits in Lotus Pose in her usual corner at the back of the class, causing her to muscles to jolt as if wakened from a shallow sleep. For a blissful while, she dipped out of time.

Hawthorn strikes the brass bowl twice more. Each time, the vibration peaks, then peters into silence. He closes their practice with an impenetrable Sanskrit chant that is nonetheless beautiful in his deep and melodic singsong voice. The last thing she does before letting light into her eyes is send a prayer of love and light to Sunil, as she does at the end of every class. It is a comfort to think that goodness may find him, wherever he is now.

At last, she opens her eyes. The studio is slowly emptying as students scurry back and forth from their mats to the props cupboard, from the changing room to the front door. All the activity reminds her of edgy squirrels in autumn, bounding and scampering, trying to outrun time. Unlike the other students, she isn't willing to give up that pleasing hum, that quiet place inside, where everything makes sense, even for her. She's in no rush to leap back into her complicated story.

She flutters her knees. Her inner thighs ache from too many hip openers. Still, she notices her body is growing supple. Soon she will be able to rest her forehead on the cup of her arches in Cobbler's Pose. Well, maybe not soon, but soon enough. Her physical transformation, however, isn't the most astonishing progress she has observed about herself lately.

During those timeless moments on her mat, somehow her life is no longer a jail, nor does she feel trapped by circumstance. While she rests on her mat in compassionate contemplation, she no longer tries to outrun her grief. Instead, she sits with it, like company, her sad friend dressed in blue. Something she was too frightened to even consider a couple of months ago, convinced that her pain was greater than she was, that if she let it out, it would sink her, the way Sunil's pain had submerged him.

Now, when alone, she discovers space. Space between herself and her circumstances. Space between herself and her grief. Space to be safe.

When she finds space, she is no longer part of a turbulent narrative. Rather, she is a step beside it, as though watching a blizzard from behind a pane of glass. Within the storm, she sees all the things that have troubled her. Yet, from her vantage point, a step away, she understands that none of these tumultuous states are who she is. Just as Sunil was not his illness, she is not her pain. None of the thoughts or feelings or situations she had found herself in since Sunil's passing are who or what she is.

Who and what she is, is indestructible.

She stands and gazes across the room at Hawthorn, who is arranging cushions and making tea. The kettle whistles as though summoning her.

"Another great class." She grins sleepily as she strolls toward the mass of colourful cushions that are piled in their usual spot by the bay window.

He hands her a steaming cup. "One ginger lemon tea for my favourite student."

"I thought you were supposed to be impartial," she teases. She sets the mug on the floor to cool.

"That's true." He blows over his tea. "But I guess it doesn't matter anymore." He places his cup on the floor and then lowers onto the cushions.

"What do you mean?"

He bobs his tea bag a few times. "I have something to tell you."

Her light-headedness clears as she detects a change in his tone. "What is it?"

"Ever since our birthday last month, I haven't been able to stop thinking about Sequoia's letter. So, I'm going down to California to scatter her ashes. My parents are coming, too. I'm giving up my classes."

"That's wonderful. But why give up your classes? Can't you find a sub?"

He chews his bottom lip. "The thing is," he says. "From California, I'm heading down to Costa Rica. An old teacher of mine has offered me a position teaching classes and work-shops to tourists at an eco-lodge. The place is right on the beach along the Caribbean coast. I've seen pictures online. It looks pretty incredible."

"Oh," she says, a bit stunned. "That sounds like an amazing opportunity." She is embarrassed by how hollow her words of congratulation sound now that she has heard them, but the news of him leaving came as such a surprise, she couldn't find any other words to reach for. "Those don't come around every day. Of course, you have to go." Something in her chest starts unspooling. "I'm just going to miss you, that's all. I've gotten used to you torturing me in class. And of course, group isn't going to be the same without you."

"I'm going to miss it, too."

Silence settles between them for a few tense moments. She tries to think of encouraging things to say, excited things, like a friend should, but instead snags her tongue on disappointments.

"That's why…" he says at last. "I want you to come with me."

"Well, of course, I'll come to California with you, if you don't think I'd be intruding. You've helped me so much this year, I'd love to be able to support you for a change."

He blinks at her. "Thank you. I appreciate it. And I'm happy to hear that you want to come to California with us. I could definitely use the support. But that's not exactly what I mean."

She looks at him, puzzled.

"I want you to come to California with us to scatter Sequoia's ashes, that's true. But when my folks go back home, I want you to stay with me, so we can go to Costa Rica together."

Seconds pass and her mind is blank. Whatever she might have been thinking or feeling before his invitation drops to the floor.

"Hawthorn," she says. "This is out of the blue."

"Can you really say that to me?"

"What do you mean?"

"Don't make it sound like it's all in my head."

"I have a husband."

"I know all about him. How he doesn't talk to you or support you or stand up for you."

"I told you those things in confidence. You aren't supposed to use them against me. That's the opposite of trust."

"I'm not using them against you. I'm just trying to open your eyes. There's so much more to life than what you've settled for."

"I haven't settled for anything."

"You've rebuilt yourself from the ground up. I've seen it with my own eyes. You've done such hard work and changed so much, it inspires me. But you're still clinging to things that you've obviously outgrown."

"My life is what it is."

"But what do you want?"

"Want?"

"Out of your life?"

"I want everything to be different. I want Sunil to be alive. I want to be able to go back in time and do everything over. But that isn't possible. All I can do is make the best of things as they are."

"You're right, everything's changed since your brother died, right down to the people you thought you knew, and yourself. There's no way back to the way things were before. So, since that's the case, where do you want to go from here? Because this holding pattern you're in can't last forever."

Time passes as she breathes unevenly. "I don't know," she confesses at last.

"Let me put it this way. Do you want to hide forever? Keep just getting by from day-to-day? Or do you want to reinvent yourself with me?"

"Nothing's ever that simple."

He lifts her chin with his warm fingers and reaches deeply into her eyes. "I'm not saying it's going to be easy. What I'm offering you is a fresh start. With someone who understands you. Someone who knows what you've been through. I'll take the burdens your heart can't take, Kavita. I'll stand by your side. Isn't that what you've been searching for? I have, although I didn't realize it until I met you."

Part of her knows he is right. That their time together has been as much about connection as healing. With him she has found a new cave to dwell in, full of light, and warm. In him, she found someone like her.

A *fresh start*, she repeats silently to herself. Is such a thing even possible in the wake of tragedy? Can anyone touched by trauma ever really start again?

"Was this part of your plan all along? Prey on the sad girl?"

"You know me better than that."

"Do I?"

"Of course," he says, his voice tender. "You know me better than anyone. Even better than Sequoia in some ways. After all, she missed all of this. But you haven't. You've been here with me."

Her cheeks flush with embarrassment. "I'm sorry. I didn't mean it. But you caught me off guard."

"Then I'm sorry, too."

She rubs her forehead. "When do you leave?"

"We leave for California in two weeks. I hope you'll still come with us. So do my parents. They really like you. They told me so. They really like you, Kavita. And I adore you. Broken pieces and all. You'll never have to hide those parts from me. I'd never want you to."

She looks into his eyes. They are dark and soft and open. Wells of empathy.

36

THE NEXT DAY, she drives up to Gatineau Park along the narrow road that swerves through the densely wooded hills all the way to the top of the escarpment. A few cars are parked at Champlain Lookout. A family of four stands by the stone half-wall, peering over the flat land below as they snap photos. A pair of cyclists dressed in bright spandex like riders in the Tour de France suck on blue energy drinks. Off to one side, a couple of teenagers lean against the wall, kissing.

She climbs out of the car and ambles to the wall with her hands stuffed inside her jean jacket pockets. She touches the smooth thread of Sunil's *rakhi*, winces for a second, and then rubs it between her thumb and forefinger as though it is a *japamala*.

When she reaches the wall, she stares at nothing for a few moments. This is the place Sunil came to think, to get away, to gaze at the hawks riding the thermals—unencumbered and free—and dream about joining them. Desperate for his council, she was drawn here, the way the weary are drawn to temple, to feel the spotlight of heaven kiss the crown of their heads and surrender the secrets of their hearts. She feels his presence in so few places anymore, but she feels him deeply here, somewhere in the poetry blue of the sky.

She hoists herself onto the wall, and swivels to let her feet dangle off the side. To the left, the gentle slope of the hillside is bright with the lushness of late spring. In the distance, at the far edge of the patchwork farmland, the river meanders from north to south, and then beyond her view.

A fresh wind rushes into her unbuttoned jacket. She folds the front panels over her waist and lifts her gaze to the lightly clouded sky. A few hawks dip and climb and loop with the air currents tracing swirls in the blue. Her eyes follow their kite-like flight.

What should I do? she asks Sunil. *Please, Bear. Tell me what to do.*

She used to be so sure of everything. So certain of the path she had chosen. But ever since his passing, it is as if the lines of her life's map have been burned away by grief. Which way is she supposed to go now?

Hawthorn's proposal kept her up last night, as haunting as restless spirits, echoing over in her mind: *A fresh start with someone who understands you. Isn't that what you've been searching for?*

She shivers, exposed. Is he right? Has she been looking for a way out of her misery all along? Did the hunger of her lonely heart lead her to Hawthorn? Is he the missing piece that is meant to fill the hollowness she carries inside like trouble? This person with whom she shares a language of loss, a connection through pain few understood, whose strange melody of Tibetan singing bowls and yogic chanting, organic farming and back-bends, drifted into her darkness just as she was leaning into the silence in search of a new rhythm to follow? Can she live within the movements of this new song? Will its resonance be enough to fill the icy sphere of loneliness she carries inside?

With an unfocused gaze, she keeps a passive watch of the hawks, distracted by the war within her. Conflicting sides tug in opposing directions—duty versus desire; staying versus fleeing; rebuilding versus starting over.

Is it even possible? To start over? Or will she simply carry her troubles with her like items in a suitcase? After suppressing them all day under the noise of a new life, will she be able to stop them from howling in the night?

Part of her fears change. This part says that it is best to stay with what she knows and continue rebuilding her life from the debris. She's been doing it and it's working. She's finding a better way.

The other part of her craves freedom, like the hawks soaring above. This part says it isn't wrong to want a fresh start. People do it every day. People start over. Sometimes things are broken—broken beyond repair. Hawthorn's family likes her. He adores her. He accepts her, broken pieces and all. Without him, this part reminds her, she might not have found a better way.

As the two sides jerk and yank, Kavita feels close to splitting. She can't deny the allure of Hawthorn's proposal, its temptation, its promise. The reckless selfishness of a fresh start. She isn't sure she has ever made a decision like it before in her life. She is accustomed to consulting her loved ones, weighing her wants against the good of the family, adjusting her wants accordingly. She has been raised to be a good daughter, and that is what good daughters do. They compromise, for the good of everyone, even if doing so makes them feel as if they are being torn from the truest part of themselves. They stay.

And she has. Stayed. But where has everyone else gone? Despite her devotion, her love, she has found herself alone.

And she is tired of it. It is exhausting, this cold.

At its heart, that is what Hawthorn's offer is. A hand to hold. A way out of winter.

He offers, so easily. The opportunity to hew herself from her past, like a tree branch, and escape downriver with the fast-flowing current. Is that so bad? Everywhere she looks, she sees failure, loss, pain. Is it so bad to want to get away from that? To start over as the person she is today? Whoever that is.

Of course, leaving isn't easy, not that Hawthorn will ever truly understand, winged-like creature that he is. Sequoia was right about that. There is Nirav to consider. The man she fell in love with. The man she married, who once seemed as essential to her as sunbeams and air. The man who abandoned her to loneliness and shame. The man she doubts she can ever forgive.

The wind blows harder. Kavita hugs her jacket around her waist a little tighter.

In the end, she always confronts the same obstacle. Filial duty, as weighty as tradition, as present as her cells, not easily dismissed, especially not by something as anaemic as her own wants.

The truth remains that her life is her family.

Their joy is her joy.

Their pain is her pain.

Their survival is her survival.

Even if her family hasn't always treated her with such care, to her, they are inseparable, like the tangled roots of a banyan. What she feels for them is more than duty—it's love. The most tangled connection of them all.

Hawthorn assumes she can deny the strength of this bond, and be like him, spin through the air as free and daring as the papery, winged seeds of a maple.

If she joins him, he has promised her good earth in which to plant themselves, a new place to grow green things that will creep over and cover the memory of all that went wrong, maybe even growing so thick one day, she might forget what was ever underneath.

Closing her eyes, she stares at the blood-orange imprints on the insides of her eyelids. The low chatter of the other visitors feels far away. She tries to remember the last time she visited the park with Sunil, the autumn before he disappeared.

They hiked around Pink Lake, with its surprising blue-green waters, straying from the trail to discover a small beaver pond. Sitting on a fallen tree, hushed with awe, they watched as a beaver swam noiselessly through the water, ever-watchful of their presence. Afterwards, they drove up to the Lookout. She might have sat in the same spot she is sitting now. Without speaking, they enjoyed the flight of the hawks.

Please, Sunil, she begs him. *Send me a sign.*

Slowly, she opens her eyes. Wincing against the midday light, she sees two hawks gliding side by side, drawing interconnected figure eights in the sky, symbols of infinity braided together on the wind.

Her body starts to tremble. The rims of her eyes shiver. As she watches the skyward dance, Kavita feels her brother's absence that is so present, the missing part of herself that is him. She can't say it is simply a hole in the heart, or the stomach, or any place in particular. Rather, the loss of him is an ever-absence, a void that can't be filled, because it isn't meant to be.

The wind gusts against her with even more force, as though the hand of life is trying to upset her precarious balance on the wall. Kavita curls in on herself, holding on fiercely, so she won't blow away.

37

PERCHED ON THE EDGE of the couch, Kavita waits for Nirav to arrive from work. A small suitcase of her belongings sits by the door, along with the cat carrier. Not long ago, she lured Coal inside with a toss of his favourite treats, and the irresistibility of his ratty blue towel, upon which he is now curled. She made arrangements for him to stay at the vet's office while she is away at Muir Woods, after which they will both have to find somewhere else to live. All she knows for sure is that wherever she ends up, Coal will be with her. Throughout the upheaval of the past year, he has been her comfort, her company, even her saviour when she thinks of that night. Not to mention, he is the only thing she has left that still feels like home.

She glances at her watch. Nirav is late. After they talk, she will call a taxi from the corner store down the street.

She expected to feel more jittery. Yet somehow, nothing shakes or quivers inside her, as if she has reached a point beyond fear and upset. Still, something about the calm is unsettling. Maybe she is experiencing the stillness that comes from resolve. From finally accepting that when it comes to her marriage, she can't control everything, she can't hide forever from the way things are. Nirav is free to act as he chooses, and she needs to know what he will do when finally confronted.

After all, what he does is who he is, and how he feels about her. Perhaps that is the reality she is ready to confront, at last.

The metal sound of the key in the lock draws her from her thoughts. Swiftly, she rises, presses her shoulders back, and braces herself with a short breath. The door shuts behind him. He doesn't call out hello like he used to, in his overly-cheerful way. They are long past that kind of effort.

Instead, his first spoken words are, "What's this?" He would've seen the carrier and suitcase by now. He emerges from the hallway, pointing his thumb at the front door. "Going somewhere?"

"Nirav, please sit down. We need to talk."

With his mouth slightly open, he drops his leather messenger bag on the floor in a noisy display and takes a seat at the island.

She lowers back onto the sofa and folds her hands over her lap.

"Well?" he asks.

"I'm going on a trip."

"Oh really? Nice of you to tell me. Where abouts, might I ask?"

"California. I'm helping a friend from group scatter his sister's ashes. I didn't tell you because it's taken me a while to decide whether or not I was going. Besides, we haven't exactly been on speaking terms." He leaves for work early and stays late and eats and sleeps in the guest room. Part of her thought it was possible he might not register her absence for days.

"He?"

"Hawthorn's parents are going too."

"What does this have to do with you?"

"He's helped me a lot this year. Now it's my turn to help him." That is what relationships are supposed to be about: give and take. Although, Kavita realizes now that she and Nirav have always struggled to find the right balance."

"How long will you be away?"

"We'll be in San Francisco for a week."

"All right, so you'll be back in a week, then."

"Not exactly."

"You said a week?"

"What I mean is, I don't know when I'll be coming back here."

What she sees on his face isn't shock, exactly. It is more like the arrival of something inevitable, something he has had his eye on for weeks, and is finally as large as a ship in front of him. "I know we've been having problems. But I didn't think things were this bad."

"Well, they are." She walls her courage around her. There is no time to waste. She needs to ask him what she has been too afraid to ask for too long. "Nirav," she says. "Why don't you ever talk about Sunil?"

His eyes flare for a moment, then close halfway. "I don't know what you mean. I talk about him plenty."

"I wish that were true. But it isn't. Didn't you love him? Don't you miss him?"

"Of course I did. I do."

"Don't say of course like it's obvious. It hasn't been obvious to me. You never so much as mention his name."

A tight-lipped pause. "I suppose I don't have anything good to say."

"What do you mean?"

Three long beats. "I'm angry."

"Angry?"

"Yes."

"With me? Have I done something?"

"It's not you," he says. "It's him. I can't speak his name because I'm too angry at him all the time."

"I don't understand."

"Isn't it obvious? It's all his fault. This mess we're in. The fact that you're depressed and can't work. That we've drifted apart. That your parents have split up. That you're fighting with my family. It's all his fault."

For several shallow breaths, she only glares at him.

"That isn't fair," she says, attempting to steady her voice. "You can't blame him for being ill. And you can't use him as a scapegoat, either. He didn't force your mouth shut all these months. He didn't make your family shun him. He didn't make you do nothing about it. He didn't make you say that you *hated* being a part of my family when we needed you the most. All of that, you did on your own."

"He's your golden boy," he snorts. "I can't do anything right compared to him."

"That isn't true and you know it."

"I don't know what you want from me."

"I want to talk to you about what's happened. I want to go through this with you. That's all I've ever wanted."

"No, you don't. You want to pummel me."

"I don't, really. I don't even have the energy anymore." She pauses. "My brother died, Nirav, and I needed you. I needed to talk to you about it. I needed your support. But instead you treated Sunil like he didn't exist. And when things went wrong with your family, you acted like that didn't happen either. It breaks my heart that you expected me to pretend, too."

"Here we go. See? All my fault."

"No, it's my fault. People treat me like shit because I let them. I should've spoken up ages ago, but I didn't. I've had this incredible secret pressing against me for months. I've been such a stranger to myself—such a mess—that I thought I'd done something to deserve it. I thought, keep your mouth shut, Kavita. You brought this on yourself, so deal with it. No one wants a mess, so shut up and take it. But it's gnawed away at me. At us. And I can't live like this anymore."

"I thought that was behind us."

"And I've been waiting for it to come to the surface."

They sit in silence, briefly.

"Listen," he says. "What happened wasn't right, all right?"

"No, it's not all right. You still don't understand how shaming it was for me, back then and even now. Can you imagine what that must've been like for me? Have you?"

He doesn't answer.

"Well, it added to my guilt. Because even though I didn't

do anything wrong, I still felt guilty for not standing up for my brother." She glances at her palm, the scar, that he has never asked about or noticed, or maybe has noticed but never asked about. "I was devastated. To be honest, on top of everything else I've been struggling with, it almost pushed me over the edge."

She pauses expecting some sort of reaction from him, but he only keeps blinking at the floor, so she goes on.

"If our places had been switched, you know I would've stood up for you. Right then and there. Like always."

Isn't it typical for men to wax lyrically about fighting for a woman's honour in songs and poems, only to fall short when the time comes to transmute words into actions. Isn't it often the case that women are the actual protectors, while receiving no credit for being strong and steadfast, loyal and devoted, to everyone but themselves.

"Look, I don't know why I reacted the way I did. I don't why I didn't say something back then."

She stares at him, unblinking. "You did say something, Nirav. You told me I was selfish. Selfish for wanting my brother's memory to be treated with dignity. All I have left is his memory."

"It's just a big misunderstanding. No one's shunning Sunil. My family just didn't want to embarrass you."

"Embarrass me? They did worse than embarrass me, Nirav."

"They didn't want you to have to face the community and feel, you know, ashamed or anything."

"Ashamed of what?"

"Sunil...taking his own life."

"I'm not ashamed of that." But something else is clear to her now. "I've never been ashamed of Sunil. But your family assumes that I am, because to them there's something to be ashamed about. Is that right?"

"Not my immediate family, no. But you know what community gossip can be like. My family figured they see us so infrequently, it would be easier on them to—"

"Not be associated with something so shameful? To save face?"

"It sounds so harsh when you put it like that."

"What else could it be? How long have you known about this?"

"It came up a while back."

"And you didn't think to tell me? After our last blowout, you didn't think I might want to know?"

"Well, you haven't brought it up since then. I thought you were over it."

"I'll never get over it, Nirav. I will never forget this. Do you understand that?"

He rolls his lips and they disappear into his mouth.

"I haven't brought it up until now because after getting shutdown so many times, it's taken me this long to muster up the courage. Besides, I shouldn't have to chase down explanations, let alone apologies."

"Listen, I know I cocked up. I see that now. I know I'm not perfect. But I want to be a good husband to you, Kavita, really I do. And I think I've done pretty well, considering."

"You do?"

"I've been here for you. Through thick and thin. I've been here the whole time."

"Like all those times I asked you to go to group with me. I even begged you."

"I supported you going."

"By not going."

"I told you, I don't need therapy."

"Maybe not," she says. "But I needed you. I needed you to hear all the things I couldn't articulate about what I was going through. I needed you to learn as I was learning. I needed to feel like I wasn't going through all the pain and the grief alone, with only a bunch of strangers to relate to. I needed you to be my husband."

"I am your husband."

"Sunil's death is the worst thing that's ever happened to me. It's probably the worst thing that will ever happen to me. I've never needed you more. And you've never been harder to find."

"I didn't leave you."

She thinks about this, and realizes, there is more than one way to leave someone.

"So, group is where you met that bloke, then?"

"His name is Hawthorn. And yes."

"Is this your way of punishing me? By going off on holiday with him?"

She has no sighs left to exhale. "Scattering the ashes of a beloved sister who died by suicide isn't a holiday, Nirav."

Coal mews in his cage.

"Kavita, I know my family hurt you—"

"Not just them, Nirav. You hurt me too. You hurt me by the things you did, and mostly by the things you didn't."

"Forgive me, my darling, and we'll start again. We'll put all this behind us and get back to normal."

"That isn't an answer," she tells him. "That's just more silence. More pretending."

The longer their conversation goes on, the clearer it is to Kavita that she isn't getting through to him. But she will try, one more time. "My pain is supposed to be your pain, Nirav. But you shrug it off like it's nothing. That's how I know you don't really know how I feel, and you don't care to. You just want the awkwardness to be over. Well, so do I. But I also want a partner that understands me. That loves me, broken pieces and all. Someone I don't have to hide my pain from because he would never want me to."

Kavita pauses, shaken, realizing the words that came from her mouth, first came from Hawthorn's.

Nirav looks at her as if she is deranged.

She rises to her feet and gazes at him with sad eyes. "If I forgive you now, Nirav, nothing will ever change between us. And if we have a future together, I need for things to change."

"Don't leave like this."

"The truth is," she says. "You left me first."

He steels his eyes. "No, Kavita. Sunil was the one who left you."

His words rake through what little remorse she has left for him. She can't bear to look at his face. She stares at the floor, dispassionate, and says, "You're wrong, Nirav. Sunil left me with you. And you left me all alone."

She walks past him, grabs her things, and leaves.

38

KAVITA STANDS SHOULDER to shoulder with Hawthorn behind a chest-high stone wall. They are surrounded by throngs of tourists, drawn to the rust-coloured spectacle of the Golden Gate Bridge. They decided to make a stop on their way back from Muir Woods after scattering Sequoia's ashes.

The wind gusts fiercely. Kavita wishes she had worn something warmer than her jean jacket. Still, she can't deny the beauty of the place. The waters of San Francisco Bay seem to reflect the bright blue of the sky above.

"It's a lovely spot," she tells Hawthorn. "I'm glad we decided to take in the view."

He squints at the iconic bridge. "It's impressive. But now that we're here, I can't help but think about all the jumpers. Ironic, isn't it? Considering what we just did for Sequoia."

"I've been thinking the same thing."

"Weird, isn't it? The world marches on, back and forth across this bridge, ignorant of the despair right under their feet. See where my parents are standing?" He signals with his chin. Their matching orange windbreakers make them easy to spot in the crowd, as they take in the sights, hand in hand.

"I see them," she says.

"Someone might've jumped from that very spot. Someone's daughter. Someone's sister." He wriggles his shoulders. "I just got chills."

A shiver runs up her neck. "Me too." She rolls her shoulders back against the ghostly sensation. "Do you think your parents are all right? Today couldn't have been easy for them."

"I think they're okay. Or at least they will be. I think today brought us some closure. We've been reluctant to scatter Sequoia's ashes for so long. But back in the woods, I can't explain why, somehow it just felt right." They had hiked along one of the less popular trails for about an hour and stopped at a thick stand of redwoods that blocked the view to the ocean. "I wasn't necessarily expecting that. It's hard to let go of someone when you have so little of them left to hold on to. But she wanted to see the redwoods. And now she's a part of them. She belongs there, in that beautiful place. We found her the perfect spot."

"She'll be able to see all the way to the ocean, just like you wanted her to."

He gazes at the bay with a faraway look in his eyes.

"Are you okay?" she asks, nudging him with her shoulder.

"I will be," he replies. "Having you here makes things easier. Thanks again for coming."

"Well, it's like I told you before. I'm happy to be able to help you for a change. You've done so much for me this year. Sometimes I feel like I'll never be able to pay you back."

"I didn't do anything, other than listen to you, and maybe give you the odd book to read."

"Which meant everything to me."

"Well, it's like I've been trying to tell you. Everything is what you deserve."

His gaze shifts from the blue waters of the bay and locks onto her face. Despite all the active air around her, she can't seem to pull in just one breath.

"Kavita?" he asks. "You look like you're about to hurl. Do I need to get out of the way?"

She pauses. Looks at him. Can't tell if he's joking or not. All of a sudden, her nerves spurt into laughter. "Only you could diffuse a tense moment like that." Smiling, she shakes her head. Only him.

"Just tell me," he says, straight-faced. "I can take it."

She can almost hear her heart thudding in her ears. Where to begin? "I want you to know how much you mean to me," she says, slowly. "I never expected to make another best friend after Sunil passed away, but that's what you've become to me. I don't want to lose you."

"Then you won't."

"I'm flattered that you asked me to join you in Costa Rica. And if I'm honest, part of me wants to go with you and see what happens. There's a part of me that wants to run and not stop, ever. But that isn't the right reason, is it?"

He considers. "If you come with me, I want it to be because there's nowhere else is the world you'd rather be. Not because you're hiding."

"The truth is," she continues. "I'm still in transition. When Sunil died, part of me died with him. I feel like I'm just getting to know myself again. Some parts of me are the same. But some parts of me are totally different. It's all so new. Does that make sense?"

"I get it," he nods. "It was the same for me. Two years later and I'm still working out who I am without my twin to bounce off of. Every time someone dies, we lose a bit of our identity."

"And I'm still figuring out who I am without Sunil. I'm still figuring out what I want."

She pauses. "For a long time after Sunil died, I thought I should be dead too. He was dead, and it was my fault, so I should be dead too. I thought that's what I deserved. But then I met you, and you helped me realize I have a life that's all my own. And it's a life worth living, even if it feels like I'm starting over sometimes. I finally believe it. That I deserve to live. And it's okay. I'm not doing anything wrong."

"Can't living your new life include me?"

"It always will," she tells him, earnestly, holding his gaze.

His eyes are dark and soft and open. Those wells of empathy that made all the difference to her. "When every other person failed me, you were there, letting me know that I wasn't alone. I'll never forget that. I know I've never told you, Hawk, but you saved my life. And I'll never be able to thank you enough."

He smiles at her with gentleness. "No, Kavita," he says. "You saved yourself. You're doing it right now. Knowing you're okay is all the thanks I'll ever need."

The fierceness of the wind pushes them together. She wraps her arms around him and buries her face in the cool bend of his neck. He holds her close, and squeezes, and squeezes. As the wind rages through her hair, he whispers into it, "You're my best friend, too."

39

NO ONE SPEAKS on the way to the marina, not even to request the radio for distraction. As Kavita drives, her father sits behind her, staring out the window passively. Beside her sits her mother, clutching the brass urn of Sunil's ashes as though it is treasure that she isn't quite ready to part with yet. When she first asked them, Kavita wasn't sure if her parents would agree to come home for the one year anniversary of Sunil's passing. She wasn't even sure if having them in the same room was a good idea. But now that they are here, she is grateful for their temporary armistice, and especially, for not having to face the day alone. As she pulls into the parking lot, her insides start to harden, as if steeling themselves against whatever might be coming next. She parks, shuts off the ignition, and looks around for Nirav's new car, which is lime green, apparently. A few moments later, she finds a car matching that description to her left.

"I think Nirav's here," she says in a neutral voice. Neither of her parents responds. She presumes they are still sore about the London incident. Shortly after coming back from San Francisco, she finally told them the truth. They deserved to know what had happened, even if that knowledge hurt them, which of course it did, particularly the question of why their son was treated with less respect than they have shown Nirav over the years, a question for which Kavita had no answer, a question that had no answer good enough, regardless.

"Well," Kavita says. "We should go meet him."

Her mother holds the urn tighter. "Maybe this is a bad idea."

Kavita places a hand on her knee. "I know it's going to be hard. But in the end, I think it'll be good for us. Remember my friend, Hawk? Well, he said that scattering his sister's ashes brought them some closure. I think we could use that."

Neither of her parents agrees or disagrees. She opens her car door with a creak. "Come on," she tells them, gently. "We'll get through this together."

They approach the lighthouse in a silent procession. In the distance, she sees Nirav standing by the lighthouse. He is dressed in a pair of tan linen pants and a loose-fitting navy shirt with the sleeves rolled up to his elbows. With his hands in his pockets, he stares across the river. No sailboats to count today. Not enough of a breeze.

Although they have started talking on the phone again, it feels strange to see him, which she hasn't since she returned from California eight weeks ago. When she moved out, she picked up her things while he was at work, but thanks to their lenient concierge, didn't have far to carry them, as she was permitted to stay in one of the guest rooms in their building, the same room her father had stayed in, while she figured out her next step. For now, she is renting a one-bedroom apartment in a building close to the river. What she likes most about her new place are its north-facing windows and eleventh-floor balcony. When she's out there, it is a comfort to gaze at the gentle slope of the Eardley Escarpment, sleeping Vishnu covered in mosses. Although she can't see them, she knows the hawks are there too, soaring above the landscape and any earthy pain, like Sunil's spirit.

"Nirav," she calls out. Startled, he looks over his shoulder, smiles guardedly, and approaches them. Kavita can sense the hesitation weighing down his steps. "Mum," he nods in greeting. "Dad."

After a few mute seconds, her mother reaches out a cheek

for him to peck. His worried expression breaks into relief. He kisses her, enthusiastically, on both cheeks, then does the same to Kavita's father, as if frightened of losing the moment and momentum alike. But when he reaches Kavita, Nirav falters.

"How are you?" he asks.

"Okay."

"It's lovely to see you." He smiles. "So lovely."

She returns his smile, silently admitting that it is good to see him too, she needs his support, today of all days, despite the separate spheres they have occupied of late.

With greetings aside, the weight of their purpose for gathering settles upon them. As she listens to the intermittent call of the gulls, Kavita gazes at the lighthouse. When crisis befell them last year, this was the place they came to escape their troubles. A place that seemed to beckon them with its memories of happier times, like a torch through the darkness, offering a promise of how things could be for them again. This place, now the last place they spent together as a family.

Kavita peers at her mother. "Are you ready?" she asks.

Her mother looks at her father, who gives a solemn nod. Then, veiling her eyes, passes the urn to Kavita. The metal feels cold against her palms. She hugs the urn to her chest and leads them to the water's edge.

Although this river isn't the Ganges, somehow it feels just as holy. Kavita can sense a hum rising off the rocks and the water; the very air seems to vibrate. Her skin is alive. Her heart is beating slow.

Cool water licks her sandaled feet. Its touch is fresh and purifying, as if it holds the memory of spring showers, the victorious end of winter.

"We should've rented a boat," she says. "I didn't think of it before. If we scatter Sunil's ashes here, they'll just collect along the shoreline."

Kavita recalls her recent trip to Muir Woods, and how Hawthorn found the perfect place to scatter Sequoia's ashes. She imagines the wind moving gently through the canopy with a silvery ruffle, lets her mind's eye travel along miles and miles of sky-blue ocean. That is what she wants for Sunil. Freedom. Transformation. She wants him to dissolve into these waters, and course as freely as only rivers can, only to rise as a cloud, reaching higher than any hawk could possibly soar.

She takes a step forward. The coolness of the river swallows her ankles. She looks back at her family. She won't go any farther if they think her idea is silly.

Nirav slips off his shoes and enters the water. Her father follows. And finally, her mother. Her parents link arms. The magic of the river has touched them already. What she has just witnessed is a miracle.

They wade out into the river as naturally as bathers at Ganga *ghats*, to where the water is thigh-deep. They organize them-selves into a shape that mimics a horseshoe. She feels the river ease against the backs of her legs, sensing the encouragement of its forward motion. Let go, the river is telling her. I am here to catch him. I will carry him, always. We are water.

A puff of fine grey dust, like incense ash, releases into the air as Kavita lifts away the lid. Then, she closes her eyes, and recalls one of the *Gita* passages Hawthorne marked for her, those simple words that gave her perspective, an understanding of *samsara*, the cosmic wheel of life, when all she could see at the time was death. *It cannot be cut or burned*, she recites silently. *It cannot be wet or withered. It is enduring, all-per-vasive. Fixed, immovable, and timeless....* She opens her eyes to the light. *Indestructible.*

With a gentle shake, she tips the ashes. A powdery cloud forms on the surface of the water, then slowly starts to drift away from them. Little by little, the ashes disappear. As she watches her brother's remains dissolve below the surface of the dark water, Kavita does what the river whispered.

She lets go. Of all the little anchors that at one time seemed forever hooked to her soul, surrendering them to the swift current, as if tossing stones, an arc of pain that shoots through the air away from her, and sinks out of sight.

What remains is all that is most precious to her.

All the love that will keep her buoyant.

40

KAVITA SITS AT THE welcome table by the entrance of the church basement. It is her first night running the table alone since she started volunteering with the bereavement group a few months ago. They expect a big turnout tonight. The last meeting before Christmas is always crowded.

Her notes are tucked inside her purse. It took her about a week to compose all the things she wanted to say about her experiences as a suicide survivor. It took another week to practise the words out loud. As she did, in front of her dresser mirror, she scarcely trusted that the healthy person being reflected back to her was her own image, just as she scarcely recognized the sound of her own voice.

Her thoughts rewind to where she had been at this time last year. As she gazes around the room, at the regulars preparing snacks in the kitchen and gossiping, the newcomers sitting off on their own averting their eyes, and all versions of mourners in between, she smiles, grateful she chose to breathe in life again that night.

She can't help but chuckle at the kitschy plastic Christmas tree twinkling beside the snacks, its wire branches heavy with red and gold bobbles, multicoloured lights, and fistfuls of chrome-shine tinsel. Some of the mourners have filled out snowflake cards to their departed and tucked them into the bare patches of the tree. Kavita hasn't written a message to Sunil yet, but might before the night is done. In the background, she catches notes of her favourite holiday song, waits for the most touching lyric, then sings along with Bing Crosby: *I'll be home for Christmas, if only in my dreams.*

Along with the cheer this time of year can bring, she can't deny the absences also brought into keen focus. Of course, there is Sunil, whose absence is always so present, but especially now when thoughts turn to family togetherness. And her parents', who aren't coming home for the holidays. And also someone she misses keenly whenever she finds herself in the church basement: her friend of friend's, Hawthorn.

She reaches into her purse and pulls out his most recent postcard. The image is an enviable panoramic of a secluded beach with turquoise waters and a solitary highlighter-yellow surfboard planted in the sand. She can expect an update every couple of weeks or so, the postcards like snapshots of his latest excursions—ziplining through the canopy, bungee jumping over a river gorge, surfing on beaches that appear too pristine to be real.

Her only regret about tonight is that Hawthorn will miss her talk. He asked her to record it and send it to him as a Christmas present, but she has always hated the sound of her voice on tape.

Still, she has so much she wants to tell him. If he were there, she would thank him for his unconditional friendship. For speaking openly with her in their shared language of loss. For helping her understand the depth of her grief was inseparable from the depth of her love. For showing her it was possible to survive unspeakable trauma and loss. Not only survive, but live, meaningfully.

She reaches into her purse again and unfolds her notes. *Then, of course, there's you, Bear. My reason for doing any of this at all. Hawthorn would have called this speech my tombstone. My way of testifying to your life.* What is a person's life if not a collection of stories held together by a worn spine? And what is the purpose of these stories if not to be shared, another word for given, and perhaps, by some gentle miracle, heard, another word for received.

"Hello," says a familiar voice, snapping her out of her reflections. Nirav stands in front of her with a plastic grocery bag in either hand, smiling, as he looks down on her. It was their turn to fetch the refreshments for the meeting.

"Hi," she grins. "They're waiting for you in the kitchen."

"Well, we're in for a treat tonight, let me tell you. 'Tis the season of gaining a stone, isn't it? I splashed out for gingerbread *and* a chocolate Yule log, if you can believe that. I was this close to giving in to the mince pies."

"I'll take gingerbread over mince pies every time."

"I suppose I could let you sneak one before the break but only because you're my missus." He gives her a sly wink.

"I wish I could, but my stomach's doing flips."

"Nervous, love?"

She drops her gaze to the sign-in sheet. She still feels strange when he calls her *love* or *darling* or *sweetheart*. *Patience*, their therapist told them last session. *It takes ten times as long to rebuild a house as it does to pull it apart.*

"You know," he says, suddenly serious. "I've been meaning to tell you, I'm really proud of you. Thank you for including me. I can't imagine missing any of this."

"I'm glad you're here," she smiles. "Now, you better get to the kitchen. Barbie has no qualms about scolding youngsters."

"One last thing." He leans over the table and kisses her. A sweet little kiss that touches the corner of her mouth. Then he scuttles off to the kitchen.

She savours a private moment of her old affection for Nirav returning, then rearranges her piles again, and plays with her retractable pen, anything to distract away from her mounting nerves. She is about to run through her speech one last time, when out of the curve of her eye, a shadow moves. She turns to look and finds a young woman dressed in a long black coat hovering at the bottom of the stairs. The young woman is holding her elbows across her stomach in a shielding way as she scans the basement with nervous flits. Kavita notices she has come to the meeting alone. It isn't hard to tell, by the young woman's reluctant body language, she hasn't committed to staying, yet.

"Hi there," Kavita calls out, brightly. "Are you here for the bereavement group?"

Their eyes meet. The squint of the young woman's eyes widens to surprise, as though she rues being discovered, as though Kavita has ruined her plan of scouting the place out and then slipping away undetected.

"If you are," Kavita continues, "then you're in the right place." She smiles even more brightly than her cheerful tone. She thinks of Hawthorn. Is this how he felt on the night she slipped away? This strange combination of hopeful and helpless. "Come in," she waves.

Cautiously, the young woman approaches the sign-in table as if treading over an old suspension bridge with untrustworthy slats underfoot.

"Hi," she says. She speaks with a softness that contradicts her apprehensive demeanour. "I'm Emily. It's my first meeting."

For a moment, Kavita peers into Emily's pale, red-rimmed eyes. The alertness they glinted with earlier has dimmed to a tender sadness. In those eyes, Kavita glimpses a part of herself, as if Emily's pupils are cut of mirrors. She remembers something Hawthorn told her at her first meeting. How he recognized the pain in her eyes.

Never breaking the bridge of their gaze, Kavita rises to her feet, and reaches out her hand in welcome. "I'm Kavita," she says.

As they shake, Sunil's *rakhi* balances on her wrist, alive with light.

ACKNOWLEDGEMENTS

My deepest appreciation goes to Inanna Publications for championing this novel, and to my talented editor, Luciana Ricciutelli, for her careful attention and insights throughout the editorial process. Heartfelt thanks also to Renée Knapp for supporting the promotion and publicity of the book, as well as never being too busy to answer a question or two. Working with Inanna has been a pleasure and an honour. Sincerely, thank you.

Many thanks to Sherrill Wark, Sonia Saikaley, and Allan Briesmaster for taking the time to read and share their impressions, as well as encouragement.

Thanks to Shyam Selvadurai for being a thoughtful and challenging mentor during my time with Humber. Thanks also to the Humber School for Writers and their support through the Bluma and Bram Appel Scholarship.

To my friends and family, thank you for supporting me throughout the years, and understanding my need to tell a difficult story. And to my writer friends, in particular, thank you for sharing this journey as only you can.

Thanks to Noodles, the orange version of Coal.

Last but never least, to Daniel, thank you for believing in this novel before a word was written, and for standing by my side.

Anita Kushwaha grew up in Aylmer, Quebec. She holds an M.A. and Ph.D. in Human Geography from Carleton University, and is a graduate of the Creative Writing Program at the Humber School for Writers. She is the author of a novella, *The Escape Artist* , which was published in 2015. She lives in Ottawa.